Family Values

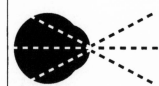

This Large Print Book carries the
Seal of Approval of N.A.V.H.

Family Values

K.C. Constantine

G.K. Hall & Co.
Thorndike, Maine

Published in 1997 by arrangement with Warner Books, Inc.

G.K. Hall Large Print Mystery Collection.

The text of this Large Print edition is unabridged.
Other aspects of the book may vary from the original edition.

Set in 16 pt. Plantin.

Printed in the United States on permanent paper.

Library of Congress Catalog Card Number: 97-93602
ISBN: 0-7838-8232-7 (lg. print : hc)

Family Values

Balzic sat stiffly in the first row of straight-backed wooden chairs in the Conemaugh County Courthouse Annex chambers of District Justice Ralph Parma, except Parma wasn't sitting in his chair. Parma wasn't even in the room. Sitting in Parma's chair, chin in one hand, bony index finger drumming his cheek, the gavel in the other hand going end over end, was a DJ Balzic had never seen before, one T. Melvin Nicklowe, who'd had to drive thirty-eight miles from his home in the southernmost district in the county just to hear this one case.

Seconds after Nicklowe had set his nameplate down on the front of the bench, and even as he was settling into Parma's chair, he explained how he felt about having to travel an excessive distance much too early on a Monday morning, especially in light of his original expectation for this particular Monday, which had been for him to be strapped into a chair on the back of a forty-foot sport-fishing cruiser while satisfying his lifelong ambition to compete in a sailfish tournament in Bimini, the Bahamas. It had been his dream since boyhood, he said, to fight a sailfish in the Gulf Stream, and he wanted everybody to understand that his dream could not have been possible without careful budgeting and planning, budgeting and planning that had begun exactly one year, three months, and two weeks earlier.

Mostly, Nicklowe wanted everybody to know that, as far as he was concerned, the ugliest words he had ever had to speak were, " 'I'm sorry. I have to withdraw from the tournament. I can't be there for the start.' 'Cause the geniuses that run the courts in this county can't find another district justice to hear this case except for good old Mel Nicklowe 'cause he's just on vacation and surely he can postpone the start of his vacation for one day, what would be the inconvenience! Never mind that there are at last count exactly seven retired district justices still alive in this county, but no, none of them can do the job. No sir! This hearing was scheduled for ten A.M. and by God it's ten A.M. — what's your problem? You been standing there with the fidgets ever since I started talking. Who are you? What's your problem?"

"Uh, Your Honor, uh, my name is Jonathan Bellerman and, uh, I am an assistant district attorney, and, uh, I'm here to present the state, uh, represent the Commonwealth, except, Your Honor, two of the witnesses, uh, that were subpoenaed, uh, including the, uh, gentleman whose chair you're sitting in, Your Honor, I, uh, respect-fully request that Your Honor just give me a few minutes to see what's holding them up, uh, to see if they're in the building, Your Honor."

T. Melvin Nicklowe became very still. His eyes turned to slits. "Wait a minute. Are you telling me that the man who's usually in this chair, the man who couldn't hear this case because he's a witness? Are you telling me that man has failed to appear — is that what you're tellin' me?"

"Uh, no sir, Your Honor. I'm just saying he's not here yet, that's all I'm saying —"

"And how long am I supposed to wait for this witness? You want to tell me that?"

"I just want to go outside and see if maybe he got caught up in a conversation in the hall, or got sidetracked, or something."

"Well you just do that, Counselor," Nicklowe growled. "You just go find your witness. But if you come back in and he's not with you? You hear me?"

"Yessir. Every word."

"You come back in here and you're alone? I warn you, Counselor, don't even think the word 'continuance,' you take my drift?"

Bellerman practically ran out of the room. The whole five minutes and thirty-two seconds he was gone — Balzic watched the second hand on the clock above Justice Nicklowe's head — were as empty as any time Balzic had ever spent. Because not only had Parma not appeared, neither had Patrolman Larry Fischetti. And if neither one of them showed up, Balzic was going to take the full weight for this screwup. And given the frustration smoldering behind the desk that served as a bench, Balzic was starting to ask himself how much worse it could be if he just stood up and slipped away.

What the hell, Balzic thought, this Nicklowe doesn't know me from Hillary Clinton. But just as Balzic began to stand, ADA Bellerman was back, flushed and out of breath and strenuously apologetic.

"Save your apologies, Counselor," Nicklowe said, banging his gavel once. "This court's in session. State your case."

Bellerman, who Balzic guessed was probably no more than twenty-five or -six, and probably no more than a year out of law school, suddenly couldn't look at Nicklowe. He stuttered his way through reading the names and numbers of the case while his eyes flitted from his forms and notes to the walls, the ceiling, the floor, the bench, his shoes. Finally, amid much rattling of paper because his hands were shaking, he said, "Uh, Your Honor, would you give me —"

"Counselor, what I'm going to give you is a piece of my best judicial advice — get on with it!" Nicklowe turned to his right and said, "Counselor, introduce yourself and your clients and give me the happy news that you're ready."

"Thank you, Your Honor," said a graying, lanky man, rising slowly. "My name is Panagios Valcanas. I represent the two defendants in this case, Missus Anne Marie Vittone, on my far left, and Missus Mary Theresa Vittone on my near left. And we are ready, Your Honor."

Nicklowe stood up and held a Bible in his left hand. "All who are about to testify here today, stand and raise your right hand and repeat after me. I, state your name, do solemnly swear to tell the truth, the whole truth, and nothing but the truth, so help me God. Be seated. Call your first witness, Counselor." Nicklowe settled back, right arm across his belly, left elbow on right hand, left hand cupping his jaw.

"Uh, yes sir, Your Honor. I call, uh, Mario Balzey."

Oh God, here we go, Balzic thought as he took the three steps from the front row of the spectator section to the witness chair, on the left of Parma's, now Nicklowe's, bench.

"Uh, would you state your full name and address for the court, please," Bellerman said, clearing his throat after every three or four words.

"My name is Mario Balzic. That's B-A-L-Z-I-C. Not Balzey. I live in Rocksburg. I respectfully ask the court not to require my street address."

"Come again?" Nicklowe said, hunching toward Balzic, brows rising, lips pinching. "You're asking what now?"

"Your Honor, I was a police officer all my adult life. I try to not make it easy for the people who don't like me to find me. I'm respectfully askin' the court's help, that's all."

"Why me," Nicklowe said under his breath,

but loud enough for everybody to hear. "All right, don't say where you live. But the court better know where you live if it needs to, understand?"

"Every official in this building knows, Your Honor." As soon as he said it, he regretted it. The hole he was in was getting deeper the longer it took for Parma and Fischetti to show up. Without them, there was only one cause for this screwup and that cause was him. And while he deserved everything he was going to get for it, he also knew that Fischetti had been the second officer on the scene and had spent as much time with the defendants as he had, and Parma had said repeatedly that they were following the rules to the letter and had nothing to worry about.

So much for not worrying, Balzic thought, glancing once again around the box-like chamber. No Fischetti, no Parma — as if anybody could have entered this room in the last ten minutes without drawing Nicklowe's attention. The room was smaller than Balzic's unheated garage, and not half as cozy.

"Would you state, uh, what is your occupation now?"

"I'm retired."

"Well before. Before you, uh, your retirement, Mister Balzic, what was your occupation?"

"I was chief of the Rocksburg Police Department."

"And, uh, how long did you, uh, were you in that capacity?"

"Twenty-four years."

"And you retired when? When did you retire?"

"Uh, my retirement date was effective December thirty-first last year."

"Now, Mister Balzic, on the morning of twenty-eight August of last year, were you in, uh, did you have occasion to be at the, in the, uh, number seventeen Harrington Avenue, Norwood Hill? In Rocksburg I mean."

"I did."

"And what brought you to that place? Why did you go there?"

"I was responding to a call that a disturbance was in progress at that address."

"No, I mean why did you go to that address? Why did you yourself go? I mean, you were the chief is what I'm asking — why didn't you send somebody? One of your men. Officers."

"It was August, and I had several officers on vacation. Nothin' unusual. Married officers have young kids, they wanna take vacations in the summer. Happens every year. But we were short-handed to begin with. The other officer on patrol that morning was already respondin' to another call, so that left either me or the dispatcher, so I went."

"And what happened, uh, tell the court, uh, what you found when you arrived? At that address."

"I could hear people shouting and screaming as soon as I got there. When I got up on the porch and knocked, the man, Frank Vittone, came to the door. Inside the house, uh, there was his wife,"

13

Missus Ann Marie Vittone, and her sister, Missus Mary Theresa Vittone, who I found out was married to Mister Vittone's brother — George, I think his name is — or rather she was separated from him and was living at that address."

"So there was indeed a fight there? In progress I mean."

"Yes there was."

"Was it a physical fight or was it a — what kind of a fight was it?"

"At that time, it was just verbal."

"Did you go into the house? And if you did, uh, what did you do? What happened next? Tell us what happened."

"I did go into the house. Mister Vittone let me in, and once I got in I found out there was this dispute, uh, which as near as I could make out was over a watch, uh, a wristwatch that had belonged to Missus Mary Theresa Vittone and she was accusing Frank Vittone of stealing it, and selling it, uh, to buy, as I recall, cigarettes, beer, and lottery tickets. Mister Vittone was saying that he had taken the watch in lieu of rent, or room and board, I don't remember exactly which. He also was saying that he'd pawned the watch, he had not sold it."

"Was that the end of this dispute? Did anything else happen? Something else?"

"No sir it was not the end. I never did determine specifically what Missus Mary Theresa Vittone was upset about. There was so much shouting goin' back and forth with all three of 'em, I think what started that particular incident that particular day was, uh, probably the owner-ship and possession of the watch. She kept saying that her brother-in-law had stolen her watch. They were also arguin' about what it was worth. There were probably some other things involved, but I think basically the watch was what provoked that dispute."

"And did you, sir, bring this dispute to an end, and if so, how so? How did you do that?"

"Well it's still not over as far as I'm concerned, but at that time, what I tried to do was I separated the women from Mister Vittone, and I thought I had them more or less quieted down out on the porch, and I was trying to get Mister Vittone to go back inside the living room, which as I recall was just off a very small entranceway, no more than a coupla steps inside the front door. I'd got him turned around, I had him facin' the couch, and, uh, I had my hands on his back and shoul-ders, and I was talkin' to him and steerin' him towards the couch when I felt somebody behind him — behind me is what I mean — and out of the corner of my eye I see this hand and arm comin' around and this big shiny thing, and it strikes Mister Vittone right behind his right ear, and he goes down, facefirst onto the couch. He also stumbled over the, uh, coffee table, which was in front of the couch. Anyway, I immediately turned, I instinctively turned to my right, and caught the person's right wrist with my left hand and took hold of her upper arm with my right

15

hand and brought her arm —"

"*Her* arm, Mister Balzic?" Nicklowe interrupted him. "Whose arm are you talking about?"

"Oh, sorry, Your Honor. That would be Missus, uh, Mary Theresa Vittone. Her arm."

"Do you want me, uh, may I, uh, may I continue, Your Honor?"

"Anytime you want to ask the right questions in the right order, Counselor, I'll be happy to let you continue."

"Uh, thank you, yes sir, Your Honor. Uh, Mister Balzic, what happened then?"

"Uh, I had her wrist in one hand, my left hand, and her upper arm in my other hand and I brought my right knee up while I was bringin' her arm down over my knee. I was doin' that to make her release the weapon — which it turned out was an ashtray — which she had used to strike Mister Vittone."

"I understand, Mister Balzic, go on —"

"I am thrilled that you understand him, Counselor," Nicklowe said, smiling wickedly. "Would you spare me the editorials and stick to the questions?"

"Uh, yes sir, Your Honor. Sorry. Please continue, Mister Witness — I mean Mister Balzic."

Balzic had to force himself to look at his notes to keep from laughing. Poor bastard. Aw fuck him, what am I feelin' sorry for him for, he ain't gonna look half as stupid as I do in a coupla minutes.

"Uh, well," Balzic said, looking at the back wall

16

and clearing his throat, "I guess I did it too hard, 'cause soon as I did it I heard the bone snap in her forearm and she started screamin' and the thing went flyin', the ashtray, it hit the floor and shattered, you know, pieces just flyin' everywhere, and the next thing I knew, her sister, uh, Missus Frank Vittone, Ann Marie, she was on my back, she was, uh, she had one arm, her left arm, around my throat, and she was poundin' on my neck and the side of my face with her other hand, sometimes she'd be slappin' me and sometimes she was hittin' me with the side of her fist like, and, uh, I didn't realize till later on she'd knocked my glasses off and cut my face right beside my eye. And then I found out when, uh, when one of the emergency medical techs with the Mutual Aid Ambulance, when he was giving me a little first aid, he told me part of my ear was missing, said it looked like it had been bitten off. Which was true it turned out, but I couldn't believe it at that time 'cause I'd never even felt that. You can see this chunk that's missing from my ear, if you wanna look."

"Yes, I can see that," Nicklowe said. "Get on with it."

"Yes sir, Your Honor. And, uh, and how did this fight end, Mister Balzic?"

"Well I managed, uh, somehow to get her off me and I handcuffed her around the leg, uh, one of the legs of the coffee table — the one Mister Vittone fell over? Or across? And then I got another pair of handcuffs from my car and I cuffed

17

her sister to another leg of that same table. And then I called for assistance and for an ambulance, and, uh, that's how it ended. Rocksburg Patrolman Lawrence Fischetti arrived in a coupla minutes, and so did an ambulance from Mutual Aid. The EMTs did first aid on everybody, and Patrolman Fischetti and I arrested them all, and then they were taken to Conemaugh General Hospital so everybody could be treated, and then, uh, as the opportunity arose we booked 'em."

Well there it was. He'd finally reached the rule of criminal procedure that was going to make T. Melvin Nicklowe a whole lot more frustrated and angry than he already was.

"When you say you arrested them all, Mister Balzic, what charges did you file, uh, specifically, against each one?"

"Uh, I'll have to consult my notes here," Balzic said, reading from the notebook he'd opened to the pages where he'd recorded all the things he had done in regard to this case and where he had not recorded the one thing he should have done. Unfortunately, nobody else had done it either. Balzic couldn't postpone the misery any longer. He started talking from the notes.

"Uh, first I charged Mister Frank Vittone with a violation of Title 18 Section 5503, disorderly conduct. Then I charged Missus Mary Theresa Vittone with violations of Section 5503; then Section 2701 period A one and two, assault; Section 2702 period A one, two, three, and four, aggravated assault; then, uh, Section 2705, recklessly

18

endangering; and uh, Section 5101, obstruction of administration of law, and 5104, resisting arrest or other law enforcement. Then I charged her sister, Missus Anne Marie Vittone, with violations of the same sections — you want me to read them again?"

"Is that necessary, Your Honor — if the court wants it in the record —"

"It's already in the information, Counselor. We don't need him to repeat everything that's already filed, do we?"

"Wait a second, Your Honor," Balzic said.

"Now what?"

"I just wanted to correct something I said. I didn't file a Section 2702 period A two against Missus Mary Theresa Vittone. She never assaulted me."

"Was this information filed correctly, Counselor? Is what's on paper different from what he's saying? 'Cause if it is, that one's gone right now."

"No sir," Bellerman said. "No sir, it was filed correctly. I went over the charges at least twice with Mister Balzey, uh Balzer — Balzic. Sorry. And with Patrolman Fischetti and Justice Parma."

"Speaking of which," Nicklowe said, making a show of looking around, "they here yet, Counselor? Especially this District Justice Parma — Ralph Parma, there's a name I'm never gonna forget if I get the worst case of Alzheimer's in medical history. I mean, as I look around the court, Mister Bellerman, I don't see them, do you?"

Bellerman shrugged and sighed and cleared his throat and looked ready to burst into tears.

"Oh, Your Honor, uh, I hope that you, that Your Honor knows . . . I cannot personally enforce the subpoenas myself . . . and present the case too. I don't think, uh, that's, uh, reasonable to expect — may I continue, Your Honor?"

"You may, Counselor."

"Uh, Mister Balzic, do you see Ann Marie Vittone and Mary Theresa Vittone in this courtroom now?"

"Yes I do. They're seated beside Mister Valcanas, to his right. Ann Marie Vittone is on the left, to my left, and Mary Theresa Vittone is on the right, to my right."

"Thank you, Mister Balzic. No more questions, Your Honor."

"Mister Panagios is it? You said you were ready. Don't disappoint me."

Valcanas stood slowly and stretched his chin upward and stuck a finger in his collar and stretched it. He cleared his throat, sniffed, and said, "It's Valcanas, Your Honor. Panagios Valcanas. And I am indeed ready, Your Honor."

"Then, Mister Valcanas, please, please proceed," Nicklowe said.

"Mister Balzic, can you hear me?"

"Yes I can."

"Good. Because I'm having a little trouble with my hearing this morning. One of my ears seems to be all clogged up with wax and everything I say sounds real loud inside my head, inside my mouth actually, if you can believe it. So I hope you won't mind if I ask you on occasion to please speak up."

"I'll try." Well, Balzic thought sourly, as if I'm not going to look stupid enough here, leave it to my old friend to find another way to double the fun.

"Good. Now, sir, I know that in the situation as you described it at the Vittone residence, you were extremely occupied to say the least. I know that domestic disputes are often the most trying and difficult situations a police officer ever encounters. I know there's potential for great harm all around, and I think I can guess that if somebody — I'm not saying who, mind you — but if somebody was on my back and pummeling me and biting my ear, I would be, to say the very least, extremely occupied. But later on, Mister Balzic, after Patrolman Fischetti — is that his name?"

"Yes sir."

"After Patrolman Fischetti arrived — there, not here. We can see, I believe, that he has not arrived here. After he arrived there, at seventeen Harrington Avenue, Norwood, Rocksburg, things were more or less calmed down, is that correct?"

"More or less, yes."

"So all the potential for harm would seem to have passed at that point, wouldn't you say?"

"Yes sir."

21

"So at that time — and I would ask you again, please, to speak up just ever so slightly if you would — at that time you would then have had plenty of time to Mirandize the defendants, would you not? I mean, you would have had more than ample time to inform Ann Marie Vittone and Mary Theresa Vittone of their right to remain silent, and their right to an attorney, and their right to have the state of Pennsylvania provide them with the services of an attorney if they could not afford one, is that not correct? After you'd placed them under arrest I mean. What I'm asking you, sir, is do you agree there was ample time between when the actual physical confrontation ended and when you supervised the transportation of these two defendants to Conemaugh General Hospital, between those two events, was there not more than ample time for you to inform these defendants of their rights? That's what I'm asking you."

Balzic rolled his eyes and shook his head twice, and thought, Jesus, why don't you just make a speech? "Yes. There was time."

"Ample time, correct? I mean, didn't the actual physical confrontation end at approximately eleven forty-five A.M. on August twenty-eighth?"

"Approximately, yes."

"And didn't the last booking — the one for Mary Theresa Vittone, didn't that booking in fact take place the following day, August the twenty-ninth? In fact, the following afternoon, at about five-thirty P.M.? Before she was discharged from the hospital August twenty-ninth?"

"Yes it did."

"So, Mister Balzic, did you personally, during that period between the end of the physical confrontation and the end of the final booking, did you yourself ever inform either Ann Marie Vittone or Mary Theresa Vittone of their rights, sir? Do you recall ever Mirandizing these two defendants?"

Balzic looked at the notebook in his lap as though he was going to find some startling piece of information that would set everything right. When he saw the same stale, painful, embarrassing omission of information, he closed his eyes and licked his lips, and when he opened his eyes again, he looked directly at his old friend and said clearly and loudly, "No sir, I do not recall that."

"You do not *recall* Mirandizing them or you did *not* Mirandize them?"

"I do not recall Mirandizing them."

"I see. Did you ever ask Patrolman Fischetti — is that his name?"

"Yes."

"Did you ever ask Patrolman Fischetti if he Mirandized these two defendants?"

"I don't recall whether I did or not."

"Now, sir, you did not go alone to the hospital to book Mary Theresa Vittone, did you? You went in the company of some other person, sir, is that not true? Would you tell the court, please, who that other person was?"

23

"Uh, that would be District Justice Ralph Parma. But he wasn't with me both days. Just the first day."

"So he was not present throughout that booking, is that what you're saying?"

"He was not, yes sir, that's what I'm saying. He just went along the first day."

"It's unusual, is it not, for a booking to take place in a hospital, number one, and number two, even more unusual for a district justice to actually participate, isn't it?"

"Yes to both."

"Now I don't claim to know everything that happens in the law, Mister Balzic. Believe me, sometimes I'm appalled by my own ignorance, but I must tell you honestly I have never heard of a district justice leaving his chambers to participate in a booking. I'm not saying it's never been done, I'm not saying it can't be done, or shouldn't be done, all I'm saying is I've never heard of it. Why did that happen — just to put an end to my ignorance, that's the only reason I'm asking — with the court's indulgence, Your Honor."

"Trust me, Counselor," Nicklowe said, scrunching forward on his chair. "I'm as anxious to hear this as you are."

Balzic dropped his chin and peered over his glasses at his old friend and smiled a smile that said, You're really enjoying this, ain'tcha? Really gettin' your jollies, ain'tcha? Well what the fuck, somebody might as well.

24

"Uh, that happened, Counselor, because on the first day, the twenty-eighth, I had been injured, and I don't mind tellin' you I was a little bit rattled. And I wanted to do it by the numbers, and I didn't wanna screw it up, and that's why I asked Justice Parma to go along. It so happened he didn't have anything to do at that time, and I needed to have somebody whose head was clearer than mine, and he agreed to go along with me, that's why it happened."

"Thank you, sir, for enlightening me," Valcanas said, rocking on his heels, his thumbs hooked into his vest pockets. "Your Honor, I have no more questions of this witness."

"And that goes double for enlightening me, Mister Balzic," Nicklowe said. "Mister Bellerman? You gonna call any more witnesses?"

"Your Honor," Bellerman said, coughing and swallowing, "I, uh, as I look around this court I see that my other witnesses, uh, the other witnesses have not arrived here —"

"Really?" Nicklowe bellowed.

"Your Honor, I can't explain why they're not here, but it's not my fault —"

"You don't say," Nicklowe said.

Bellerman stood there shaking his head and throwing his hands up and letting them fall feebly against his sides.

"Mister Bellerman," Nicklowe sang out, "any chance you're gonna maybe snap your fingers and pull some other witnesses out of your briefcase? Any chance of that?"

"Uh, I don't know how to answer that, Your Honor."

"Mister Bellerman, you got one last chance for an explanation."

"They were subpoenaed, Your Honor. They said they would be here, I don't know where they are, it's not my fault they're not here, I'm not supposed to, uh, you know, go out and drive them here."

Nicklowe, hunching up his shoulders and spearing Bellerman with his gaze, said, "At this very minute I'm already missing the first day of competition in Bimini, which in case you've forgotten is in the Bahamas, from which competition I had to withdraw. I've already missed the first three days of my vacation — did I mention I was supposed to be on a plane that left at ten fifty-five Friday morning — did I mention that? I'll consider myself real real lucky if I get to Bimini by midnight tonight, and right now I don't even know why I'm goin' 'cause I know damn well I won't be able to get on a boat, and everybody's gonna say, why'd you bother? Why'd you come down here? And I'm not gonna have an answer for 'em, but the guy whose chair I'm sitting in, this guy who was a subpoenaed witness, this guy who I was led to believe resides in this town, close enough in fact that he could walk here, this guy can't find it in his agenda of professional events to get here on time! Mister Valcanas, you gonna say anything I hope?"

"I was just waiting to see what Mister Bellerman was going to say, Your Honor. Yes sir, Your Honor, I move that all charges against my clients be dismissed for the reason that they were not informed of their rights under the Rules of —"

"Yes yes yes," said Nicklowe, pounding his gavel in rhythm with his words. "Dismissed. Ladies, good-bye. Go home. Just one reminder. You got lucky this time. As for the rest of you, I hope I never see any one of you again as long as I live. But if I do, I warn you. I've got a great memory for faces. Believe it. As for you, Mister Former Chief of Police, do I have to say anything to you?"

"No sir, Your Honor, you don't," Balzic said, heaving a great sigh and standing and heading for the coatrack to get his raincoat. "Sorry, kid," he said as Bellerman tried to get past him. He wasn't sure why he said it.

"Oh give me a break, okay?" Bellerman said, flushing, trying to keep his papers and notes from spilling out of his briefcase and trying to shuffle around Balzic. "I was supposed to be in Judge Vrbanic's court ten minutes ago and I'm a lot scareder of him than I am of that, that — could you please get out of my way, please?"

"Yeah, right, go," Balzic said, and stepped aside and turned around and glowered at Valcanas and the two Vittones. "Okay, lay 'em on me, may as well get it over in one whack."

"Lay what on you?"

"Oh come on. For crissake, I've been walkin' around on eggs since last August. If you're gonna do it to me, Panagios, do it now."

Valcanas shook his head. "If you're talkin' about a civil matter, my friend, you're talkin' to the wrong lawyer. My representation for these charming ladies ends right here."

"Oh don't you worry, Mister Ex-Chief of Police," Mary Theresa Vittone said, her head rocking from side to side, "there's plenty of lawyers in this world. We'll find us one, you can bet your ass on that."

"Yeah," said Ann Marie Vittone. "We'll find us one. They got lots of lawyers in Pittsburgh. They don't all live around here. And they ain't all your friend like him." She pointed at Valcanas with her thumb.

"Clear the court," Nicklowe said. "I don't need much of a reason to cite you all for contempt. I'm saving that for Justice Parma. Believe me, it wouldn't take a whole lot at this point to include you all in my citation. Last warning: clear the court."

"Gimme a coffee," Balzic said, slumping onto a stool in Muscotti's.

Vinnie the bartender put his hands on his hips and pulled his chin back into his neck. "Coffee! The way you look, coffee ain't gonna do it. Maybe I put a little Sambucca in it, huh?"

"Just gimme the coffee, okay? Cream, sugar."

"Cream? Hey, you want cream go to a fuckin' restaurant. We're lucky we got milk here," Vinnie said, pouring the coffee into a heavy white mug and setting it in front of Balzic.

28

"Cream, milk, whatever. And some of that white sandy-lookin' stuff, sugar, huh?"

"Some guy was in here lookin' for you," Vinnie said, going to the refrigerator in the small kitchen beyond the end of the bar and returning with a paper carton of two percent milk.

"What guy?"

"Whatta I know what guy. Said he was tryin' to call you, you don't answer your phone or you don't have no answerin' machine, some bullshit. Told him you wouldn't know how to work an answerin' machine."

Balzic stirred the milk into the coffee and sipped it. "You oughta go on television, you know that? You could be the next Ofra. That's what everybody wantsa do anymore, listen to some talkin' machine. Talk talk talk, that's all ya hear. It's everywhere. Turn on the fuckin' radio, try to find some music, if it ain't some asshole talkin' about football or hockey or baseball or who's on strike, who ain't on strike and why — like they know —"

"Hey Mario, what'd you call her?"

"Huh? Call who?"

"What'd you say she was? O-fra?"

"Ofra. Yeah. What?"

Vinnie leaned across the bar. "It ain't Ofra. Read my lips. It's O-prah. Say it, O-prah."

"O-prah, O-fra, Oufra, Ouprah, what the fuck's the difference, that ain't the point."

"Yeah yeah, right. And the point is?"

"You. You'd fit right in there on television. Or

radio. All you do is talk anymore, non-fuckin'-stop. And that's apparently what the world wants. Somebody talkin' at 'em constantly. Used to be you could occasionally be alone with your thoughts. Used to be I could walk in here, order somethin', you'd give me some shit, hey, I expected that, but after a while, you know, you'd bring me what I ordered and eventually you'd leave me the fuck alone. Now I come in, I get the fuckin' history of the world since yesterday. Gimme a break."

Vinnie, arms folded, listened to Balzic's harangue, and then said, "Hey. You wanna be alone with your thoughts, huh? Be my fuckin' guest. I don't need this shit. Take your own fuckin' messages from now on, answer your own fuckin' phone, I ain't your fuckin' messenger boy. I look like Ma Bell? Huh? Federal Express maybe?"

"Okay okay, Jesus, what guy?"

"Ohhhhh. Now all of sudden I got a purpose. All of a sudden I got a seat on your bus now. No shit."

"What guy, what the fuck, come on."

"What guy, whatta I know what guy. Guy comes in, says he hears you're spendin' a lotta time in here since you retired. I said you ain't spendin' no more time in here now you ain't workin' than when you was workin'."

"What'd he want?"

"He wanted you, what the fuck do I know what he wanted. Here he comes anyway. Ask him your-

30

self what he wants."

"Huh?"

"Oh. And the coffee ain't free, you know? Lately you been actin' like I make coffee here like it's a public fuckin' service or somethin'. It ain't. It's sixty-four cents."

"Huh? This guy comin' here?"

"Yeah yeah, him." Vinnie looked at the tall man in the camel-hair wool topcoat stepping lightly and quickly around Iron City Steve, who'd picked that moment to slide his stool backwards in preparation for launching a lecture.

Vinnie held up both hands, palms up, and then pointed both at Balzic. "There's the man you're lookin' for."

"I've been tryin' to break the laws of gravity for most of my life," Iron City Steve sang out to the bottles on the shelves above Vinnie's head. "I thought the noblest ambition I could ever have was to be a gravity outlaw. I get high, I get higher, I get highest. I load up my six-gun. I throw down on gravity. I get the drop on gravity. I got gravity on its knees. It's down there, shakin' in its boots. But still, I don't fly. High as I get, still . . . I don't fly."

"Hey!" Vinnie shouted, hustling down the bar until he was opposite Steve. "You gonna start already, you're gonna do it on the fuckin' sidewalk, I'm not gonna tell ya again. Siddown and shuddup or you're gone, you hear me?"

Steve slipped laboriously onto his stool, in- haled mightily, and said in mock whisper, "I

31

been gone since 1964."

Vinnie softened suddenly and said, just loud enough that Balzic could hear, "I know, I know. It's okay. It's all right. You'll be okay, just settle down a little bit, that's all."

The tall man in the camel-hair topcoat had reached Balzic but was looking back at Steve and Vinnie. Then he turned to Balzic and said, "I almost missed this. I almost never learned there were places like this. People like him." He was smiling as though he'd made some great personal discovery. He pulled off his black leather gloves, put them in his left hand, and extended his right hand to Balzic. "You Chief Balzic?"

Balzic extended his fingers limply, hoping this guy wasn't going to express every righteous molecule of his character by the power of his handshake. "Ex-chief."

"But you are Mario Balzic, correct?"

The man's grip wasn't a vise exactly because Balzic hadn't allowed him a shot at more than the fingers, but it was enough to sting the first two joints on each finger.

Balzic withdrew his hand and stretched his fingers several times between his knees, thinking that one of these days he was going to get smart and keep his hand at his side. He looked the man over and guessed that what he was wearing could have fed a family of four for six months. At least. His tie alone was probably worth a week's worth of groceries.

"What'd you pay for that tie?"

"Beg your pardon?"

"The tie. How much?"

The tall man's brow rose. He dropped his chin and cleared his throat. Then he put his gloves in his pocket and took off his topcoat and looked for a place to hang it.

"There's hangers on the wall beside the kitchen door," Balzic said. He pointed over his shoulder with his thumb.

The man hung up his coat and then came back smoothing his suit coat and hair and sat on a stool so that he was between Balzic and everybody else at the bar. "I don't know how much the tie cost. It was a gift. The shirt, on the other hand, I order myself by the dozen. They cost three hundred dollars."

"Per dozen or per shirt?"

"Per shirt. Would you like a more complete accounting?"

The man was not in the least offended, as Balzic was hoping he might be. Would've been easier to blow him off. On the contrary, the man seemed to be enjoying himself.

"Nah, I think that's enough. Yeah, I'm Balzic, who're you?"

The man reached inside his coat, found a business card, and handed it over. Balzic read, "G. Warren Livingood. Deputy Attorney General, Commonwealth of Pennsylvania." Below that were two addresses, one in Harrisburg, the other in Philadelphia, along with two phone numbers and one fax number for each address.

Balzic looked at the name and then at the man and said, "Livingood, huh? I guess so." He tried to hand the card back but Livingood wouldn't accept it.

"Keep it, please. I'm going to ask you something and I don't expect an answer now. I do expect to come back in two or three days, but you never know, so you might want those numbers."

"Yeah. So?" Balzic put the card on the bar and leaned back. "What're you gonna ask me?"

"Chief Balzic —"

"Ex. Don't forget that ex. That ex is very important."

"I think I understand," Livingood said.

"I don't think you do, but go 'head anyway," Balzic said, studying Livingood and his tanned, manicured fingers, French cuffs with gold triangle cuff links, the tiny red flecks in the charcoal-blue wool of his suit, the three-hundred-dollar bluish-gray shirt with the white collar and white cuffs.

"You don't think I do?"

"Well, you're one step below cabinet level in Harrisburg and you didn't come at me with a subpoena, so what else would you be wantin' to talk about, huh? You got some job in mind, either you or one of your bosses. And somebody told you, Christ knows why, that I'm the chooch to do it. And I'm tryin' to remind you of the ex, that's all."

"As an exact matter of fact, I do want to ask you about a job —"

34

"If I gotta drive more'n an hour one way, forget it. I hate drivin'. Drivin' scares the shit outta me anymore."

"We'll provide you with a car and a driver if you like."

"Well see, that's even worse. Then I gotta talk to somebody I don't know. I gotta pretend I'm sociable. Like now. What's this about?"

Livingood cleared his throat, smiled politely, and said, "I can't say I wasn't warned. Okay. Here it is. We've got a stinkpot going in Wabash County. The lid's off and the stench is spreading very fast. You remember the murders that happened on Deer Mountain? Wabash County?"

"Vaguely, yeah. That's old stuff as I recall."

"Seventeen years old, but it won't go away. What we have is a history of mistrials, trials, convictions, appeals, convictions overturned, more mistrials, more trials, more convictions, more appeals, ad nauseam. One of the two cons has now petitioned for a post-conviction hearing on grounds that he was convicted on perjured testimony."

"That's what they all say."

"Yes, well, unfortunately, in this case, it may be true."

"In a lotta cases, it's probably true. So what's special about this one?"

"Well, what's special is the state has already spent so many taxpayer dollars — to be candid, I don't think anybody knows how much. Just incarcerating and transporting the two cons to

35

court has topped four hundred thousand, that much can be documented. I'm not going to tell you how much their legal costs have been, but believe me, they have used every legal service the state provides. And one of them, of course, is still using them. The other one insisted he'd given up, but now along he comes and says he's willing to recant about the other con's involvement. And so it starts all over again.

"I'll tell you more complications in a moment, but what I want you to understand now is that I've been given the task of bringing this mess to an end. My boss, the AG, has decided that it's long overdue for a conclusion and that I'm the one to make that happen. I think you understand that we're all rising on a tide of opposition to the costs of government in general, but most certainly in the area of criminal appeals, a lot of people are just fed up. There are legislators from the rural counties who've been screaming at us to get everybody off death row one way or another, and the cheaper way as far as they're concerned is to execute them. But it's not just them. Everybody's apparently had more than enough already —"

"Let me interrupt you here, Mister Livingood —"

"Warren. May I call you Mario?"

"Yeah that's okay. Uh, this thing is comin' back to me now, and what you said before, about it's a stinkpot? I remember it now. One of the two guys convicted was the son of a cop, am I right?"

"Right, exactly."

"He's the one wants the p-c hearing, right?"

"Right again. But this time, he's got not only the accomplice who's been deposed that he's willing to recant, we also have a deposition from the only other witness there has ever been, who now claims he wasn't even in Pennsylvania when it happened. He now claims he was visiting his aunt, his mother's sister, in Ohio, at the time he had said numerous times in and out of court that he was present during the murders. And of course now his aunt is dead, conveniently or inconveniently depending upon your point of view, which would have been the best reason in the world to ignore him.

"However, somehow or other he's managed to come up with what he claims is his copy of a citation for public drunkenness in that town in Ohio on that very day. The document is being examined by the state police at their labs at Troop A — or is supposed to be. I haven't heard anything yet."

"Sounds like to me somebody has a problem."

"Well if it were only that, we would be able to deal with it as soon as its authenticity is determined. But he's also now claiming that his original testimony was beaten out of him over a period of three days by a police officer. Two police officers. And that the beating was witnessed in part by the then district justice who subsequently got himself elected district attorney, and he also claims the beatings took place with the full knowledge and cooperation and subsequent cover-up of the then district attorney who is now a judge of the Common Pleas Court of Wabash County."

Balzic shook his head and laughed. "Does it get worse?"

"Believe it or not, it does, yes. One of the police officers who allegedly coerced the testimony is now himself doing ten to twenty for second-degree homicide, and he himself has now appealed for a post-conviction hearing on the ground that there was a conflict of interest between his lawyer and the prosecuting attorney because they had once been in partnership together, would you believe."

"And what, he's makin' noises like he *did* coerce the witness?"

"He's making lots of different noises. Because," here Livingood sighed heavily and said to Vinnie, "I'd like a cup of coffee, if you wouldn't mind, please. And another for Mario, please? Do you want another?"

Balzic shook his head. "I got a feelin' I'm gonna need a little somethin' else here. Soon as I think of what, I'll ask, but I don't want any more coffee. Already got a shitty taste in my mouth."

Vinnie filled another mug and set it in front of Livingood, who paid with a fifty-dollar bill.

Balzic winced.

"What's the matter?" Livingood said.

"Uh, none of my business really, but, uh, you think it's cool for a deputy AG to pay for coffee with fifties?"

"It's all I've got," Livingood said, shrugging.

"Bartender didn't seem to care."

"Yeah, well. Count your change, that's all I can tell ya. Where were we?"

"Well, as if what we have isn't enough, there is a literary type involved, who for reasons quite beyond me, seems to have attached himself to the cop. Which by itself is neither here nor there, but the cop now one day wants to cooperate with us to get his post-con hearing moving, and the next day he wants to listen to tales of how much money there is to be made in bookstores and movie theaters and on television and he gives us this blank stare when we say 'post-conviction hearing.' I've talked to him twice myself and he just loves, as he puts it, 'to jack me off.' Interesting term. I always thought it was 'jerk,' but around here everybody says 'jack.' "

"Actually, if you listen close enough, what they say around here is 'jag.' "

"Really? Even more interesting. I love words, the way they grow and change and decline. Anyway, last time I talked to him, I came away with the distinct impression he's trying to get somebody to declare him certifiable. Which is probably another way he might be trying to work the system if his post-con hearing doesn't turn out the way he wants it to. What I'm trying to say, Mario, is I need an objective, impartial, trained investigator — and this is the most important part — one who won't bullshit me."

Balzic laughed. "I woulda bet large money 'bullshit' wasn't in your vocabulary."

"You would've lost, wouldn't you? That's beside the point, which is, Harrisburg is full of trained investigators. Especially in my department. But most of them make a show of being impartial or objective. What I mean is, they're as impartial and objective as they think you want them to be. They're all political animals, in other words, which goes without saying I suppose. I mean if they weren't, they wouldn't have gone to Harrisburg."

"I'm gonna bet somethin' else."

"What?"

"You're not in this for the money, are ya?"

"Actually, not that it's any of your business, and despite the way you're trying to steer this conversation away from you, half my salary goes to Big Brothers, Big Sisters of Philadelphia, and the other half goes to a Shriners children's hospital for burn victims. But I'm not slumming if that's what you think. You might not believe this, but I'm getting an education. I worked the Main Line in Philadelphia, as I had been trained to do and as I was expected to do, until it occurred to me one day that if I didn't do something else I was going to die way before my time and the cause of death would be excruciating boredom. Sometimes — I know this is going to sound ridiculous, but I assure you the feeling is genuine — sometimes I feel like I ought to be paying the state for the excitement. Really. I mean that. I know, I know, it sounds very very suspicious. But it's true. I'm having the time of my life. Other times, working for nothing is payment enough, believe me. Like with this mess. But it's never dull. Not to me.

"Back to the point, however. I'm taking a couple days off to visit friends in Pittsburgh. They're leaving Thursday for Morocco, and they're letting me use their place while they're gone. But until they leave I'm just going to visit with them. What I'm saying is, I'll be back Thursday. Will you be here, do you think? Or at home?"

"Hey, wait a minute here. You're offering this to me because why? You heard from somebody I was not a political animal, is that why?"

"In a phrase, yes. But that's not the main reason —"

"From who? Who told you this? This reputation I got, by puttin' my head up my ass as far as politics goes, this has spread clear to Harrisburg? I don't believe this."

"Well, all I can say is what I know I've done. I've looked for somebody who didn't have a political history — not that that's the primary consideration, believe me. I just thought it would make for a cleaner investigation, that's all, starting out with someone who has no debts, no scores to settle, and believe me, that's not easy to find in a state capital. I'm not going to play games with you. The man who told me about you, who insisted that I meet you, is an old friend of yours. Or so he claims. Walker Johnson."

"Shit, he's been retired longer'n I have. He's runnin' a pistol range out in —"

41

"Not anymore he isn't. He's been a special investigator for us for more than a year now. And I've worked with him a lot. As soon as he found out what I was looking for, he immediately said your name. And he kept saying I might find better investigators maybe, ones with better pedigrees, but I wasn't going to find one as smart, as honest, and as less likely to bullshit me. Almost his exact words. And the more people I talked to about you, the more I heard the same thing."

"Yeah, well, nothin' like backassward praise. The thing that cost me my job is now suddenly the best thing I got to recommend me? That's funny, no shit. But from where I sit, that's the wrongest reason in the world for you to want me. You want somebody who's free of politics, but it also sounds like you want somebody who understands it, and I may be good on the first half, but I'm no good on the second. I mean, if I was pressed, I might be able to tell you who was connected to who in this county politically, but you get me outta here? You put me in Wabash County? You kiddin'? I'd need steel underwear and a magnet in both hands to find my ass."

"Johnson said you'd say something like that. But see, if you don't mind my saying so, you're jumping to a conclusion here. You're thinking about the judge and the DA, right?"

"Sure. Aren't you?"

"Yes of course, but not where you're concerned. I've got people who'll work on that side of it. Including me. You won't have to go near them."

"Oh."

"Anyway, forget about the word *politics*. I was wrong to lead you that way. It's an obstacle. Just think of a family, many siblings, much rivalry, much gratitude for certain behavior, much animosity for certain behavior, much guilt, much resentment, much ambition, much greed for security or love or money, many appetites for certain foods prepared certain ways, many associations with certain foods with love, security, approval, disapproval for and with the people who prepared the foods, or paid for them, that's all politics is. Nothing but a family extended to a clan extended to a tribe extended to a territory. Nothing more, believe me.

"Instead of Balzic or Livingood, it's Democrat or Republican, and Depublican or Remocrat. An extended family to be sure. Believe me, when I first arrived in Harrisburg, I was dragging along all these stupid prejudices — not that a prejudice is ever anything else — I was dragging all this baggage I'd heard all my life about Democrats. Where I came from nobody even used the word when they talked about them. I began to believe my genetics actually made it impossible for my mouth to form the word *Democrat*. But once I got to Harrisburg, once I saw that without nametags it was impossible to tell one party affiliation from another, I began to study them like they were any other group. Affiliation was the keyword for me.

43

Filia means brother. You can't talk about a brother without thinking family. You just can't."

Balzic mulled this over for a long time, all the while studying the well-tanned face of the man who'd been lecturing him. Livingood was either the best con man Balzic had ever met or he was the real article, a man having the time of his life working in a culture he never knew existed until he'd plunged into it headfirst.

Finally, after a long moment, Balzic said, "You know, I been lookin' at you for a while now. I can't figure out whether you're forty-five or fifty-five or what."

Livingood threw his head back and laughed, exposing very white, very even teeth. "Johnson warned me, I'll give him that. Here I sit, giving you my best definition of politics, and you're sitting there guessing my age. What difference does that make?"

"I always like to know how old people are, 'cause that way I know when they start talkin' about somethin' whether they ever lived through any of it or whether they're gettin' it outta books or movies or off the tube."

"Oh, Mario, surely the person with the most knowledge of an event is not the one who was most directly involved in it. Who has a better overall view of a football game, for example? The linemen, or the people sitting fifty rows up?"

"I personally can't stand football. But to answer your question, no doubt the guy sittin' fifty rows up got a better view, but if he was never in a game

44

himself he wouldn't have a clue what's goin' on down there, I don't care how good he could see it.

"Lemme give you a different example. I been readin' court decisions about arrest, probable cause, search and seizure, and stuff like that, all my adult life. Every one I ever read, I knew the person who wrote it had never done the thing he was writin' about. All those decisions and opinions were written by people who had never spent one fucking second of their life doin' what they were writin' about. What's more, they weren't writin' 'em for the poor bastards who had to change what they did because of what was written. These things, they were written for other judges, for other lawyers, people who had time to sit around and bullshit about it over coffee. They weren't written for the people who had to change the way they acted because of what was on the paper. Which in my opinion is the biggest single reason everybody's so pissed off about law enforcement right now. And that's why I wanna know how old you are. I wanna know whether you were alive when somethin' happened, or whether you just saw it in the movies. It's a personal thing, that's all."

Livingood nodded, smiled, and held up his hands, palms up. "Well. I guess I know what you think of my profession. Sometimes I'd have to agree with you. But we need to talk about this another time. Right now, back to my original purpose. Will you think about taking the job?"

45

"Well hell, you gotta give me more information than what you've given me so far. Who do I report to?"

"You report to me. No one else."

"What kinda records do I keep and how do I keep 'em?"

"Talk them into a tape recorder is my advice. You don't have one I'll get you one. Record everything that way, don't put anything on paper. Send the tapes to me, I'll have my staff type them out."

"Where do I send them?"

"For the next couple of days I'll be at this address in Pittsburgh." Livingood picked his card up off the bar and printed another address and phone on the back and handed it to Balzic. "Afterwards, send everything to Harrisburg."

"I have to carry a piece? If I do, forget it. I didn't carry one the last twenty-four years, I'm not gonna start now."

Livingood laughed. "Strictly Q and A. No guns, I promise."

"Okay, so, uh, how much am I gonna get paid?"

Livingood stood up, went and got his topcoat, and put it on. He came back and said, "I'm sorry. I keep forgetting. I've had to learn more than once how rude it is to act as though money's not important. You'll be paid thirty-five dollars an hour, plus expenses, uh, including a car and driver if you want one, which I take it you don't. You use your own car, you get twenty-six cents

46

a mile, or whatever the going rate is, I'm not exactly sure. All meals, all lodging, just submit documentation, nobody's going to question it. Believe me, whatever you spend will be less than the shell off one peanut compared with what's already been spent."

"Thirty-five an hour?" Balzic said, his mouth dropping. He was delighted to be collecting his FOP pension. Two thousand dollars a month for doing nothing, plus all of what Medicare didn't cover, was as near to financial heaven as he thought he was ever going to get. Or deserved to get. And now a stranger had walked up to him and offered him — how much? He tried to act like people paid him thirty-five dollars an hour every day.

"Hey, Vinnie," Balzic said after Livingood had left, "how much is thirty-five times eight?"

"See what happens when you don't pay attention in school? Whatsamatter with you? Two-eighty. What, that chooch offerin' you a job or somethin', huh?"

"Somethin' like that. Wonder if that would cut into my pension. If you're younger'n seventy, you make money it cuts into Social Security, right? Am I right or not?"

"What the fuck do I know? I look like I'm on Social Security to you?"

"Never thought to ask about that. If it screws up my FOP pension I can't do it. Shit. Sounded kinda interesting. Get me outta the house anyway. Christ knows, I don't find somethin' to do outside the house pretty soon, Ruthie's gonna divorce me, or kill me. Fucker never did tell me how old he was."

Driving home from Muscotti's, Balzic debated how to tell Ruth. She wanted him out of the house, she didn't want him back in law enforcement. She loves me, she loves me not; she wants me home, she doesn't want me in the house; she wants me to help around the house, she doesn't want me taking her jobs away from her; she wants me to cook, she doesn't want me to rearrange the pots or the spice jars; she's glad I'm trying to learn how to bake bread, she doesn't think I need to buy flour every time I go to the Food-4-Less just 'cause it's forty cents cheaper than the Giant Eagle. Oh man, how come nobody ever gets you ready for anything important? Nobody ever gets you ready to be a husband after the honeymoon's over, nobody gets you ready to be a parent after you bring the kids home from the hospital, nobody tells you the hardest part of any job is dealing with the people you have to work with. Jesus, I wish I was starting over. All the things I would've done different. . . .

"Everybody says that and everybody lies," Ruth said. "You just want to think you would've done something different." She dumped the clothes hot from the dryer on the kitchen table and started to fold them.

"I would've read a lot more," Balzic said. "I would've asked a lot more questions. I

wouldn't've been so goddamn proud of my ignorance, man, what a joke that was. Don't ever let
anybody see you don't know how to do something, hell no, they'll see ya with your pants down,
see your little pee-pee hangin' out there, see how
small it is."

"I know I shouldn't be the one telling you this,
Mar, but you were very concerned with how small
your pee-pee was."

"Who was talkin' about me? Me? Concerned?
Bullshit."

"Oh, really? Then tell me how come you didn't
ask all these questions you think if you had it to
do over again you would ask? C'mon, I wanna
hear this."

"I wasn't ever worryin' about the size of my
joint —"

"Well you're the one who said that just now,
not me. You're the one who made the connection
between being afraid of asking questions, being
afraid of looking foolish or ignorant, and the size
of your pee-pee. That wasn't me said that. I'm
just repeating what you said."

"I wasn't talkin' about myself specifically. I was
talkin' generally. That's how most other guys
strike me. That's how they've always struck me.
That's why they act the way they do. Don't wanna
ask anybody anything. That's the problem I had
in the beginning with every guy I ever hired."

"But it didn't bother you, oh no. Not you."
Ruth piled folded towels and washcloths in her
left arm and set a pile of folded underwear and

socks on top of that and headed off for the bath-room and bedroom.

"Whatta ya mean it didn't bother me — I just said it bothered me, but it didn't bother me spe-cifically about the size of my peanuts. I was speakin', uh, whattayacallit, symbolically. You tryin' to tell me now there was a time I was actually worryin', I mean out loud? About the size of my peanuts? That I don't remember."

"You don't remember lots of things, Mar. You remember what you want to, and what you don't want to, you don't. A highly selective memory, that's what you have."

"Aw well shit, who doesn't? Everybody does that. You're no different. You're the same as me about that."

"Don't try to turn this around on me. I didn't start this, you did."

Balzic rubbed his mouth several times and cleared his throat.

"What's the matter with you?" Ruth said, clos-ing the underwear drawer in the chest on her side of the king-sized bed and coming around and holding out a stack of his shorts and T-shirts to him.

He took a long time fumbling around putting his underwear away, and when he turned around she was looking at him with her tongue against her upper teeth and lip.

"What?"

"I said, 'What's the matter with you?' Now you turn around and say, 'What?' You want to tell

50

me something, tell me. What do you want to tell me?"

"What makes you think I wanna tell you anything?"

"You're following me around, that's what. When you don't want to talk to me anymore you go some other direction. Wherever I'm not goin'. That's what. You followed me in here, so? What?"

"Uh, yeah, guess I did. Follow you," Balzic said, chewing the inside of his lips. "Uh, you know how we seem to be, uh, you know, gettin' on each other's nerves a lot lately?"

Ruth snorted a laugh and rolled her eyes. "Getting on each other's nerves? Is that what you call it? Jesus God, Mario, we've had some of the worst fights we've ever had and we're 'getting on each other's nerves'? In our whole married life, we never had fights like we've had since you're home all the time."

"Hey, I'm not home all the time, I go out."

"Mario, there you go. Stop being defensive. When I said you're home all the time, that was not an accusation. That was a statement of fact. And you immediately respond, God, the first words out of your mouth, 'I'm not home all the time. I go out.' I wasn't starting anything, Mario. I'm not accusing you of staying home, okay? Staying home is not a crime. I was merely trying to tell you when it was — you know? — *when* we've had our problems? I was trying to set a time frame for you. I'm agreeing with you, and you're trying

— oh shit, never mind. I swore I wasn't going to do this anymore. Just tell me what you want to tell me. Please? Just say it."

"Aw man, I hate this. I hate these conversations, you said, I said, you meant, I meant, you think, I think —"

"Just tell me what you want to tell me, okay? Please? You followed me in here. That's my clue. That's what tips me off you want to tell me something. For God's sake, tell me."

"Okay okay, I'll tell ya. I was in Muscotti's today, Vinnie tells me some guy's lookin' for me. He no sooner says it'n this guy comes in, uh, he's dressed like he stepped off the cover of some men's fashion magazine. Got this great tan, fingers all manicured. Introduces himself, gives me his card." Balzic didn't know how to say the rest.

"And?"

"Well, see, turns out he's a deputy attorney general. For the state, you know."

"And?"

"And, uh. We started talkin', you know? He introduces himself. And uh —"

"He did that already."

"Did what? Huh?"

"Introduced himself. You said it twice. Why don't you just say it, Mario. Just say the words. Say it, 'He offered me a job.' "

"Huh? How'd you know that? What, he call here? Vinnie would never've called you'n told you that. That guy call here?"

"Nobody called here, Mar. Nobody is spying

52

on you. I do not have agents out behind your lines reporting on every conversation you have, either with other people or with yourself. God, Mar, you were paranoid enough when you were a cop, you're worse now. What else do you think I think you'd have such a hard time trying to tell me? The only thing you could possibly have a harder time talking about is sex."

"I do not have a hard time talkin' about sex, what're you talkin' about?"

"Stop it! Forget about sex. I'm sorry I said the word. I'm sorry I said anything — never mind. Forget about that — tell me about the job he offered you. I know he offered you a job. I know that's what you're stumblin' around about. Tell me about *that*. Please. Please?"

"Man, these conversations get tougher all the time, I swear."

"Mario? The job? Just tell me one thing: are we gonna have to move? 'Cause if we're gonna have to move, I'm telling you right now the only place I'm moving to is Florida. I'm not moving someplace else in this state. I'm not gonna do all that work packing, just to move to some other place I'm gonna freeze. I can freeze right here in Rocksburg."

"No we ain't gonna have to move. I'm nowhere near sure I wanna take this job, but for sure if I do, that's not even a consideration, movin'. I'll do it from right here. Just have to drive, that's all. But I don't even have to do that if I don't want to. He says they'll give me a car — with a driver if I want one. But see, that ain't the thing. The thing is, this thing he wants me to do, it's a mess. It's like seventeen years old."

"So what's the job? What do they want you to do? What kind of a mess?"

"It's just a routine job, that's all."

"Routine? It's a real mess but it's routine? What does that mean?"

"Routine, routine, you know, interviewin' people. Like that. Some con wants a post-conviction hearing. It'd just be drivin' around interviewin' people, that's all."

Ruth leaned forward and peered up at him. "Routine? Some con, nobody in particular, just some con, he wants a post-conviction hearing and the state attorney general sends one of his deputies and this deputy walks into Muscotti's and offers you the job to interview people, and it's just routine? So why're you looking so down about it? Is it 'cause you think it's going to upset me?"

"Well, hey, you know, we had some real go-rounds about me not bein' a cop anymore. I mean, you remember those. You *do* remember those, right? Practically beggin' me to quit."

"Of course I remember. But this doesn't sound like what you used to do. Maybe I'm wrong, maybe you're leaving something out. You haven't told me a whole lot so far, you know? *Are* you telling me everything?"

"Hell no I'm not tellin' ya everything but that's 'cause I don't know everything. I think the guy was straight with me. I told him I'm not carryin' a piece, I told him I hate drivin', I told him I hate politics. He said it's a straight-ahead investigation of the facts, nothin' else. Only thing is, the grounds for the post-con appeal are a lot more recent, but all the rest's older'n dirt. And some cops are involved. A judge, too. Also a DA. It's in Wabash County."

"So if that's all it is, what're you hesitating about?"

"I don't know, it's, uh . . . ah that's bullshit, I do know. I didn't know how you were gonna take it. And I also don't know how it's gonna affect my pension. Guy offered me a lotta money. Thirty-five bucks an hour plus expenses."

They both fell silent, looking at each other, trying to read each other's eyes and face and body.

Ruth sat on the edge of the bed and said, "Are you waiting for my reaction?"

"You know that's exactly what I'm waitin' for."

She canted her head and picked lint off the quilt she was sitting on. "If it screws up your pension, what I think might not matter."

"C'mon, c'mon, don't screw around with me here. I can make one call to an FOP rep and find out about the pension. I wanna know what you think. What I think is — if you wanna know what I think before you say what you think — what I think is, all the noise and steam we been givin' each other, I think you oughta be jumpin' up and down happy over it. But lookin' at you now, I can't read ya. So you gotta say somethin'."

"Well it's up to you. It's got to be your decision —"

"Nah nah, nothin' doin'. Don't be weeniein' outta this. C'mon, don't do that. I wanna know what *you* think, not who's gonna make the decision. C'mon."

"Okay. Since you put it that way. What I think is, if one of us doesn't get out of this house for at least half the day, and pretty soon, we're going to wind up not being friends anymore. And I would hate that. Nothing I can think of would make me sadder. Or more scared. Or madder. Or more lonely. But I'd be lying if I said I liked the idea of you going back into the kind of work you used to do. I don't like that. At all.

"You say it's just routine, just interviewing people and you make it sound like it's nothing. But interviewing people like you do it and interviewing people like people have been doing it to me, God, when you do it, every time you ask somebody a question they could jump in your face. And I know you know that. Who knows it if you don't? But for me to think you're suddenly going to get offered some other kind of job, that's just stupid. Not at this stage of our lives.

"And God knows nobody's knocking down the door to hire me. I've been to five interviews — God, five, that's all it's been. Feels like a hundred and it's only been five. Shit. I don't even want to think about them. They were so, oh God, talking to people younger than Emily about a job, about what can I do. Mostly about what I don't know how to do. Anyway, where was I? Oh. So if anybody looks like they're going to get out of this house so we can keep on being each other's best friend, what can I say? You're the one. You're the one who's got something people want to pay for. Not me."

"Aw you're startin' to sound a little poor baby there, you know?"

"I'm not poor baby. It's the facts. You have skills to sell. You have ability, you have experience, you have a reputation, why else'd that guy come to you? He didn't come to me. That's not poor baby. That's the truth."

"So are you sayin' you're not gonna get all crazy on me if I take it?"

"What a way to put it, Mar, Jeez, thanks."

"Aw shit. Now who's gettin' defensive? Okay, so that wasn't the best way to say that. Lemme think. Okay, here. So are you saying you would not object if I gave this serious thought and eventually I decided to do it, is that what I'm hearin'?"

"Thank you. Yes. That's what you're hearing. I would not object. In fact, just the opposite. I'm encouraging you. Really. You need to do something, and I think what you would do would be very good for us. Because obviously, we have a whole lot to learn about how to live with each other. And I think nothing would be better for us than to spend part of the day apart so that when we do see each other, maybe we could get glad again, get happy again to see each other.

'Cause I think we've forgotten how much we used to miss each other. And now we never get a chance to miss each other. You never get a chance to feel how glad you are to come home. And I never get a chance to feel how glad I am to see you. So yes. Not only would I not object, I hope you do — take it. Honest. Take the job."

"Well. One nice thing. We ain't like a lotta people around here. We don't have to think about doin' it for the money. That's one thing I guess we should be glad for."

"Amen, Mar. Amen."

"So, uh, whatta you think? You up for a foot rub?"

"Oh God, my left foot hurts so bad."

"Hey, kick them booties off, cakes. Doctor Goodfoot is in."

Early Thursday morning, as promised, Deputy Attorney General G. Warren Livingood called Balzic at home, and they arranged to meet in Muscotti's within the hour. Livingood said he was still in Pittsburgh and he figured it would take him at least that long to say his good-byes to his hosts and to make the drive out. It was nine o'clock when Balzic hung up.

At five after ten, Livingood strode into Muscotti's, wearing dark blue: topcoat, suit, tie, socks, all some shade of navy blue. Only his shirt and teeth were white. The rest of him, phenomenally to Balzic, seemed tanner than the last time they'd met.

"You go to those, uh, tanning joints?"

"Beg your pardon?"

"Tanning joints, you know. Where you go there and lay down under special lights, get all tanned up? Like I know whether you lay down. For all I know they tie ya on a spit and barbecue ya."

Livingood found that very funny. He held up his right hand and looked at it. "Actually this is, uh, a residue of five very wonderful days in Boca Raton. That was two weeks ago."

Balzic shrugged. "I haven't been outta the States since I got outta the Marines."

Livingood started to laugh, then caught himself, leaned forward, and said gently, "Boca Raton's in Florida."

"Oh. Sounded, you know, Spanish. Figured it was in Mexico or someplace."

"Well it's certainly Spanish. My Spanish is practically nonexistent, but I think it means mouth of the rat. Whatever that means. Probably some geographical configuration that struck the Spaniards' fancy way back when. So. You're taking the job. Good. I'll tell you where all the records, or copies, I should say, of the records are kept. I warn you: there's a small mountain of print to get through —"

"Not so fast," Balzic said. "This is it? I'm hired? In a conversation in a saloon? Trust me, I don't do official business in saloons anymore. I made my last mistake doin' that right there." He pointed at the floor behind Livingood. "I suspended an officer, he was standin' right there.

Man, was that a mistake. FOP lawyer called me, said he was gonna do me a favor, he was gonna come to my house and chew me a new ass, he wasn't gonna do it in public. So he did. Came to my house, sat down in my kitchen, drank my coffee, chewed my ass for ten minutes about how unprofessional I was to do that and how goddamn lucky I was the officer didn't wanna pursue it. Worked out okay, the officer got another job in another state, but, man, for about ten minutes there I felt pretty stupid. So, uh, it's nice you feel comfortable hirin' me and all that, but if it's all the same to you, I want somethin' on paper. I mean, what happens three weeks from now you get hit by a car? You said I'm gonna report only to you, right? Isn't that what you said?"

"That's what I said, correct."

"So three weeks from now, I'm still reportin' to nobody but you, you get rear-ended by some drunk, you get whiplashed into a coma, then what? I mean, you're a political appointee, right? Am I right?"

"Exactly right."

"So say the governor fires your boss. Where's that leave you and me?"

"Life goes on, my friend. If I've learned anything in this job, I've learned that nobody's indispensable."

"My point. So?"

"And it's well taken. Believe me, you will be hired officially. You will take an oath. You will

60

get a shield. You will get a contract. Signed by my boss. We will sign it together. Whatever makes you comfortable. I apologize if by starting to talk about the particulars I made you in the least dubious about my professionalism, or my integrity. Or yours. If you prefer I will say nothing more until we get these other, very important matters taken care of. Is that what you want? We can do it right now. We can go to the DA's office, I'm sure they have a spare Bible we can use. I've got your shield in my briefcase, which is in my car, but we can pick it up on our way. I can have my boss fax a contract here, I'm sure the DA's fax machines work, it's up to you. And if you don't like the looks of fax machine paper, I'll have a contract messengered here this afternoon. Believe me, the one on fax paper will be as valid as the original."

Balzic nodded and said, "Okay, let's go."

And so they went to the Conemaugh County Courthouse, to the DA's office, where Livingood swore Balzic in as a special investigator, Attorney General's Office, Department of Justice, Criminal Division, Commonwealth of Pennsylvania. After the swearing, Livingood handed Balzic a gold shield in a black leather case, congratulated him, and told him where to send a mug shot so it could be affixed to the official ID card that would occupy the other half of the case. They sat around making small talk with one of the DA's staffers, waiting for the fax from Harrisburg. And when three copies came, Balzic and Livingood signed them all and faxed them back.

"No point sitting around here," Livingood said. "No telling when the AG'll get around to signing those. I mean, I know you know that I have full authority to make this contract with you. I just want you to feel comfortable that the AG is also going to sign it, but I'm not foolish enough to predict when he'll get around to doing that, that's all. So let's find someplace to talk."

"Okay if we go back to Muscotti's? You're not gonna find anyplace in this building. Not unless you wanna sit in the lobby, and everybody and his brother can hear every word you say down there."

"Muscotti's is fine. I love places like that. Let's go."

Once back there again, over coffee, Balzic thought about those words, *I love places like that,* and he debated with himself whether to say something or just let it go. Livingood probably didn't have any idea how that sounded, probably would fall all over himself apologizing for it, but Balzic couldn't help feeling that Livingood would be apologizing for reasons he didn't understand. Aw fuckit, Balzic thought. Let it go.

When they got settled over coffee at a table against the wall in Muscotti's, Livingood said, "So, now that you're hired, how soon do you think you can get started?"

"That depends how fast you get my bona fides straightened out."

"No, what I meant is, how soon can you start

62

reading? Remember? The mountain of print I told you about?"

"Mountain of print?" Balzic said. "Oh. The transcripts of the trials."

"Yes, not only every trial, every hearing, trial, mistrial, appeal, every deposition. I don't know how fast you read —"

Balzic shook his head. "I'm not gonna read it."

"You're not?" Livingood's brows rose. "Well. That's interesting. Why would you think you need not read it?"

"Well why would I? I mean, from what you said a coupla days ago, the principal problem that came up was the witness — the only one who was not a perpetrator — and this guy now claims he's got a citation for drunkenness that proves he was in Ohio at the time the murders happened so, uh, I mean, that document is being investigated, right?"

"Even as we speak, right, yes."

Balzic splayed his hands. "So if the answer's yes, I mean, if that citation's righteous, why would I have to read anything? I mean, why would you even bother to hire me if the document's righteous, that doesn't make sense."

"Well, logically, yes, that's true. But we can't build a puzzle with one piece. Besides which, I examined the document myself, and while I'm no expert by any means, not in any area of criminology, believe me, certainly not in any of the tests that the state police lab people are doing.

But I'm reasonably sure the citation is, as you put it, bullshit."

"Yeah? How're you certain?"

"Well instead of me answering that, you tell me what you would have done."

Balzic shrugged. "First thing I would've done, I wouldn't've sent it to the lab. I'da called the PD in Ohio and asked 'em to check the numbers and dates on their citation books. If it's a phony, it woulda been out of sequence, either the number or the date, or both, case closed. Whose idea was it to send it to the lab? What do they think the lab guy's gonna do?"

"The previous investigator. The one you're replacing. Who was hired by my predecessor, a man who really didn't have anywhere near the background in criminal work he'd let on."

"Oh. Well. Lotta that goin' around."

"Unfortunate, but true, yes. As far as I'm concerned, however, trying to get lab verification of that document looked like doctors ordering every test remotely associated with a set of symptoms just because each test eliminates one more cause of potential liability. Might be wise for an MD who's having trouble keeping up his malpractice premiums, but, from my point of view, it's just more time wasted. And more money."

"Uh, I probably shouldn't be sayin' this here, but, uh, I mean, lookin' at you, you know, you don't sound like you got a whole hellofa lot of criminal experience yourself."

"I don't. Believe me. But I never pretended

that I did. Anyway, that's why I hired you. So tell me, please, I'm very interested. Why don't you want to read the case record?"

"Look, you start readin' how other people did an investigation, no way you can dodge their prejudices. And we all have 'em, I don't care what anybody says. 'Cause that's how we get to be who we are. Point is, I'm comfortable with my prejudices, 'cause they're mine and I know they're mine. I read this, uh, this mountain you're talkin' about, I'm dealin' with other people's prejudices there, but I don't know what they are. And people have strange prejudices, man.

"I don't wanna bore you, but lemme tell ya about this call we got one time, some people said they hadn't seen this guy for a while. Lived in a row house in the Flats, that's a neighborhood down by the river, mostly Slavic people livin' there. Anyway, I open up the guy's front door a crack, I smelled somethin' dead right away. Got inside, man, that place was a junkyard. Newspapers up to the ceiling, old shoes, old clothes, cans, bottles, magazines. There were places you could put your feet down, that's all the floor you could see.

"Couple days later, landlord sent people in to clean it up, they found somethin' like two hundred thousand dollars, no bill bigger'n a twenty. Money stuck everywhere. They'd open up magazines, every coupla pages they turned, there'd be a five, a ten, a twenty stuck in there. This was 1958. I'm talkin' serious money. And all his neighbors could say was oh how poor he was. But my point isn't what his neighbors thought, or what I thought.

"It was what *he* thought. Because no matter how much money he had, this guy, in his mind, he was dirt-floor poor. Only relative I could find was his sister, and she nailed it, she said, 'My brother would rather live destitute than be destitute.' Told me how they'd been real poor when they were kids and then after he started makin' a livin' for himself, he lost all his savings when his bank folded in 1929. So he trapped himself. Wouldn't put his money in a bank and he wouldn't spend it. Now that's what I mean by prejudice. That man let what happened to him blind him to what money was for. Had this huge pile of money, could've lived any way he wanted, but what he saw had nothin' to do with what he was convinced he saw. The oldest con there is, but that doesn't make it any less true.

"So I'd be wastin' my time readin' that stuff. Afterwards now, after I talk to everybody, then maybe it might make sense to read it, but no way I'm gonna read it before."

"You *might* read it afterwards? You're not *sure* you would? That's interesting. Why not?"

"Look, if I do it right, if I find out what you need, I mean, you have to go one way or the other, right? Up or down, either the guy has grounds for a new trial or he doesn't, right? I mean, that's what the p-c hearing's for, right?"

"Right."

66

"So what I'm gonna do for you is collect information so you can make that decision, right? I mean, we're not tryin' the case here, the guy's just askin' for a new trial? Right?"

"Right."

"So I'm not gonna pretend I'm up on all the rules of procedure about p-c hearings, but I think you're gonna tell me sooner or later that the rules are pretty much the same as a prima facie test at a prelim, right?"

"Not quite. But close enough, yes."

"Well, there ya are. So, uh, where's the con who wants the hearing, where's he?"

"Matter of fact, he's right here in this county jail. Up until last week he was in Pittsburgh."

"Oh, great, good."

"Great? Why?"

" 'Cause I hate Pittsburgh."

"You hate Pittsburgh?" Livingood laughed until he coughed.

"Not the city, no. The state correctional facility there. Depresses the shit outta me. Only place ever depressed me more'n that was a Marine Corps cemetery. On Iwo Jima. Least that was outside. But I don't even like drivin' in there to Pittsburgh. I don't like parkin' there, I don't like goin' through the metal detectors there, I can't stand the smell of that fuckin' place. I hate the noises there."

"When were you there last? It's been remodeled, you know. More than once. I'm told it doesn't look anything like it looked, as recently as ten years ago."

"It has? I didn't know that. Ah, I don't care, just the thought of that place, I mean, to me, I get in there, honest to God — I don't have to get in there, just thinkin' about that place makes me queasy. You don't know how glad I am to know he's out here. This joint's still so new, still smells like paint and concrete, you know?"

"Well I see that you are honest at least about your prejudices. Johnson said you were different. You are that. So. Anything else you want to discuss right now?"

"Well, I wanna know where everybody else is. Addresses, phone numbers, directions."

"Okay. That's easy. Anything else?"

"Yeah. How often you want me to report? Every day, every other day, when? You said I can talk it into a recorder, right?"

"Right. You have a recorder or do you want me to get you one?"

"Nah, I have one. Just need new tapes and need to plug in my battery recharger, that's all."

"Sounds to me like you're on your way."

"Nah, no, nothin' doin'. Before I go to work, I'm gonna have a letter in my pocket, you know? From you or your boss. And I'm gonna know that you been callin' around, establishin' my bona fides. I don't wanna get my balls busted by some corrections bureaucrat. I mean, so far, all I have is a shield and an empty ID case and a memory that you swore me in. I know the people in the county jail here, that's no problem, but all the principals can't be here, can they?"

"As a matter of fact, the witness — the one who says he was in Ohio? — he was supposed to've been transferred from Wabash County today. No. Friday. Tomorrow he'll be here. But I heard somebody say they were going to house him in the old county lockup, not the new one. But that's right here in town, isn't it? The old one? I was told it was."

"Yes it is. About three blocks from here. I thought they were only usin' it for DUIs and deadbeat dads. What about the cop? The one doin' ten to twenty?"

"He's in Southern Regional. He was in Huntingdon, but apparently somebody recognized him a couple of weeks ago, so he had to be transferred. So, really, all the principals are right here."

"You forgot one."

"I did?"

"Yeah. The shooter, right? The one who says he's gonna recant — where's he?"

"You're right, I did forget — oh, well, sorry, he *is* in Pittsburgh."

"Aw c'mon man, get him transferred, pull some strings, bully somebody, I'm not jokin'. I don't care they remodeled it, I really really hate goin' in there."

Livingood shrugged. "I make no promises."

"You don't have to promise, just try, okay? You got three, four days at least. It'll take me that long to get around to all the others."

"Why? There's only the three of them and they're all right here. I thought it would take you a day and a half maybe."

Balzic cleared his throat and looked at his shoes, trying to think how to say it. "Look, I'm not gonna read anything, I already told you that, but I am gonna wanna talk to Walker Johnson about this, if nothin' else, find out who was in charge of CID on this thing, understand?"

"Yes. Of course."

" 'Cause his prejudices I understand. Why isn't he doin' this, by the way?"

"Because he has plenty of other things to do."

"You sure that's the only reason? Weren't there some state cops involved in this?"

"Of course there were."

"No no, I don't mean that way. I know there were state cops investigatin' the murders, I'm talkin' about somethin' else."

"Then you should probably talk to Johnson."

"He didn't shy away from this thing?"

"It was never presented to him. I told you, he has other things to do."

Balzic studied Livingood for a long moment, wondering whether to push it about Johnson. Finally he said, "Look, it's gonna take me a while to figure out how to approach all these people, it's not gonna be, you know, heigh-ho heigh-ho it's off to work I go. Anyway, I still lost my bona fides when I retired, so even though a lotta these people know me, they're still gonna wanna see somethin' better'n a shield. I mean they know

I'm retired. Word gets around, you know?"

"Not anymore you aren't," Livingood said.

"Nah wait, you don't understand. I don't like bein' jagged off and I don't like jaggin' people off. If I'm goin' to interview an inmate in a prison, I know how those people are 'cause I'd be the same way —"

"Those people?"

"Corrections people. I show up with a shield and I'm not on anybody's visitor sheet, I don't care how well they know me, I'm not gettin' in. And I'm not gonna stand around explainin' and waitin' for somebody to call you when you still haven't put a signed contract in my hand and you still haven't called them, told 'em I'm comin' and why, you get me now?"

"Oh absolutely. And I will do those things. As soon as I get to my car phone I will call my secretary and dictate a letter and she will make copies and they will be faxed or express-mailed to all the right people. And you will have one. And then I will call them and tell them you're going to make the appointments, okay? Acceptable?"

"Okay. Fine. I'll give you a couple days and —"

"Couple days? No no. I'll have this taken care of within the hour. No, you give me until this afternoon, then you start making your appointments and tomorrow you go to work. Start keeping your time now."

Livingood stood, extended his right hand, and said, "Welcome aboard, Chief. I hope you'll be

71

patient with my lack of experience."

"Hey, I'm sure you know things I never even thought about knowin'. We'll be all right. Only one thing," Balzic said, right hand still at his side.

"What's that?"

"Take it easy with the iron-man grip, okay? I got a little arthritis in my fingers, you know?"

"Oh, certainly. Of course. I didn't hurt you, uh, before, did I? Tuesday?"

"Yeah you did. Gave me a two-aspirin handshake there."

"Oh I'm sorry. I wondered why you, uh, so, uh . . ."

"Why I just give you the limp fingers? Yeah, I try never to give anybody a real shot at me, but, uh, you got me pretty good anyway."

"Oh I really am sorry. Never happen again, I promise."

Balzic shrugged it off. He was already back to worrying about whether Walker Johnson was really doing something else.

On his way home, Balzic stopped at Lebrand's office supply store and bought three six-packs of sixty-minute tapes and four double-A batteries he figured he'd need until his rechargeables were ready. He also bought paper for his notebook, though he didn't know why he'd bothered because his handwriting had become so illegible he'd taken to a kind of pidgin printing, which while legible enough took much too long to do.

Once home, before he thought about lunch, he

hunted up his rechargeable batteries and re-charger, and plugged the recharger into a wall outlet on his side of the bed, popped the batteries in, and slid it under the bed. Then he put the batteries he'd just bought into his recorder and tested it and opened the packages the tapes came in and put the tapes in a sturdy envelope. He remembered a briefcase, one he hadn't used in years, and he thought it might be in his closet. He had to get on his knees and move many pairs of shoes and several boxes full of notebooks from the most recent cases he'd worked.

The briefcase was there, against the back wall of the closet, moldy on the back and down two sides, and so was the only thing in it, a blackjack. He took them downstairs, washed them with sad-dle soap, and dried them with an old towel. Up-stairs, he put everything including the blackjack into the briefcase, and started to walk out toward the kitchen but caught sight of himself in a mirror. He looked at himself for a long moment. He shook his head and started to laugh, and he was still smiling when he walked into the kitchen and found Ruth and asked what she had in mind for lunch, if anything.

"My stomach's all funny," she said, rubbing it and looking in a cupboard at some canned soups.

"Least you're gettin' some laughs out of it," Balzic said. "I smell sardines. You just eat some? We got any more?"

"I finished the last can about ten minutes ago."

"You think maybe that's why your stomach's doin' jokes?"

"Maybe it was the scallions."

"Take a couple Titralac, you'll be okay. What else we got here? I don't know what I'm hungry for."

"I don't want Titralac," Ruth said. She looked at him for a long moment. "Don't you think you should tell me something?"

"Huh? Tell you what."

"It's Thursday. I heard the phone this morning. I heard you talking to somebody. You've been gone since quarter to ten. Isn't there something you want to tell me?"

Balzic drew his chin back and scowled. "What? What'd I do now?"

"It's not what you did. It's what you haven't done. Are you going to tell me you've been sitting around Muscotti's all morning but you didn't see that guy from the attorney general's office?"

"Oh yeah yeah, course I saw him. Been with him all morning. Since ten o'clock anyway."

"And?"

"I took the job. Yeah. I'm on the clock right now."

"Oh Jesus Christ, Mario, did you — do you think maybe I might want to know that?"

"Well you knew I was gonna take it. I mean, what the hell were we talkin' about a coupla days ago? In the bedroom, right? Remember?"

"That was — our conversation in the bedroom — that was you were offered the job. That was

— that conversation in the bedroom — that was I had no objection to you taking the job. That was not a definite absolutely yes you had taken it! And that was Tuesday! Remember? This is Thursday?"

Balzic threw up his hands. "I took it, I took it. I went to see the guy this morning, he swore me in, we went down the courthouse, they zipped a contract back and forth in their fax machines there, and then, uh, we went back to Muscotti's, we said how it was gonna work, and, uh, then I went and bought some tapes and batteries and notebook paper and then I come in here and you're tellin' me your stomach's all funny and now you're all pissed off at me again 'cause I said somethin' wrong or I didn't say somethin' or I did somethin', Jesus Christ, Ruth, I mean what the fuck. I mean I'm gonna get outta the house now, you won't be trampin' on me every time you wanna sweep the rugs, I thought this was fine with you —"

"Mario, listen to me. This *is* fine with me. But I would like to be told *when it was time* for it to be fine with me. And the only person who could have told me when it was time is you. And you didn't. You come dancin' in here sniffin' around 'cause you think you smell sardines — and you don't say one goddamn word about what you been doin' until I have to drag it out of you! Jesus, you make me crazy sometimes!"

Balzic let his hands fall against his legs. "Look, I'm sorry I didn't tell you —"

"I don't want your sorries! I want you to think a little bit about me before you go off on your own, living your own private life inside your head there. 'Cause if you're not gonna think about me when there's gonna be a major change in our lives because of something you're gonna do, then maybe . . . God, why don't you see these things? I'm not asking so much, do you think I'm asking so much? I mean, Mar, do I? If I do, tell me, 'cause I don't think I do." She had backed against the sink and was hugging herself.

Balzic blew out a long sigh and shook his head. "I don't know. I just, you know, I mean I figured we already talked about it. So, takin' the job, shit, that was like a formality, that's all —"

"That's all! My God, Mar, what have we been doing for the last three months? I mean, after we got home from Florida, what have we been doing? You being here, God, our lives turned upside down —"

"Upside down? Me? Just bein' here? Jesus, that's some way to put it."

"There is no other way to put it!"

"Aw come on."

"No no. Listen," Ruth said, trying hard to find the words. "Listen, Mar. I lost something I didn't even know I had, something I didn't even know I wanted. I didn't even know it was something I could want. I mean, when your mother died I thought I was gonna go crazy bouncing off the walls in here, but, God, afterwards, I found something I never knew I had —"

"What, what? Tell me already, Jesus."

"I lost my privacy."

"Lost your what?" Balzic was incredulous.

"My privacy, yes. I found myself here eight, ten, sometimes, twelve hours a day, by myself. Alone. And I really loved it. It was something I never knew about, Mar. Mar, don't look at me that way. Please. I'm not telling you I want to be alone, I'm not tellin' you I don't want you here —"

"Well if you ain't, it sure as hell sounds like it."

"No no no, that's not what I'm saying! Please listen, Mar. There are things I do — did, I mean, I didn't do them — I don't do them when you're here."

Balzic stared at her. "You do things when I'm not here? What things?"

"Mar, you're starting to get really mad, I can see it. You're taking this the wrong way — try to listen and see if maybe you can put yourself in my place for a while, just for a little while, that's all I'm asking."

"I'm not gettin' mad, goddammit. Sometimes, Ruth, honest to Christ, sometimes you act like I'm the biggest asshole in the world — just tell me what you're tryin' to tell me, okay? And if I can put myself in your place I'll do it and if I can't I'll tell ya —"

"Okay," she said, running her tongue over her lips and sighing. "I, sometimes when you're not here — uh, do you remember what I used to do when I was little?"

"I didn't know you when you were little —"

"I know you didn't know me when I was little — wait a minute! This is something I told you about. I'm wondering if you can remember what it is, that's all."

"Why don't you just tell me what it is, okay? Don't give me a test, I hate that."

"I wanted to dance, Mar, remember? I wanted to take lessons, but my parents couldn't afford lessons, so I never got any. But after Ma died and when you weren't here, uh, before you retired, I had the whole house to myself. Oh, God, you're looking at me like I'm some crazy woman —"

"Just stop that right now. I am not lookin' at you like you're a crazy woman. Just tell me what you wanna tell me —"

"Okay, all right. When you're not here, when I found myself alone here, I turned the radio on and, uh, I danced." She shrugged and held her shoulders up for a long time and shook her head and finally let her shoulders drop.

"You danced?"

"Yes."

"And so, what? 'Cause I'm home now you can't do this anymore, is that what you're tellin' me?"

"Yes."

Balzic snorted. "Well excuse me, but that doesn't sound like it's my problem. That sounds like it's your problem. I mean if you wanna dance, hey, dance — I ain't stoppin' ya. This is the first time I heard anything about it."

"But to do it I have to have music."

"So?"

"So you never play the radio. You almost never play any of our records. Anytime you listen to music, which is mostly the blues 'cause that's what you mostly listen to anymore, I mean, if you wanna do that, you put a tape in your Walkman and I never hear it. You go downstairs and I hear you playing your harmonica, but I never hear what you're listening to."

"So what're you tryin' to say?"

"I'm trying to say that when I found out I had the whole house to myself, I turned the radio on, and I turned it on real loud, and I danced to the kind of music I felt like dancing to, that's what I'm trying to say."

"So whatta ya sayin'? I turned the radio off? I mean, who turned the radio off? Me or you? I didn't pull the plug on the radio. You sayin' it was me just bein' here, huh? Just because I was here, huh? I made you not turn the radio on?"

"Yes. Exactly."

"Oh come on, what the fuck, I didn't even know you wanted to do this, uh, this dancin'. You never said anything to me about it. And this whole conversation started 'cause you got pissed at me 'cause I forgot to say anything about takin' the job, remember? At least I think that's what we were talkin' about."

"Right right, that's exactly right —"

"So now you're pissed at me 'cause I didn't tell you somethin' about me, on top of which you're

79

also pissed at me for bein' here 'cause that inter-feres with you dancin', which is somethin' you never said a word about till now, but I'm sup-posed to know how much I changed your life 'cause I'm home and you can't play the radio. Is that pretty much it? Or is there somethin' else? I musta done somethin' else since I come home today, Christ . . ."

"Mario, stop shouting. You're shouting, and I told you I don't want to be shouted at anymore."

"I'm not shouting!" he shouted. And then he took two deep breaths and lowered his voice. As quietly as he could manage, he said, "Listen, Ruthie, I ain't stoppin' you from doin' things you wanna do. I never knew anything about this dancin'. I mean, you can't hold somethin' against me if I don't know about it. I mean, I'll take the rap for not tellin' ya I took the job. I shoulda told ya, no argument, I shoulda. But, hell, I don't have any experience at tellin' ya about stuff like that. I already had a job when we got married and I never got another one. Remember?"

"I remember very well," she said.

"So I didn't — you know, I didn't have any experience. I know, I know, that's no excuse. I mean, me bein' here has caused us some mondo problems, so I shoulda figured out that not bein' here anymore would cause some more prob-lems —"

"It's not that it's gonna cause problems, Mar. It's just that this is another major major major change for us. Again. And I wanted you to rec-

80

ognize that. And tell me without me havin' to drag it out of you —"

"Oh. Yes. Right. Like you told me about dancin', right? Is that how you don't wanna drag it outta me?"

"Mario, cut it out, you're bein' a real wiseass now."

"Well, Ruthie, maybe that's 'cause that's what I feel like right now. 'Cause, see, I have this little tiny problem with all this, uh, this, uh, whatever it is I do that's suddenly invadin' your privacy. I know it's just a little thing, but it happens to be true —"

"Oh God, Mar, you should see how you're looking at me —"

"Hey, if I look pissed it's 'cause I am pissed. Which doesn't change this one thing I'm talkin' about, which is — and I'm tellin' you just in case it mighta slipped your mind — you're not the only person who lives here. I live here too. So while I'm at it, hey, you want me to move all the pots and pans back where they used to be? Fine, just say the word —"

"Cut it out, Mar, we worked that out already. I don't care that you moved the pans —"

"How 'bout the spice jars, huh? You want me to put all the spice jars back where they used to be? Just say the word."

Ruth hugged herself tighter and looked at the floor and shook her head. "Mario, we've been through all this. I'm glad you're cooking more. I'm glad you're learning how to bake bread. I'm glad you're doing a lot of things I used to do. I don't want to fight those fights all over again about where the pots and pans would be easier to get to, or whose job it is to do anything around here, read my lips, I do not want to fight those fights all over again. I just want you to recognize that your being here was a major change in our lives. Both our lives. And now there's gonna be a major change again, and I want you to recognize that, that's all I'm saying. And I would've known that you recognized it if you had just told me about it, that's all I'm saying."

"That's all, huh? All I woulda had to do was tell you?"

"That's all."

"So okay. I'm telling ya. I took the job. I could start right now if I found out I had my bona fides in order. But I'm gonna tell you somethin' else right now. This job's only good for a couple weeks at the most, maybe not even that. I don't see it goin' beyond two weeks, and that's gonna be stretchin' it. So we're gonna be right back where we are in two weeks, far as I can see. So if you wanna play the radio loud so you can dance, you better start figurin' out how we're gonna work that. There's just one thing I want you to know."

"I know it, Mar. I know it already, you don't have to say it."

"Well I wanna say it, okay? 'Cause I want it to be out in the open where we can both see it, okay?"

"If you wanna say it, go ahead."

"I would never turn the radio off. I would never tell you to stop dancin'. God, Ruth, if you don't know that about me, if you don't know I'd try to make it easier for you to do what you wanted to do, whatever it is, I mean, Jesus, then we need to see a pro 'cause we can't fix what's broken here."

"It's not broken, Mar. It's just got some dents in it, that's all. We can fix it."

He believed her words. It was her tone and expression that worried him. It was still worrying him when he called Conemaugh County Detention Center to find out if his name had been put on Lester Walczinsky's visitor sheet yet.

Going through the metal detectors at the new Conemaugh County Detention Center, Balzic set them beeping, which got the attention of the corrections officer standing in the small, window-enclosed office to the right, just inside the front door. The CO told Balzic to step back through and place everything metallic he was carrying in one of the trays on the table between the detectors. "Unless you have a weapon. If you do, please step forward now and place it in the box I'm opening. Otherwise, go back through and try it again."

"Don't have a weapon," Balzic said, setting every metal thing he had on him in the plastic tray, coins, keys, pens, wristwatch, tape recorder, and Swiss army knife. He passed through the detector again, silently this time, and carried the tray over to the open metal box set into the wall just below the windows of the CO's office. Then Balzic took everything out of the tray except his knife and keys. The CO pushed a button that closed and withdrew the box, put Balzic's keys and knife in an envelope, and passed a property sheet back out for Balzic to sign. Balzic put his shield and his contract inside the box with the signed property sheet and waited.

After the CO had given the contract a quick once-over, he said, "What's your business here, sir?"

"I'm here to interview an inmate. Lester Walczinsky. I confirmed that with the deputy warden of operations about an hour ago. He said he'd put me on Walczinsky's visitor sheet. Am I on there?"

"One second, sir. Mario Balzic? With the attorney general's office?"

Balzic nodded.

The CO set shield and contract in the tray and sent it back out, and said, "Just let me check and make sure they're bringin' him and where they're bringin' him to." He picked up the phone and spoke briefly into it and then said to Balzic, "They're bringin' him to the interview room at the end of the corridor on your right as you face that wall on your left. You familiar with the electronic doors here, sir? You been here before?"

"Only once since I got a tour before it opened. I stand in front of the door at both ends of the corridor, right, and somebody checkin' me out on the monitors opens 'em, right?"

"That's correct, sir. Well, the interview room you want will be at the end of the first corridor on your left as you exit the corridor, and it will be the second room on your left. There'll be a CO waitin' for you. He will want to inspect that tape recorder. He may even wanna pat you down."

Balzic shrugged, thanked the CO, and walked to the far wall and stood by the door leading to the corridor on the right. Almost at once it was buzzed open, and he stepped into the narrow corridor and headed for the other end, the door shutting behind him solidly and heavily with a hiss from its pneumatic arm. At the other end of the corridor, there was a TV camera above the door. He looked over his shoulder and saw another camera above the door he'd just come through. He waited at the far end until that door buzzed open, and then he stepped out into a slightly wider corridor, with glassed-in rooms on both sides. Two of the rooms were each occupied by eight or so inmates who looked to Balzic like they were involved in some therapy session, or a Junior Achievement meeting, or a high school equivalency course.

The rooms were oddly shaped, set at odd angles because the whole building was a series of octagons poking out of the central tower where he was now, and this tower was itself an octagon. A CO, young, his shirt bulging with muscles in his arms, shoulders, and neck, was standing outside the door to the second room on the left. He said, "You with the state attorney general?"

"That's me."

"See your ID please?"

Balzic showed shield, contract, and driver's license, and studied the inmate studying him back on the other side of the windows on Balzic's left.

"You're here to interview an inmate, is that correct?" the CO said, handing Balzic's ID back.

"Right. Lester Walczinsky."

"Your man's right there. Would you empty your pockets, please?"

Balzic did, and held everything out for the CO to inspect. The CO took the tape recorder, asked how to open it, and gave it a quick inspection after Balzic told him how. The CO returned Balzic's recorder and said, "You need anything, there's a button on the wall right about six inches above the end of the table there, you see it?"

Balzic nodded.

"You need anything or when you get ready to leave, hit the button. Otherwise, you're locked in, understand?"

"Yeah. Uh, is he a smoker, Walczinsky? Allowed to smoke in there?"

"That's up to you, we got no policy about it. Supposed to get one. Word is some asshole who don't have to work here thinks we oughta go smokeless. But if you can stand the smoke, it's up to you. Oh, one more thing. He won't respond to that name, Walczinsky. Made a huge fucking deal out of it when he got here. I forget what he wants to be called, but he won't answer to Walczinsky."

"Oh. Okay. Thanks for tellin' me," Balzic said, going in after the CO unlocked the door. He put his tape recorder on the table and draped his raincoat over the back of a chair opposite Walczinsky, as the CO was closing and locking the door.

Balzic sat and studied Walczinsky, who, like many other cons, was muscular from years of lifting weights, but not bulky so much as ropy, sinewy, with thick veins in his hands, arms, and neck. His wavy brown hair was graying, and grew down to the top of his shirt collar. His cheeks were sunken and deeply lined. He had a bluish cast to his face where he shaved, and he had piercing brownish-black eyes, eyes that blinked seldom and wavered even less seldom from Balzic's eyes. It was a look Balzic had seen many times in his life, first among Marines on Iwo Jima, and later among coal miners who'd survived a roof fall, or firemen who'd had a floor drop out from under them or a roof come down on top, or women who'd been gang-raped or had been beaten for years by men they'd thought they could trust.

Balzic had also seen it many times among cons, especially those who'd done time locked away from others, no matter by what bureaucratic euphemism it was called: special housing, or re-stricted housing, or isolated housing, or solitary confinement. Balzic believed there was nothing to compare for creating that look artificially than purposely forcing a con to stare into a mirror that wasn't there. The look had a name, different maybe in different parts of the country, but Balzic knew it as the thousand-yard stare; and once he'd seen it on Iwo Jima, once it had been seared into his memory there, he recognized it everywhere else he saw it. And once he'd seen it, he didn't care whose face he saw it on or where they were when he saw it, his heart went out to whoever was behind that stare despite everything else he knew about that person. It was one of his prejudices, one he was comfortable knowing about, but one he knew he couldn't let get out of control here or he might as well be interviewing a bag of gravel.

"I hear you're not answerin' to your name these days, is that true?"

"Who are you?"

"My name's Balzic —"

"I know what your name is. Deputy Attorney General Livingood told me that when he told me he was sendin' an investigator and I should cooperate. So I'm cooperating. But I still wanna know who you are. You showed your shield and your papers to the screw, but you didn't show 'em to me."

Balzic thought that over for a moment, then put his shield, contract, and driver's license on the table for Walczinsky to read. He took reading glasses out of a case in his shirt pocket, put them on, and spent a long time hunched over the contract. When he straightened up he said, "All this says is you were hired. Doesn't say who you are."

"How much history you want?"

"How much you got?"

"Well, I was a police officer from 1947 to 1993. And for twenty-four years I was chief of the department in Rocksburg."

"So you were mostly an administrator. Mostly you were not an investigator."

"I did my share. In a department my size, everybody did everything."

"Yeah? Well see, what I need is an investigator who did more than his 'share.' What I need —"

"Stop right there. I was sent here, not by you, but by a deputy attorney general 'cause he wanted me to interview you."

"I understand where you think you're comin' from," Walczinsky said, his gaze unblinking, unwavering. "What you have to understand is, I petitioned the Court of Common Pleas of Wabash County for a post-conviction hearing as is my right under Pennsylvania Rules of Criminal Procedure. The attorney general or any of his deputies, they didn't file that petition. I did. And it is my right to have those facts which I allege in my petition, it is my right to have them investigated by proper and competent authorities acting in my behalf because I am not, as you can see for yourself, in any position to investigate those facts by myself.

"And before you try to stop me from sayin'

anything else, Mister Balzic, I want you to know that for the last seventeen years I've read a lot of books and I've talked to a lot of people about the law. I don't have any degrees 'cause I never wanted to pass the tests. I never even graduated from high school. But I know when I'm bein' fucked with. I'm an expert. And I also know what to do about it.

"You work for the state. That means it's the state that's payin' you. But right now you're working for me. Because the state is working for me. Because the state has no choice about working for me. That's why I have every right to discuss your credentials as an investigator. So you tell me what they are."

"On-the-job training," Balzic said.

"What?" Walczinsky's mouth fell open. He canted his head incredulously.

"Plus I read a lotta books. And I talked to a lotta people. About the law. So, uh, except for the on-the-job training, I got the same credentials as you. Ain't that some shit, huh? Whattaya think?"

Walczinsky closed his mouth. He stiffened in his chair for a moment, then let out a long breath through his nose. Then he settled back, worked his tongue around a tooth for a moment, and said, "How many murders you investigate?"

"Enough."

"How many?"

"I never counted 'em."

"Well count 'em."

90

Balzic thought for a while. "I can't. I'd be guessin'. Anyway, murder's not accounting, not for me. And, as for people talkin' about any kind of crime numbers, far as I could tell, they always had some budget they wanted to increase or decrease, dependin' which way they were gonna get more out of it. Oldest scam there is, some police chief who wants new equipment? All he has to do is scare everybody about how, uh, how crime is a river risin' faster than his department can fill sandbags. And nobody cooks numbers better'n those bastards in Washington. They're the pros. Far as I'm concerned, when it comes to numbers, FBI oughta stand for Federal Bureau of Imagination. So if you've read so many books and talked to so many people, Mister Walczinsky, uh, why do you think the number of investigations has anything to do with the way anybody does 'em?"

"My name's Walin. That name you called me, that's my old name. My new name's Walin. Spelled just the way it sounds. And I didn't say anything about the quantity havin' anything to do with the quality. I just know as a general rule administrators don't know what investigators know. And you said you were a chief. For twenty-four years. That's all I'm goin' by. And thanks for takin' the trouble to learn my new name."

"Walin, is it? You're welcome, Mister Walin. Listen, I'm sure we could sit here for hours, goin' back and forth about our views on crime numbers, but, uh, why don't you just let me do my job, okay? And you can decide later on whether I meet your qualifications. I don't measure up, you can file another motion, write another petition, whattaya say?"

Walin hesitated, then shrugged. "Like I got a choice. Go 'head."

Balzic nodded, started his recorder, and identified himself, the date, time, place, purpose, and other person involved in the interview.

"So, uh, you had no alibi witness, right?"

Walin shook his head and smiled in spite of himself. "Man, you get right to it, don't ya?"

Balzic shrugged. "From what I heard, all the rest of the facts are written down about half a dozen times. At least. So what we both know is you got convicted 'cause somebody said you were someplace doin' somethin' you shouldn'ta been doin', and you didn't have anybody to stand up and say you were someplace else doin' somethin' else. So if I'm sittin' where you're sittin', the only thing I'd wanna tell me is, I know somebody who's gonna say I was somewhere else when this bad shit went down. I mean, these other people comin' forward now? What good are they gonna do you? This guy that says now he was in Ohio, and the other shooter? Now they say they're gonna testify —"

"Hold it. The *other* shooter?"

"Yeah. There were two shooters, right?"

"I don't know how many shooters there were. I wasn't there."

92

"Well I probably didn't say that the way I should have —"

"Yeah, right."

"As I was sayin', these people comin' forward now, I mean, everybody has reasons, but everybody's gonna know that. You say you got convicted on perjured testimony, least that's what I was told, I didn't read the petition myself. Was I told right?"

"Partly right. The rest was, I wouldn't let my counsel investigate my alibi."

"You wouldn't? Is that what you said?"

"Yes, I wouldn't. I didn't know . . . I was stuck. I wanted to do somethin' but I couldn't do it . . . I didn't know how."

"Did you include this on your petition? That you had an alibi but you, yourself, you didn't want your counsel to —"

"I just said that, didn't I?"

"I know what you said. I'm tryin' to figure it out. So I'm straight here, you did not write that on your petition?"

"Maybe you should've read it."

"If you're straight with me I don't need to read it. I mean, you're the guy who wrote it. What do you wanna fuck around with me for? I'm the guy who's been sent here to find out whether you should get what you're askin' for, now you're gonna play games with me, does that make sense to you?"

Walin shrugged.

"Hey, man, you better do more'n shrug. 'Cause

93

if I'm you? And I had an alibi? I'd wanna make sure I was doin' everything I could to cooperate with me — the guy who's gonna check it out. I mean I sure wouldn't be countin' on a guy who'd told as many different stories as this Patter. And I sure as hell wouldn't be countin' on the guy who stood up in court — how many times? Three? Three times this dirtball said I was the shooter?"

"Four."

"Okay, four. The guy who —"

"Hold it. It isn't 'the guy who.' That bastard's got a name."

"Scumacci. Hubert. I know Hubert. Unless there's more'n one Hubert Scumacci, believe me, I know him. Very well."

"Right. Hubert Scumacci. World's greatest fucking liar."

"Okay we have the same guy. Lemme see if I can guess what he said. Sure, he was there, absolutely, but all he did was drive the car, he wasn't the one pullin' the trigger, right?"

"Right."

"He had a gun but it wasn't even loaded. He emptied it before he went in the house, just to make absolutely positively certain he wasn't gonna shoot anybody. How'm I doin' so far?"

"Don't stop now."

"Uh-huh. But now he says not only were you not there, but the guy who was there, the guy who was the actual factual shooter now, according to Scumacci, what, he's dead?"

"Something like that, yeah."

"So now this guy who fingered you four times in court, this guy now says he's gonna swear this croaker did it, and you're sittin' there believin' he's actually gonna do that? Scumacci? You're the guy who's read all these books and talked to all these people, and you know when you're bein' fucked with, and now you're gonna tell me you're gonna put the rest of your time into the hands of these two guys who're suddenly gonna do something they have no history of doin' — tellin' the truth?

"But you're gonna play games with me about your alibi. What did you say — you were stuck? You wanted to do somethin' but you couldn't — is that what you said? Mister Walin, I'm not you, and you're not me, but let's not bullshit each other here, okay? I wouldn't trust either one of these two guys, Patter or Scumacci, either one as far as I could throw this building. If I'm you, I'd have somethin' else to tell me. And the only thing that makes sense is, you know somebody who can say you were someplace else, and not only is he gonna say that, he's also gonna prove it, and, even more important, not only can I find him, but I can persuade him to say so at your hearing. Otherwise, we're just goin' through the motions here, are we not?"

For the first time, Walin averted his eyes. Then he said, "Her. Not him. Her."

Balzic leaned back and blew out a sigh, his cheeks bulging. "Uh-huh, okay," he said, nod-

ding. "Don't stop there, Mister Walin, I'm listenin'."

Walin cleared his throat, several times. He still
could not look at Balzic, and he was swallowing
hard.

"I thought . . . I thought this was gonna be a
lot easier. I thought it . . . I used to get through
my time in RHU thinkin' about gettin' even —"

"RHU?"

"Restricted housing unit. Solitary."

"Go on."

"I used to get through time there, only thing
got me through time there, I'd be . . . I'd be
thinkin' about eatin' my revenge up with a spoon
like it was whipped cream on top of a hot fudge
sundae . . . thinkin' about how I'd feel, and what
I'd say, and what he'd look like, and what he'd
say, and mostly what he'd feel. I used to jack off
thinkin' about givin' him a heart attack. Thinkin'
about how I'd done what I'd done . . . and that
was what I was really doin' the time for. . . ."

Balzic was lost, but he didn't want to interrupt,
and wouldn't unless Walin drifted too far away.

"Almost from the first time, everything I ever
did, I did it to spite him. All the houses I burgled,
all the cars I stole, all the dope I sold or stole or
smoked, it was all to get him. But I never shot
anybody. I never murdered anybody. I would've
never murdered anybody over a key of pot, I
mean, that's just so far out of who I am, that's
not even a nightmare on the worst night of my
life. Stole the pot? Absolutely. Smoked it? Right

again. Bet on it. I smoked up as much as I sold. As much as I stole. I loved pot.

"I don't care whether you understand this. I don't care whether anybody understands it. Pot was the best friend I ever had. After my mother died, pot was the only family I ever had. I smoked my first joint when I was eleven years old, and I was a stone junkie before that day was over. I mean it. I had found my drug of choice. Pot, man, first, last, and always . . . for whatever ailed me. P, O, T. Primo opportunity time. Priceless option treasure. Profit overflow titillation. Perfect outlet tornado. Personalities obsessions tyranny. Precious outpouring tears. Penitentiary . . . oppression . . . truth. That's all I can think of right offhand.

"I haven't had any weed in seventeen years, whether you can believe that or not, but I dream about it at least once a week. Used to be every night. When I first got in, every single night, for the first six months there was not a night went by I didn't have a dream about smokin' weed. That's why I quit smokin' cigarettes, 'cause every time I lit up a Camel, it reminded me of how much I didn't have pot, and I knew if I didn't start thinkin' about somethin' else? Within a year? I'd be eatin' my own shit."

"What time are you doin' now, Lester?"

"That's the first time you didn't call me mister. Why'd you do that?"

"If it offends you I won't do it."

"Don't evade the question."

"I thought maybe we'd reached a first-name basis."

"That's bullshit. That's bullshit cop psychology. I hate havin' my intelligence insulted that way. And that's beneath you. Which makes it a bigger insult."

"Okay, Mister Walin, I say again. What time are you doin' now? You doin' thirty-nine? Or twenty-two? Or eleven?"

"All of 'em at once. That's what I learned here. Time past is time future is time now. That's all any of us have is now. What time am I doin'? That was a good question, man. Time goes back, goes way back, and every time you were, you are when you think you are. You can be eleven when you're twenty-two. You can be eleven and twenty-two when you're thirty-nine. You can be the first memory you ever had and the last memory you had a second ago and the last memory can be the first one. 'Cause when you have nothin' but time, time is what you want. You get an appetite for it. You get such a fucking hunger for it. You get a squeezin' in your guts for time was, and for time that's yet to be. God, that's why I miss pot. I knew a guy, his name for pot was 'was.' 'Let's go score some was,' that's what he used to say. When he was high, every thought he thought, before he could say it, it was gone. Couldn't even say it was gone. All he'd get out of his mouth was, 'It was.' And then he'd just start laughin'. About nothin' he could say 'cause he couldn't remember what it was. *It was.* Fucking hilarious."

"So, uh, while you're compressing time, Mister Walin, what time are you now?"

"Thirty-nine. Goin' on forever. But I can't wait anymore. Waitin' without an end, man, there isn't a word for what kind of crazy you get when you have to wait without an end. Waitin' without an end, every second's a razor cut across your mind. I'm dying, man, dyin' . . . of eighty-six thousand four hundred razor cuts a day. I need some help. Can't do it by myself. I need help."

"I will help you," Balzic said. "But you have to tell me who she is."

"No, man, that's not what I mean. You have to help me say it. I've done seventeen years 'cause I couldn't say it. I wanna say it. You don't know how my gut is squeezin' to say it. I need help sayin' it." Throughout this last plea, Walin had not looked at Balzic once. His head was down, his shoulders hunched high.

Balzic reached across the table and tried to lift Walin's chin. Walin recoiled like he'd been touched by a power line.

"Don't do that! Don't ever touch me. Don't ever do that again."

Balzic settled back in his chair and thought and thought and thought.

"You said your mother died?"

"Now you're gettin' it," Walin said. "Now you're gettin' it."

"Did she?"

"Said she did."

99

"When did she die?"

"You tell me."

Balzic turned down the corners of his mouth and canted his head. "I'd say, lemme think here, I'm slow with arithmetic. Uh, 1967? No. Sixty-six."

"Bingo," Walin said flatly, sitting up straighter, picking up his chin, and looking at Balzic once again.

"You were eleven."

"Bingo again."

"And your father remarried, right?"

"Right again."

"He's a cop."

"Why do you have to ask? You knew that before you got here. But to give you an answer how much of a cop he was, nobody can say it better than the new boys. Twenty-four seven fifty-two."

"Never took the badge off."

"New boys say somethin' else. They say, 'He had one on his underwear.' Relentless. Cop of all cops."

"How'd your mother die?"

"I don't know. Honest to God don't know. He came and got me in school. I was in Missus Edmondson's room. Sixth grade. Hated her. Hated her fat little kid. He was in the same room. First time I got busted for auto theft, this woman I hated, she called me up, asked me if there was anything she could do for me. I hated her and I thought she hated me, and there she was, standin' up when the public defender tried to tell the judge

I wasn't all bad. Unbelievable. Only teacher ever tried to do anything for me. Anyway, I was in her class, principal came in, called me out — didn't say anything, just pointed his finger at me. Got out in the hall, there was my father standin' there, said we had to go home. Said my mother got sick real fast and she wasn't here anymore. Next thing I remember, I'm gettin' dressed up to go to the funeral home."

"He hit her a lot?"

Walin snorted. "Why you askin' that? The question ain't, did he hit her a lot? The question is, who was he? And the answer is, there were only two cops in the department, and he was the chief. The question is, who was she s'posed to call — whether he hit her five times or five thousand times, that's the question — *who was she supposed to call?*"

Balzic cleared his throat and sighed and thought some more about what to ask next.

"He still the chief?"

Walin shook his head and dropped his gaze again. "He's not anything now. Can't walk, can't talk, can't feed himself . . . wears diapers. Can't wipe his own ass. If I had a million dollars, I'd give every cent of it to bribe everybody in the Department of Corrections to just let me look at him for five minutes. Just to let him look in my eyes. I don't care how stroked out he is, man, he'd know. He'd know I know how small he's feelin'. How small . . . scared. I wouldn't have to say a fucking word."

"So, uh, after your mother died —"

"After he killed her."

"Thought you said you didn't know."

"That's what I said. But that's not what I know. In my bones? I know what he did. 'Cause he loved to get you in the stomach. He'd time it right when you'd exhale, and then he'd let you have it right below the breastbone with the middle knuckle on his right hand. That was the way he always started. What I think is, she tried to double over and back up at the same time, 'cause I'd seen her do that a lot. He probably was aimin' for the same place and she was duckin' down and he got her a little higher on the chest. Least that's as close as I can figure it out. I've read about people dyin' after they were hit in the chest. Especially if you aren't very big, a kid or a small woman, which she was, a real sharp blow to the chest interrupts the rhythm of your heart. It's what's called an arrhythmia. Real erratic beating of the heart. Which sometimes causes cardiac arrest. There's a lot been written about that."

"Oh I have no doubt it's possible," Balzic said. "But what, no autopsy?"

"He was the chief, man. If he said it was a heart attack, and if it looked like a heart attack to the people in the hospital, who was gonna say anything else? The neighbors? We didn't have any neighbors. Closest house was four hundred yards away. Don't look at me like that. Who was I supposed to say it to? Huh?"

"What's on the death certificate?"

102

"Says cardiac arrest."

Balzic thought some more about what to ask. "So who's gettin' ready to say something now?"

"Think, man, c'mon, help me out here," Walin said, getting more animated by the second. He was rubbing his palms together and on his thighs and his breathing was getting shallow. "This is what I'm doin' time for. You keep askin' me, what time am I now, what time am I now. That ain't the question, what time am I now. What time am I doin', that's the question. I'm sick damn near to death of doin' time for this shit I didn't do. But I'm still too scared, man, God, you have no idea how scared I am . . . I'm too scared to stop doin' the time for what I did. C'mon, man, you're close, don't quit on me now. I can't do it by myself. I could do it in a second if I had weed. But I don't. You have to help me, man."

"I'm tryin', son. But I can't do this alone. I don't know everything you know. I'm smart but I'm no mind reader. You've got a problem here, but if you want me to help you, you gotta help me. This woman who's gonna come forward, what's her name?"

Walin's eyes were suddenly brimming with tears. "What do you think her name is?"

Balzic wanted to throw up his hands in disgust, wanted to slap Walin, wanted to tell him to stop playing this damn game, but he caught himself. "You think I know her name?"

"Sure you do, man. You know it. Just think.

It's the name . . . it's the name . . . I can't say."

Balzic couldn't do anything for a long moment but shake his head. "Jesus. Missus Walczinsky."

Walin dropped his chin and started sobbing and nodding and laughing and cheering. "Bingo, man. Fucking bingo!" It took him some minutes to control himself; he was wiping his eyes and nose on both sleeves.

"So, uh, now that I gave you the name, are you also expectin' me to say what happened? Or are you gonna give me a little help with this?"

Walin smiled at Balzic. His eyes were puffy and red and he was inhaling mucus and clearing his throat, and tears were still rolling down his cheeks, but he was smiling. He said, "You got that part, I mean, man, that was the hardest part."

"For you, son, not for me."

"No, uh-uh. The hardest part for me is sayin' what I did. To her. Gave her a hundred miles of bad road."

"You did somethin' to her? And he found out? Or he caught ya, which?"

"I didn't do something *to* her, man. I mean, I set out to. I planned it out. I was . . . I was . . . oh shit, I still can't say it."

"Listen, put that aside for a minute. Tell me about her. When she married your father, how old was she? Where'd she come from? Whatever you can remember."

"She married him, uh, they got married when I was, uh, first time I did time for burglary. I was on the farm, the juvenile center, it used to be on a farm in Wabash County, and I, uh, I was doin' six months. And when I went back home, she was there. And he never said a word about it. Course he never said a word about anything the whole six months. It was like everybody died, not just my mother. Only he didn't. Die."

"How old were you?"

"Fifteen."

"How old was she?"

"Eighteen. I'm not sure. She was a senior in high school when I was a freshman, couldn't've been more'n four years older'n me."

"And?"

"And she was, you know, she was real curious about pot. Real curious. And so I . . . I planned it out. I mean, I didn't sit down and write out a plan or anything like that. I mean it was just somethin' that just immediately started cookin' in the back of my head, and it was never very far away. It took me a couple years to get around to it — 'cause I was really enjoyin' thinkin' about it . . . plus everything else I was doin' then, it just all revolved around pot, buyin' it, smokin' it, sellin' it, stealin' it. But it was always in the back of my mind, I was always thinkin' what I was gonna do. 'Cause she kept sayin' how she wanted to try pot, she heard all this stuff about it, but she was always afraid, 'cause she didn't trust the other people she knew who did it but she thought she could trust me. And I just kept her out there, you know, on the end of my line, reel her in a little bit, let her run for a while. Thing was, I was gettin' to know her. And this plan I had to, uh, to humiliate him . . . without him ever knowin' it . . . it started, uh, to get away from me. Gettin' to know her, that wasn't part of the plan. See, 'cause in my bug-size brain, in all my pot fantasies, what I wanted to happen was for her, you know, to fall in love with me . . . and I was gonna use pot to get her, 'cause I thought, curious as she was about pot, once I got her started on it, she'd come to love it the way I did, and since she was afraid of doin' it with people she didn't trust, and since she trusted me, and since I'd be her connection, it was, hell, you know, one, two, three."

"What happened?"

Walin puffed out his cheeks and shook his head. "Oh man, she told him."

"She told? *She?*"

"Yeah. See, what I didn't find out till a long time later, you know, like years later, I found out her father had been doin' the same thing to her. Same thing mine did to my mother and me. Don't know why I never thought of that, but honest to God that never occurred to me. I thought that shit only happened in my house, I didn't think it happened in anybody else's house. And so, when she spilled it out, I mean, we were eatin' — it was one of the few times I ever ate with the both of them together. And we were sittin' there like somethin' out of *Leave It to Beaver,* and she just blurted it out. And he just backhanded her right over backwards, and I was gone, soon as he came

106

up out of his chair, man, I was runnin'.

"But he didn't come after me. He just stayed there and beat her ass until his arms got tired. And she never made a sound. And when he got tired, when he finally quit, she got up off the floor, she went over to the kitchen sink, washed her face, got all the blood off, and then she went over to him, knelt down on the floor, and gave that bastard a blow job. I was standin' outside the kitchen window watchin'. The whole thing. And when I saw this really sick fucking look that perverted bastard had on his face after he came? And when I saw how she looked at him? These big cow eyes? Man, I had to smoke three joints just to get through the rest of that day. Big ones."

"And so," Balzic said, "from then on, what? You were absolutely gonna humiliate him?"

"Oh yeah. Absolutely. From then on, I went on a campaign. Every time I sneaked back in to get some more of my stash or my money or my clothes or whatever, I worked her, man. I worked her hard. But the harder I worked her, the more I found out about her, the more I started likin' her. And the more I liked her, the crazier I got about him . . . thing was, I was so scared of him and so furious, so fucking obsessed with gettin' him for what he did to my mother, I mean, everything just got all fucking tangled up in my mind. It was a rat's nest. I hated him, I liked her, I needed her, needed to use her to get him, the more I knew I needed to use her, the more I used her, the worse I felt 'cause I couldn't help myself

107

— I mean she was really nice to me. And she was so fucking helpless around him, I just couldn't make it make sense. Like, when he ignored her for more than three days, if three days went by that he didn't smack her around? Man, she baited him, she fuckin' agitated him, man. She would provoke the shit outta him, did everything but poke him with a stick. She told me she couldn't help it, said she didn't know how to act if somebody wasn't beatin' her ass. She used to ask me to do it. And I couldn't do it. I mean I just could not do that shit."

Balzic let this sink in. "So what could you do?"

"What do you think?"

"You made love to her. In his bed."

Walin hung his head and sobbed.

"And that's the time you're doin'?"

"She wouldn't make the bed," Walin said through his sobs.

Balzic thought carefully before he spoke. But he thought it was worth saying. "She wouldn't make the bed, is that what you said?"

Walin nodded and sobbed some more.

"Well, hell, son, she was usin' you as much as you were usin' her."

Walin gazed up at Balzic and, after a long moment passed before he could get control of his voice, he said, "Uh-uh, man. I was smarter'n her. I knew what I was doin'. She was runnin' on empty. I had a full tank. That's the . . . the lowest, the coldest thing I ever did . . . to anybody."

"So now what? Now she's not runnin' on empty,

is that what you're sayin'? Now she understands what was goin' on? What, she been in therapy or something? Why's she comin' forward now? More important, what kind of proof does she have?"

"Oh man she doesn't have the proof. I have the proof. The day it happened? The day those two guys got smoked? That was the first day of deer season, 1977. Monday after Thanksgiving. My father never missed an opening day of deer season in his life, not since he was old enough to drag a gun into the woods. That was the day I had planned out to nail him. 'Cause he knew she was ballin' somebody and he knew it 'cause she baited him with it. But what the fuck, he loved it. He loved the whole sick fucking scene. But if he suspected it was me, he never let on, 'cause he never came after me. So I *wanted* him to know. I *wanted* him to know it was *me*, not just some anybody. Me.

"So after I balled her, I gave her another joint and I talked her into gettin' the paper and holdin' it up between us, and I went and got this Polaroid I stole somewhere, held it out arm's length and took about a whole roll of film of us, naked in his bed, with her holding up the front page of the paper.

"It was this little dinky-ass weekly paper, man, but every year, every deer season, they put out this special paper for the opening day. And they delivered it Sunday night, so everybody'd have it the night before the morning deer season opened. It was full of pictures from last year, guys posin' with their deer, macho shit like that, and there was my father's picture, right in the middle of the front page, from the year before. What I forgot was, right behind us on the top of the headboard was a clock. And in every one of those pictures, man, there's the clock advancin' every minute for every picture I took. 'Cause that's how long it took with that Polaroid for the picture to develop. Sixty seconds.

"But after I took 'em, I don't know what happened to me, I just . . . I couldn't do it. I lost my guts. I was too scared of him. I mean, after I'd planned the whole fuckin' thing out, after I used that poor woman who loved to get her ass kicked, after I went through all that, I lost my guts. I thought, you know, I mean . . . all I could think about was my mother.

"That was the last time I was ever in my father's house. No way I could go back. But somehow, don't ask me how 'cause I don't know, she finds out I'm livin' with this guy Jimmy Cipolla, and she starts callin' me every day, when am I comin' back, when am I gonna bring her some more weed, what'd I do with the pictures, she wants to see the pictures, she wants to see me, and on and on, this goes on for like two weeks, and every time I answer the phone, I'm tryin' to tell her, listen, I'm history, forget it, forget the pot, forget me, and especially forget the pictures 'cause I know what she wants 'em for, only I don't have the guts for that anymore, so no way was I gonna let her have 'em. So finally I told her I burned 'em, which I didn't, but that's what I told her, and she believed me."

"So what did you do with them?"

"I'm coming to that," Walin said. "I'm living with this guy, Jimmy Cipolla — I said that, right? Anyway, we had this apartment right outside Johnstown. I'd been dealin' with him off and on for a coupla years. Never had any problem with him, so I move in with him and we're dealin' out of there. Place is full of pot, pipes, papers, scales, baggies, roach clips, we were sellin' everything. Goofy fucker even got about a gross of T-shirts he had printed up said 'Legalize pot' on the front, and on the back it said 'Take a narc to lunch.'

"We're sittin' there this one day about two weeks later, we're ouncin' out about a pound of primo weed we ripped off from a coupla kids in Johnstown, and he starts tellin' me he heard about this deal went sour a couple weeks before and two guys got shot, killed. I'm goin', yeah, who? And he's goin', wouldn't surprise me we got picked up 'cause I'm not gonna believe who it is. 'Cause it's two guys we did about maybe ten deals with over the previous four, five months. He tells me their names, Jimmy Stevens and this Portiletto somethin', and I'm goin', no shit, man, that's terrible, lotsa people saw us together, you're right, we're gonna get picked up for sure.

"So we finish doin' what we were doin', get all this pot in baggies, in ounces, halves, and quarters, we clean everything up, we sweep the rugs, mop the floors, we get everything picked up and put away, and the whole time we were talkin' about where we were when these two guys were supposed to've got dusted. Then he says he's gonna go out to Pitt-Johnstown campus and do some business, and I told him I'm gonna crash out for a while, and so off he goes, and I crash out, and the next fuckin' thing I know five state cops're comin' through the door. Turn me over in the bed, pin me down, fuckers all over my back and arms, got pistols against the back of my head, got cuffs on me, and they're readin' me my rights for the murder of these two guys and I'm goin', you're crazy, you guys are out of your fuckin' minds, you got the wrong guy.

"And every time I say I don't know anything about this, here comes another one back into the bedroom with more of our shit, holdin' it under my nose, sayin', 'What's this, huh?' They found our scales, they found the baggies, the roach clips, the pipes, the T-shirts, and this is the stuff they were sayin' makes me out to be this big-time pot dealer and these guys were killed over some pot deal. Meanwhile, I found out later on, this asshole claims he saw me kill 'em, this fat fuck Scumacci, he's such a pig even the Pagans didn't want any part of him —"

"The Pagans? The motorcycle gang?"

"Yeah yeah, they wouldn't even sell that fucker crank, nobody wanted to deal with him, but this fat prick pulls my name out of thin air and gives me up. That's their case. His word and all the drug shit they find in my apartment. Mine and Jimmy's. They tore the whole place apart, while they had me layin' on my face on the bed, they tore everything up, tore all the stuffin' out of the furniture, trashed the place, but the only things they took were the pot stuff. They never found the pictures. Or if they found 'em, they didn't know what to do with 'em, so they didn't take 'em.

"So a week goes by, I'm in the county jail, Jimmy Cipolla calls me up, he's scared out of his mind, he can't believe what happened to me, he says he went back to the apartment that night, thought maybe those kids we ripped the pot offa came back with some friends and did that. Then somebody livin' in the building told him the cops were there. And then he hears why they got me locked up. So he asks me what I want him to do with all my stuff, my clothes, tapes, tape player, everything, I say what do I care, that's the least of my problems. But I ask him if he found the Polaroids. He says no, but he wasn't looking, did I want him to look. I say hell yes, that's my alibi, find those fucking pictures, I need 'em, please find 'em! He goes, he'll check it out.

"And that's the last thing I ever hear from him. Never hear another word from Jimmy Cipolla until two months ago, he walks into my cellblock in Huntingdon. Seventeen fuckin' years later, he gets busted for drugs, winds up on my cellblock, tellin' me what he did with my stuff."

113

"Wait, wait. You sayin' that if he'd've found the Polaroids you would've used them?"

Walin hung his head. "I don't know what I'm sayin'. I don't know what I would've done. Honest to God I don't."

"So what'd he do with your stuff? He musta put it somewhere."

"Oh yeah, sure. Stashed it in his old man's house, some little town outside of Butler. He's apologizin' to me all over the place, he was scared to death, he thought I was gonna kill him, said he thought I'd think he was some kind of rat fink 'cause he never tried to get in touch with me again, said he was too scared he was gonna get busted same as me."

"You trying to tell me you think if I find those pictures you're home free?"

"No no, absolutely not, I know that. Not with them alone. I'm not stupid. But if she says when they were taken? And where we were? And whose bed we were in? And how far that was from where those two got killed? That's four miles at least —"

"Four miles? That's supposed to impress somebody?"

"Hey. It's in the record — at least four times it's in the record — that when that shit went down was exactly when I was in bed with her takin', uh, you know, takin' what I thought was, uh, takin' pictures."

"If you're countin' on the pictures showin' the clock behind you, c'mon. Clocks're set every day in every way. And you're gonna try to get some-

114

body to believe you didn't know the clock was back there? Huh?"

"C'mon yourself, man. Her testimony by itself isn't gonna do it, the pictures by themselves aren't gonna do it, but both of them together? I got a shot. Especially since that creep Scumacci is sayin' I wasn't there, and that Patter, that lyin' sonofabitch, since maybe for the first time in his life he's talkin' the truth."

"Listen, son, I told you. I would not be countin' on either one of those two to do what they say they're gonna do. So, uh, where does Cipolla's father live, what's his address?"

"Oh. He lives in Chicora. It's right off the turnpike, you get off the Butler exit, it's the second little town you come to. A couple miles, that's all."

Balzic got out his notebook and pen and waited. He looked over the top of his glasses at Walin and said, "Get off the turnpike at the Butler exit and look for the second town?"

"It's a real small town. Used to be a company town. Mining village, you know. Can't be more'n like, three hundred people live there, if that many."

"What's his first name?"

"I don't know —"

"Oh come on for crissake."

"No wait. I don't know his name. But Jimmy told me his sister's livin' with him now. She's takin' care of him. He's too old to live by himself. And her name's Charlotte Michaels. Jimmy's father was born there, and after his wife died, he went back there. And then Jimmy's sister, I guess, after she got divorced from this Michaels guy, whoever he was, she went to live with her father. You're not gonna have any problem findin' her, man. You're a cop. You know how to find people. Christ."

"Anything else you wanna tell me?"

"No. That's it."

"No? How about your father's address? He still livin' in his house or is he in some nursing home? How about his wife? Where's she livin'?"

"I don't know."

"You don't know?" Balzic was incredulous. "Whattaya mean you don't know?"

"I don't, that's all. I don't know."

"Then how do you know she's willin' to come forward?"

"She told me."

"She told you? How? She visit you, she call you, how did she tell you?"

"She called me."

"She called you here? Or she called you in Huntingdon?"

"Huntingdon."

"Huntingdon, huh? So, uh, when did she say she was gonna come forward?"

"When she told me about him — about his stroke. Or strokes, I don't remember how many she said he had — if she even knew."

"Just for the record here, you two kept in touch, am I right? Over the years?"

116

Walin avoided Balzic's glance and hung his head again.

"C'mon c'mon, yes or no. What's goin' on here, Lester?"

Walin put his left hand up to his mouth and started biting the side of his thumb. He put his thumb sideways in his mouth and bit it and then drew it away. His heels and head were bouncing. His breathing was getting shallow again.

"She's been writin' to me, you know, ever since . . ."

"Ever since what?"

"Ever since I got convicted."

"So what're we talkin' here, Lester, huh? Love letters? Huh? One way, Lester? Or both ways?"

Walin bit hard on his thumb and then thrust it out and threw both hands up. "No. What the fuck, whattaya think? Jesus Christ, man, you think you can do this shit alone? Huh? Maybe there's some guys who can do this alone, but I'm not one of 'em. I'm not Superman. I'm just me. Jesus Christ . . ."

Balzic shook his head and pushed the button on the wall to signal the CO, then he said what time it was and that he was concluding the interview. He stopped the recorder, stood up, put his topcoat and cap on, and waited.

When the CO arrived to unlock the door Walin stood and said to Balzic, "Uh, one thing, huh?"

"Yeah?"

Walin extended his right hand hesitantly. "Thanks. For, uh, for helpin' me, uh, get that out. You don't know how hard that was. I'm really ashamed of that. Of, uh, you know. . . ."

Balzic shook Walin's hand weakly and said, "I do know. Well. I'm sure somebody'll be talkin' to you, maybe Livingood, maybe me again, somebody else maybe, I don't know. For what it's worth, I hope what you told me checks out, and I, uh, I hope the sleepin' gets a little easier for ya. Good luck, Lester."

On his way home from the detention center, Balzic detoured by the Triple-A auto club office and got a new map of the state. His had been taped so many times that many sections along the folds were unreadable. Then he went home and called Butler information, asking for a phone number and address for either Charlotte Cipolla or Charlotte Michaels in the village of Chicora.

"The only Cipolla we have listed, sir, is James Senior. And his address is a post office box."

Balzic said that was fine and wrote the numbers down, hung up, and called James Cipolla Sr. While he was waiting for an answer Ruth yelled to him from the bedroom that a registered letter had come for him from the attorney general's office and that it was on top of the refrigerator. He opened it and found his ID card and his contract signed by the attorney general. With the phone cradled in his neck, he stretched the cord to its limit and went into the dining room and opened the top drawer of the china closet, looking for a strip of ID pictures he'd had taken for his last Rocksburg ID. He found them, cut one off, and went back into the kitchen and found some glue and fixed the mug shot to the AG's ID card and put it in his case.

After the eleventh ring, somebody picked up and a creaky old voice said, "Nobody's home. This is a record. At the sound of the beep, give your name and number, maybe we're gonna call you back. Maybe not. Beep."

Oh Christ. "Mister. Cipolla, hold it, don't hang up! Mister Cipolla?"

Too late. The old man had hung up within two seconds after he'd given his imitation of a beep.

"Hey, Ruth, can you hear me? I gotta go someplace around Butler, I don't know how long I'm gonna be."

She came out of the bedroom and said, "Did you eat?"

"Nah, I'll get somethin' on the road," he said, blowing her a kiss, and heading back out to his car. May as well act like it's just another day at the office, no big deal. But once out in the car and driving, he was half a block away before he realized he'd forgotten to log in his time and mileage. He stopped suddenly and pulled over to the curb to do that, provoking a long horn blast behind him. He gave his best *mea culpa* shrug as the car pulled around him, and the driver, a very tiny, very old woman, whose jet-black wig was too far down on her forehead, glared at him and shook her finger.

By the time he pulled off the Pennsylvania

119

Turnpike at the Butler exit, it was snowing, big, fluffy flakes that melted as soon as they hit the car or the road. He asked the toll-taker for directions to Chicora, got them, and after driving about four miles on Route 8 he turned right onto a two-lane macadam road, pitted with such serious potholes that he was forced at times to slow to less than twenty miles an hour.

Chicora materialized out of the blowing snow after he'd driven about a mile up a slight but steady grade, all the while steering around holes. Sometimes the macadam had broken down into patches of gravel six and seven feet across. Chicora was fewer than fifty houses set along two streets on the side of a hill, houses that had once been owned by a mining company that had taken what it wanted and then left. The former company store was now a combination fire hall, post office, and video rental business. Next door was a franchise convenience store, with three gas pumps in front, six hoses on each pump. And that, as far as Balzic could tell, was Chicora.

He parked in front of the post office, went inside, and asked the woman behind the counter, the only employee, if she would be kind enough to tell him where James Cipolla Sr. lived. He showed her his ID case and gave her the man's box number.

"Oh, he lives in the second house from the end on the right as you go up the hill —"

"On this street?"

"Yes. On this street. But I can tell you now,

he won't answer the door if his daughter isn't there, and I know she isn't."

"Where is she? Charlotte, is that her name? She workin'?"

"Yes it is. And she is, working. Won't be here for another twenty minutes at least. Picks up her mail right before I close. I close at three-thirty. And no use of you trying to call him, 'cause he won't answer the phone unless you just let it ring and ring and ring, and then he tries to pretend he's an answering machine." She studied Balzic for a moment. "Can't imagine what he might have done that would require somebody from the attorney general's office to, uh . . . my, my."

Balzic looked at her and thought, what the hell, lady, you want gossip you're gonna have to get it from somebody else. He thanked her and was already going out the door before she could push it further.

He hustled through the snow, head down, into the convenience store, where he surveyed the refrigerated cases of sandwiches and the roller grill of hot dogs. He passed on all of them. Bought a cup of coffee for sixty-nine cents and a couple of packs of peanut butter crackers for another ninety cents and took a seat in the one booth that had an unobstructed view of the post office. The coffee wasn't bad, but the crackers were stale and he'd had enough after three. He tried to talk the clerk into taking back the second pack of crackers and refunding his money.

She wouldn't do it. Said her manager told her

the most important thing was to make sure her register tape was right. He'd showed her what to do if she had to refund money, but she'd forgotten, and she knew if she tried she'd mess up, she always did. She was sorry, but this was only her second day on the job, and she didn't want to do anything to upset her boss.

Balzic listened and smiled and said it was okay. Then he went back to the booth and looked through the window and the big, fluffy flakes of snow swirling outside at the post office and waited.

At three twenty-nine, a metallic-blue Dodge Omni with a badly dented left front fender stopped in front of the post office. A woman got out, hurried inside, and hurried back out, her left hand full of mail. She got back into the Omni and started up the hill. Balzic hustled out and followed her in his car.

He parked behind her when she parked and was out of his car before she was out of hers. He approached her with his ID case out, asking if she was Charlotte Cipolla.

"Used to be, yeah. Who're you?"

"Take the case, ma'am. Read it. Make sure my face matches that picture."

She read it, handed it back, and said, "Yeah. So?"

"You have a brother? James, Jimmy?"

"Yeah. So?"

"Is he incarcerated now? In the State Correctional Facility at Huntingdon?"

"This is about Jimmy?"

"No. This is about something Jimmy was supposed to've put in your house here. Property that belonged to another person. Would it be all right if I came inside? It's a lot colder here than it was when I left home. Okay if I explain inside?"

"Yeah, I guess. Come on." She led him up the three steps onto the porch and then inside into the boxy living room that had been turned into a bedroom. She frowned at the empty bed, hurried into the kitchen, calling out to her father that she was home and where was he and was he all right. Then she came rushing back past Balzic, dropping the mail and her purse on the floor and shedding her coat.

"Upstairs," came a feeble voice.

"Oh my God," she said, throwing her coat across the back of a stuffed chair and scurrying around Balzic. "What do you mean upstairs? How did you get upstairs? What's wrong with you? What the hell're you doin' upstairs?"

Balzic saw her bounding up the steps and then heard her saying, "Oh Jesus, Daddy, what're you doin' up here? How'd you get up here? Are you tryin' to make me nuts or what? What if you fell?"

"Wanted to see somethin'."

"What?"

"Somethin'."

"What? What?"

"Somethin' different."

"Hey, mister?" she called out. "Can you c'mere and gimme a hand, okay, please?"

Balzic went up and found the old man on the edge of the bed in what was obviously the daughter's room. She was trying to lift him, but he was not helping. His glasses were cocked wrong on his face so that the left lens was up around his eyebrow and the right one was down on his cheek.

Balzic straightened the old man's glasses and said, "Here ya go, Mister Cipolla, put your arm around my neck, okay?"

"Be careful, be careful, he's all bones," she said.

"You just help me get him up and we'll make it okay, I'm not gonna squeeze him."

Balzic eased him off the bed and crept him down the steps and then settled him into bed in the living room, his daughter asking repeatedly why he'd done it, why he'd gone upstairs.

"TV's broke," he said when they got him situated on the bed. "Can't hear nothing."

"It's not broke," she said, picking up the remote control. "Look, you had the mute button on. See that word up in the corner there? That's mute, can you see that?"

"I can see. I got glasses. Can't hear nothing."

She pushed the mute button and the jingle and voices of a soap commercial exploded in the room.

"Too loud," he said, wincing. "I ain't deaf."

She put the remote in his hand and said, "Here. You fix it the way you want it. You know how to do it, don't pretend like you don't. Jesus, Daddy, you're makin' me nuts."

Shaking her head, she led Balzic into the kitchen and pulled an accordion door across the opening separating the two rooms. It helped only slightly to buffer the noise.

"He wants to see something different, Jesus God. He hasn't been upstairs in I'll bet it's been two years."

"He here by himself? All day?"

"Yes. And don't look at me like that. Before Jimmy got arrested — not arrested, that's not what I mean — before he got sentenced, we had somebody coming in every day. Jimmy paid for that. But all his money's gone. It was gone last week. And I can't afford it. Anyway, this is none of your business, what do you want?"

Balzic told her as briefly as he could what he was doing there. When he was finished, she shook her head and said, "I don't know — Jimmy put somebody's stuff here? I don't know what you're talking about. Jimmy put something here, in this house?" She shook her head skeptically. "It's not in the house here, my God, we don't have room for anybody else's stuff in here. As it is, I don't know what to do with Jimmy's stuff. Maybe what you're talkin' about, maybe it's in the shed in back, in the backyard. If it's anywhere, that's where it is, it sure isn't in here. I haven't moved anything out of there, so that's the only place it could be. Only reason I ever go in there is to get the lawn mower out. You wanna look in there, go ahead. It's not locked."

125

Balzic buttoned up his coat again, went out through the door in the kitchen, and immediately as he stepped away from the house found himself walking uphill. About twenty yards away was the shed, its roof tilted to the left and developing a swayback. Balzic got the door open after a couple of moments of fiddling with the handle, and peered into the dusty darkness. He moved an electric lawn mower aside, fumbled around for his Mini-Mag flashlight, got its beam adjusted, and swept the interior. Straight ahead, caked with dust and covered with cobwebs, were two footlockers and two duffel bags.

He batted away the cobwebs and hauled bags and footlockers into the yard and the light. Everything was padlocked, but the plates securing the locks on the footlockers came out in his hands with one tug. After seventeen winters in this shed, it was a wonder the lockers had held together; they looked to be made of nothing more substantial than pressed-wood chips. The bags had so many holes from rodents and insects feeding on them that Balzic could rip the locks off them with not much more force than he'd used to get the plates off the lockers.

A quick look at the trays in both footlockers left no doubt that the contents had once belonged to Lester Walin. Both trays and one locker were filled with nothing but cassette tapes that had been copied from other tapes, and the first one Balzic picked up had the initials LW printed on the label next to the words Creedence

126

Clearwater Revival. Every tape he picked up had the same initials somewhere on the label.

The other locker was full of clothes, mostly socks, underwear, and T-shirts, most of which celebrated beer or marijuana or some rock group or some concert. The snow was falling thickly now and starting to lay. He went to the back door of the house, knocked, opened it, and called out to Charlotte Cipolla if she had any plastic garbage bags.

"Yeah. Do you want some? How many? What do you want them for?"

"I need four at least. Needa carry this stuff out to my car and I'm afraid when I pick it up, the bottom's gonna come right outta everything. I'd sure hate to have that happen when I was halfway through your house. There's all kinda dust and cobwebs and rat droppings, stuff like that."

When she brought the bags and handed them over, she said, "Aren't you supposed to have a search warrant or something? How do I know you're not taking something that belongs to my brother?"

"You can come on out and look at it if you want. If it looks like it belongs to your brother and you don't want me to take it I won't. But I don't need a warrant, ma'am. You invited me in, and then you told me where to look."

"Well what if I didn't?"

"Then I'd have to go get a warrant. So thanks for invitin' me in. But I'd be real surprised to find any of this stuff was your brother's. It hasn't been

127

touched in years and years. C'mon out and look at it if you want. I don't want you havin' any doubts after I'm gone."

She shivered and shook her head no. "That's all right. Too cold. Too muddy."

He went back into the yard, slipped the plastic bags over each of the lockers and duffel bags, and carried them back through the house and to his car, while she held house doors for him. He thanked her twice, then wrote his name and phone number on a piece of notebook paper and left it on the kitchen table. He wished her luck with her father, and then left.

Back home, he backed his car up to the garage door, remembered to log his time and mileage, then hauled all four garbage bags into the garage. He yelled up the steps to Ruth that he was home. He spread old newspapers over the floor of the garage, went upstairs and changed into some grungy clothes, yelled to Ruth that he'd be downstairs for a while, and went back down and worked his way through all the clothes in the other footlocker, the one that wasn't full of cassette tapes. He unfolded every item of clothing, shook it or turned it inside out, hoping for something to drop out. Nothing did.

Then he opened every one of the cassette tapes. No pictures. He'd worked his way through a half dozen pairs of jeans and a couple pairs of running shoes and reached the bottom of the second bag. Naturally, he thought. It's the Murphy's Law of Searching: anytime you have to look through dirty, smelly, grubby, nastified stuff, the thing you want is going to be in the last place you have to look. At the very bottom of the second bag, under a folded-up, mildewed, black motorcycle jacket, Balzic found a plastic, gallon-size, Ziploc bag.

Balzic could see the Polaroids through the plastic. He took them and counted out eighteen of them. He then looked carefully at each one, and found them all, except for two, to be more or less as Lester Walczinsky/Walin had described them: a younger Lester with longer hair and a droopy moustache, naked behind a newspaper while on his left, caught in various stages of giggles and laughter and also naked, was a plain woman with straight, short, dark hair. In the other two snapshots, only her hand was visible as her left index finger pointed at the blanket on top of the bed, shots taken presumably to show Police Chief Walczinsky that the frolic had indeed happened in his very own bed.

The banner headline atop the newspaper the woman held across their chests said, "Good Luck, Hunters." Right below the headline was a picture that took up almost all the space above the fold, a picture of a grinning man on one knee beside a dead buck. He was holding a rifle in his left hand and the buck's antlers in his right. Balzic couldn't read any of the rest of the print on the newspaper, but if Lester Walczinsky was telling the truth, that grinning hunter in the picture was his father.

Balzic put the Polaroids aside and went through

the rest of the contents of the plastic bag. Wasn't much there of interest that Balzic could see except for two vehicle operator's licenses, one for an automobile and the other for a motorcycle. The one for the auto showed a sober Lester Walczinsky looking pretty much as he looked in the Polaroids. The other one, for the motorcycle, showed him in full beard but was identical in every other aspect to the auto license except for the name. It said Lester Waldon.

Balzic shook his head. Lester Walczinsky in a car becomes Lester Waldon on a bike becomes Lester Walin inside one or another of the state's correctional facilities.

"God, what's all that stuff?" Ruth said after poking her head into the garage.

"Lotta years of mildew and dust and rain and snow and rat crap and God knows what else."

"Smells awful. You gonna be ready to eat soon?"

"Don't know. Hungry enough to eat an hour ago. But I gotta inventory all this stuff, I'm gonna be doin' that the rest of the night, so whenever you want me to come eat, just gimme five minutes to wash up, and, uh, I'll be there."

"Nothing alive in that stuff, is there?"

"Hope not. Some pictures are pretty lively. Course I guess that would depend. Some guy thinks they're maybe gonna corroborate his alibi. But I have to talk to somebody else. That person backs him up about what these pictures show, I think maybe he's got a claim. We shall see.

What're we eatin'?"

"Penne and marinara with those mushrooms you like."

"Portobellos? Oh good. Good good good. If it's ready, hey, I could eat right now."

The next morning Balzic was awakened by Walker Johnson returning all the calls Balzic had made to Johnson's home phone, his pistol range phone, and to the phone numbers Livingood had given him.

Sleepy as he was, Balzic shook himself awake by putting Johnson on hold on the bedroom phone and going into the kitchen and splashing cold water on his face and picking up the phone there. He came right to the point.

"How come you're not doin' this, Walk?"

"And good morning to you, sir. And how are you this fine day? I'm fine myself, thanks for asking."

"Hey, good mornin', okay? I been tryin' to call you since Tuesday night. Where are you, where you callin' from?"

"I'm in a motel in Reading, or just south of Reading. Or at least I was when I went to sleep last night. What're you so all outta joint about?"

"Me? What am I outta joint about? This job you're tryin' to get me, that's what."

"Tryin' to get you? I thought you took it."

"I did. I just woke up, I don't know what I'm sayin' yet."

"Well when you get woke up, hell, you could

131

say thanks, Walk, for gettin' me outta the house. You're welcome. It was nothin', really. Do it for anybody."

"Gettin' me outta the house? How d'you know about that?"

"Oh listen to him. How do I know? Foolish man. Why do you think I got into the pistol-range business?"

"What the hell do I know, you wanted to hear gunfire all day. So?"

"So what?"

"So if hearin' gunfire all day wasn't enough to get you outta the house, how come you're workin' for the state now?"

"Hey, pal, real hard to say no to thirty-five bucks an hour, especially when your wife's lookin' for a job."

"You just lost me. If you're already outta the house, why's she lookin' for a job?"

"No, listen, she was lookin' for a job, that's all, couldn't stand bein' in the house anymore, whether I was there or not. Plus, she wanted to buy some stuff, and she didn't have the money, and here comes Livingood offerin' me this job, I got this brainstorm, see. Offered her ten bucks an hour to run the range, you know, sell ammo and rent earmuffs while I'm on the road, which still leaves me twenty-five an hour to pay the rest of the bills. Plus my pension, don't forget. So now my wife's makin' four-eighty a week before taxes, and I'm the guy signin' her checks. I'm tellin' you, she gets any happier I'm gonna have to rent her some toy-boys. Honest to God, Mario, I make any more money, I'm gonna start votin' Republican. 'Nother year of this, I'm gonna start talkin' trickle-down theories."

"Yeah, well, I'm sure you're just all delighted as hell to be alive and havin' fun, but I still, you know, there's one thing still botherin' me."

"Which is?"

"How come you're not doin' this?"

" 'Cause I'm doin' somethin' else. I'm callin' from Reading, remember? Least it was last night —"

"Stop clownin' on me, Walk. Is that the only reason?"

"What're you gettin' at?"

"There were some state guys involved in this Deer Mountain shit, weren't there?"

"Mario, state guys're involved in damn near every homicide that's not in Philadelphia or Pittsburgh —"

Balzic chimed in, "Yeah, right, in every municipality that doesn't have the manpower or resources to do the investigation on its own, blah blah, hey, I may not know all the words exactly, Walk, but I know the melody, that's not what I'm talkin' about."

"Well what are you talkin' about? What're you askin' me?"

"What I'm askin' you is, am I gonna be wishin' two weeks from now I never heard of Deer Mountain? Or any of these state people?"

"Because of who's involved? State guys?"

"Yeah, exactly."

"Mario, Jesus, you need to do some routine maintenance on your paranoia control center, man. I'm not even sure I know where Deer Mountain is. Oh oh, wait wait wait, I do know where it is. That was Troop B, yeah, but without checkin' the case file, I couldn't even give you a name to call. Wait, yes I can. Rohrbacher. Yeah, he was sergeant in charge of CID there for a while. I don't know that he worked this case. But far as I'm concerned, I don't care what you find. You find a pile of dirt, I'll lend one of my old shovels."

"You sure?"

"Cross my heart and hope to fart on my hundredth birthday. C'mon, man, take the money and run, make your missus happy, make yourself happy, you're not gonna tell me you *like* sittin' on the couch watchin' TV, I'm not gonna believe that in a thousand years."

"Hey, you can't blame me for wantin' to make sure, can ya?"

"No I don't. And I won't."

"So, uh, you think, this Rohrbacher would talk to me, huh?"

"Don't see why not."

"Can I use your name?"

"I don't know how much good it's gonna do you, but sure, be my guest."

"You don't know him, is that what you're sayin'?"

"Oh no I know him, yeah, we worked some

cases together, sure, but, you know, beyond that, I don't know him, never socialized with him. But he'd probably remember me, yeah. I don't think I ever crossed him. Mario, since when do you need me to give you names? Huh?"

"I'm just lookin' for maybe some shortcuts here, that's all. Okay, Walk. Thanks for callin' back. I appreciate it."

They said good-bye, and Balzic hung up. He showered, dressed, made himself a quick breakfast of coffee and toast with peanut butter and marmalade, and then drove to the municipal parking lot behind the courthouse. From there, he walked to what was now being called the "old" county jail.

Dependent upon the age of the speaker, the "old" was relative about which county jail was the oldest the speaker could remember. The first one Balzic remembered had been situated next door to the courthouse, a three-story, sandstone building with fewer than thirty cells, no hot water, no central heat, and no indoor toilets. Guards, inmates, visitors, and officers of the court alike sweltered in summer, froze in winter, and complained about it year round.

A year after Balzic became a cop, in 1948, the then county commissioners declared their jail to be outmoded, outdated, and unsanitary and ordered it demolished to make room for a county office building, which they could not have done had they not already built a jail designed to house more than three hundred inmates. That steel,

135

concrete, and red brick testament to punishment had been built twenty miles from Rocksburg in the center of what had once been a two-hundred-acre dairy farm. At its opening it was hailed as state-of-the-correctional-art.

Twelve years and three county commissions later, however, that state-of-the-correctional-art facility was being called the biggest white elephant in modern Conemaugh County history because there were still eighteen years of debt left on the bond that had been issued to pay for a facility that had never been more than a third occupied.

Everybody who wanted to be elected or reelected to county office had an opinion about what to do with that jail, but what the county commissioners did was sell it to the Pennsylvania Department of Corrections, which itself desperately needed more cells. The commissioners completed the sale after they'd purchased an abandoned self-service laundry on advice from penal consultants who convinced them it could be converted for the right price to a jail that was more than adequate for county needs. Only trouble was, when that decision was made, it was 1968, and more and more people were being arrested for using illegal drugs; on the day the converted laundry opened its jail doors in 1970, the warden greeted a hundred inmates, four more than the ninety-six cells the consultants had said would be adequate.

By 1980, Conemaugh County was housing an average of one hundred prisoners a day in jails in rural counties all over the western third of the state at an average cost of twenty-five dollars per day per prisoner. By 1990, the number of prisoners housed in those same rural jails was up to two hundred a day and the average cost had risen to nearly forty dollars per day per prisoner. While the state of Pennsylvania kept building additions to Conemaugh County's old jail, so that it now housed more than nine hundred inmates, Conemaugh County's latest board of commissioners, elected in the fall of 1989, were running through a storm of suits and countersuits about the change orders the prison board absolutely had to have in the newest state-of-the-correctional-art county jail, the one that was going to replace the converted laundry which had replaced the jail that was now the state's Southern Regional Correctional Facility.

The "old" county jail Balzic was walking to was the converted laundry, which, rather than being abandoned as had been predicted when the newest county jail opened, was still very much in use, housing DUIs and deadbeat dads on work-release. It was still in use because the newest county jail, within months after its opening, had already filled 366 of its 386 cells, and the other twenty cells were empty only because the painting contractor was trying to figure out why the paint wasn't drying in them. The prison board was accusing the painting contractor of sabotage because they were withholding ten percent of his pay on the grounds that he'd violated the time clause in his performance bond, which he said was ridiculous because the longer he had to deal with the problem the more it was costing him out of his own pocket. But every time the prison staff tried to put cons into those twenty cells, half of them wound up in Conemaugh General Hospital, complaining of vertigo and nausea, thus costing the county even more money. Each time that happened, the *Rocksburg Gazette* editorialized that it could not imagine a more fitting symbol for the waste and inefficiency of government bureaucracy than watching paint dry.

Balzic tried not to think about it too often, but when he did, he marveled over the fact that while the population of Conemaugh County had diminished by almost nine percent between 1970 and 1990, the number of cells in the county had risen by nearly 250 percent, from four hundred to almost fifteen hundred. Southern Regional, which as the county jail had three hundred cells, now had nine hundred as a state facility. The laundry, converted originally to house ninety-six inmates, with the addition of dormitories made out of three trailers bolted together and set up in what had been the exercise yard, was now housing almost 140. And then there was the newest county jail, with its 386 cells, only weeks away from double-celling — even if the paint dried. Balzic knew in his heart, as did many other law officers he'd talked to, that the drug convictions which had begun as a bubbling creek in the 1960s had turned into a whitewater river in the 1990s, and were giving every indication of bursting both prisons and treasuries. The sorriest thing Balzic had heard about this cell-filling frenzy was the lament of a construction worker, as reported in a Pittsburgh newspaper, that he was glad for the steady employment but he hadn't worked on anything but jails in the last ten years and he'd slept better when he used to work on schools.

As Balzic stepped into the foyer of the old laundry and hit the button beside the main entrance, he thought that maybe somebody needed to rethink the whole idea of incarceration as punishment. Maybe the Quakers had been wrong. Maybe when they opened that penitentiary — what the hell was the name of that one? Was that Graterford? Christ, he couldn't remember anything anymore — was that the one in Philadelphia? Well, maybe when the Quakers opened it, there really had been some reason to believe that penitential things would happen inside. But as far as he could see, the scant number of jailhouse conversions taking place now wasn't anywhere near enough to justify the expense of housing all the rest of the cons who had no interest in repenting. Besides, every time a corrections bureaucrat denied an inmate the right to practice some other religion besides Christianity, it seemed to Balzic that all talk of repentence suddenly got hollow. When Black Muslims and Native Americans wanted to practice their religion, they invariably had to get a court order first. It seemed to

Balzic that jailhouse conversions were fine — as long as they were Christian.

Ah what the fuck do I know, he said to himself, as the door buzzed open and he stepped into the claustrophobic maze of corridors and offices inside. Who the hell do I think I am, Balzic grumbled to himself. Sure no warden. Never been, never wanted to be.

He handed over his ID case and his contract from the state AG's office to the CO working the door and the gun box and said, "I'm supposed to be on Edgar Patter's visitor sheet. Warden told me this morning he'd talk to somebody down here about it. Did he do that, is that true?"

"Yes he did. Talked to me. Lemme go see if we got some room. There's a coupla state cops talkin' to another inmate. We're kinda short on space here. Uh, didn't you used to be chief here?"

"Yes I did. Do I know you?"

"Aw we met a coupla times, you probably don't remember. I just moved onto steady daylight. Always used to work in the back at night. Hang on, I'll be right back."

Balzic tried to place the tall, roly-poly CO sidling down one of the narrow corridors away from him, but couldn't make him. In a moment Balzic forgot about him, caught up as he was in the sounds of the place, the doors opening and closing with that unmistakable heavy metal clang. Suddenly he was reminded of the night he was surfing channels when he'd come across MTV and a show called *Heavy Metal* something or other, or maybe it was called *Headbangers Ball*. He recalled being gripped by fascination at the wild-haired, tattooed, half-naked young men screaming and punishing their instruments. Standing here now, after forty-five years of listening to heavy metal doors open and close, he suddenly wondered if this was what "heavy metal" and "headbanger" music was about, and wondered how many of the kids who played it had a clue and how many were copycats. Somebody must have a clue in the beginning, he thought, just like some of the British rock 'n' rollers who acknowledged their debt to the black bluesmen and women who'd come first. . . .

"Down the corridor, left at the end, then straight. He's in what used to be the law library, you remember where that is?"

"Huh? Oh yeah. I can find it. Thanks."

"Hey, Chief, I don't wanna insult ya by pattin' ya down, but, uh, I have to ask, you know. You didn't start carryin' a piece, did ya?"

"Just these," Balzic said, handing over his keys and Swiss army knife. He watched the CO put the keys and knife into a brown envelope. The CO then tied a ticket to the envelope and tore off the bottom half of the ticket and handed to it Balzic.

Balzic hurried to what had been the law library. He hated being in these corridors, which were so narrow two people had to turn their shoulders in order to pass. In the law library, there was enough room to feed his delusion that he was not locked in, but he knew he had to concentrate and focus on the business at hand with Patter or he was going to have a hard time. As many times over the years as Balzic had taken naps in one of the cells in the basement lockup in City Hall, he'd never overcome his fear of small confining spaces. Hated flying for the same reason. Couldn't get out of the plane until somebody else opened the door. Couldn't get out of here for the same reason. Suddenly he had the urge to choke the "therapist" who'd first theorized that the way to overcome your fears was to confront them. . . .

"You Edgar Patter?"

"Yes," said a gaunt, pale man sitting on the far side of a metal table where he could watch the door. He was in his late thirties to early forties, balding from front to back, and looked like he could go a week between shaves. He wore a heavy sweatshirt under the standard-issue blue jumpsuit with short sleeves. His hands were jammed in his pockets, and while his thin upper body was relatively still, both his heels were bouncing. He had many pencil-thin scars over the left side of his face starting at about where his hairline used to be and going down to his jawline. The deepest scar angled from the top of his cheekbone downward into his nostril, where a part of his nostril was missing. Balzic wondered whether these scars were the result of a traffic accident or whether somebody had made a couple of swipes across Patter's face with broken glass. Balzic reached automatically for his ear and tugged and rubbed the spot where Anne Marie Vittone had taken a bite out of it.

Balzic introduced himself and set his bona fides on the table for Patter's inspection, and then he took off his topcoat, draped it over the chair, set his recorder in the middle of the table, turned it on, said the time, date, place, and purpose of the interview, and identified himself and Patter. Then he said, "Anything I can get for you before we start? Coffee, cigarettes, can of pop?"

"Blanket. Fuckers say it's sixty-five degrees in here. They lie. More like sixty. Shoulda brung it with me."

Balzic opened the door, spotted a CO in the corridor, and asked him to see if he could find a blanket.

"You might be right about the temperature," Balzic said, putting his topcoat back on when the CO brought a blanket.

Patter wrapped the blanket around his shoulders and pulled it tight around his neck by grabbing a handful of cloth and burying his hands in his lap.

"Ready?"

"Ready as I'm ever gonna be."

"Okay. Just for my information, what're you in for this time?"

"Perjury."

Balzic laughed. "You kiddin' me?"

"What's so funny?"

"You actually got convicted for perjury?"

143

Balzic couldn't stop laughing. "Hey. I've been a cop for a lotta years, believe me. But every time there were two people gettin' in each other's faces? I don't care what it was about, I knew one of 'em was lyin', maybe both, but one for sure, I *knew* that. But in all those years, I can't remember, Christ, I mean I used to threaten everybody with perjury but I never once busted anybody for it. Christ, that's funny."

"Glad you think it's funny."

Still laughing, Balzic said, "You musta told some big ones, Mister Patter. I mean it, you musta been on steroids when you told 'em. Human growth hormone or somethin'. So, uh, who was it, I mean, who was it actually decided to spend time and money prosecutin' you for perjury?"

"DA in Wabash County."

"And why was that?"

"Wait a minute, I thought you wanted to talk about Walczinsky."

"I am. And we are."

"So?"

"So what? You think I'm not interested in why you were busted for perjury? And who brought the charges? Who prosecuted you? What they proved to a jury you lied about? Did you have a jury, by the way?"

"No I didn't have a jury by the way. Fuckers railroaded me on this, if you wanna know. Same motherfuckin' DA who used to be a motherfuckin' district magistrate and the same motherfuckin' judge who used to be the motherfuckin' DA, that's who railroaded me, you wanna know."

"So what you're saying is, if I understand you right, is you may have changed your story about these two killings on Deer Mountain, but you did not lie, is that correct? Is that what we're talkin' here? Huh? The two murders, right? That you were one of the two witnesses who swore Lester Walczinsky was the shooter? We're talkin' the same thing, right?"

"That's what I'm talkin' about. I don't know what you're talkin' about."

"See, I just wanted to be sure we were talkin' about the same thing, okay? So, this is the thing, uh, you may have changed your story three or four times about this, but none of these times you were lying, is that what you're tellin' me?"

"That's exactly what I'm tellin' you."

"Uh-huh. What were you doin' then — if you weren't lyin'?"

"C'mon, man, what the fuck you think? I was tellin' 'em what they wanted to hear."

"Very good, Mister Patter, now we're gettin' someplace. Telling who, exactly, and what, exactly, okay?"

"Look. In '77, I was up on federal possession charges —"

"Possession of what?"

"Possession of pot, marijuana, you know? Possession with intent to distribute, all that shit. I got busted with a lotta weight. They were talkin' serious time. You know the drill, don't shit me you don't. I hear somebody's lookin' for somebody. Okay, so maybe I was an asshole. I was young, I was scared, I wanted to get the fuck outta the federal system, 'cause, right or wrong, I'd heard a lotta bad shit about the federal system, and I didn't want no part of it.

"And anyway, those fuckin' federal narcs were tryin' to turn me like every hour. Every hour, a new one'd come in seemed like, ask me who I was doin' business with, and where, and when, and how much, the whole routine. Finally one of 'em says somethin' about Portiletto and Stevens. Hey, bingo, I says to myself. I know them two, I says. Fuck yeah, I did all kindsa business with them two.

" 'No kiddin',' he says. 'Hold that thought,' he says, he'll be right back. He don't come back for like two hours and when he does come back he got these two state cops with him. So I'm figurin' all kindsa things, I'm schemin' every scheme I ever heard of tryin' to stay one jump ahead, you know, and they're askin' me all kindsa questions about these two assholes, this Portiletto and this Stevens. So I'm answerin' 'em, I'm tellin' 'em, yeah, yeah, I was in the pot business with them two for like two years — which was partly true, I did do some business with them — but these are *state* cops I'm talkin' to now, understand? And this one federal narc who's really been tryin' to turn me ever since I got picked up, all of a sudden he ain't sayin' nothin', and I'm thinkin', you

146

know, hey, I work this right, I can skate, man. I can kiss these federal motherfuckers good-bye. And then the one narc, he gives 'em a wink and a wave and out he goes, and then the other one, like five minutes later, he's gone too.

"And I'm sittin' there, and these two state cops are takin' turns feedin' me information about all these deals I mighta, I maybe, I coulda been doin' with these two, these assholes, this, uh, Portiletto and Stevens. And I'm goin', yeah, yeah, right, I was there, absolutely, I seen that, that was the day we moved two keys, right? Where was that did you say, Officer? Oh yeah, I remember now. Yeah, that was, uh, that was the day we sold them two keys to that asshole on the Pitt-Johnstown campus, right? Absolutely, I remember now. You wanna repeat his name? What? George somethin'? Oh I didn't know his last name, I just knew him by Georgie Boy, that's what they all called him, and they didn't introduce me or nothin', what the fuck, who uses their right name in the drug business?

"Blah blah blah, it goes on like 'at for maybe two hours. Nah, it wasn't November twenty-fourth, I thought it was probably the twenty-fifth, but if you say it was the twenty-fourth, hey, it was the twenty-fourth. Where was it? On Deer Mountain? Oh yeah, of course, absolutely I know, what am I, stupid? Yeah, right, we were up in this, uh, in this, what was it? Oh cabin, yeah, is that what it was? Oh right, a cabin on Deer Mountain, right, yeah, we were supposed to meet in this cabin and I was gonna trade 'em two pounds of pot for these two pistols, yeah, right, that was it, absolutely.

"And the next fuckin' thing I know, this cocksucker, this sonofabitch, he puts his notebook down, he leans across the table, he gets right in my face, he says, 'So you were present when Stevens and Portiletto were killed, is that right?'

"I go, whoa wait a fuckin' minute, what killed, what're you talkin' about, killed who?

"And these two motherfuckers put me through the worst fuckin' nightmare of my life, man. No fuckin' letup, man, no rest, no sleep, no food, no water, twelve fuckin' hours, man, those two cocksuckers had me handcuffed to the fuckin' table, wouldn't let me go to the bathroom, man, I wound up pissin' myself twice — not once — twice I pissed myself and they stand there fuckin' laughing at me, do I need a diaper, am I toilet trained, ha ha ha. Cocksuckers.

"But just when I'm thinkin' it's never gonna end, I'm gonna fuckin' die right there, hey, the motherfuckers finally bring me a Pepsi and a pack of cheese crackers and put me in a cell and let me go to sleep, man, and I'm thinkin', hey, it's over, I made it. I give 'em a lotta shit they wanted to hear, what the fuck, they want somebody for these murders, fuck, I'll give 'em somebody, what the fuck I care, I ain't goin' through twelve more minutes of this shit, never mind twelve hours. I'm gettin' outta this, I don't give a fuck who I gotta give up.

148

"So the next day — I think it was the next day, but I don't know how long they let me sleep — here they come again, only this time they don't say nothin', same two bastards, they're not sayin' a word, they take me down, put me in a car, drive me some fuckin' place I never been in my life, some fuckin' cabin up in the mountains somewhere, all I know is we're in Wabash County 'cause I seen the sign when we crossed the county line, but other'n that I don't know where the fuck we are. Way back in the woods, end of this road, road's nothin' but dirt, they pull up in front of this cabin. Fuckin' log cabin. Like fuckin' Abraham Lincoln was gonna come strollin' out.

"And we get out, they're still not sayin' a fuckin' word, nothin', they just start walkin' me around. Walked me around the whole outside of this cabin, didn't say one fuckin' word. And then we get back around to the front again, and they start up onto the porch and I see this little tiny piece of yellow plastic, it ain't no bigger'n a fingernail clippin', it's stickin' on a post on the porch, and I go, oh shit — to myself I'm sayin' this, I didn't say nothin' to them. I ain't no fuckin' genius, but I knew what that was. That yellow tape you guys put around someplace when you want everybody to stay out.

"And it didn't take no genius to figure out they sent somebody in there first, ahead of us, to take all that tape down for my benefit, and I'm thinkin', hey, this is where all this shit went down we were talkin' about yesterday. This is where those two assholes got their ticket punched, and I start sayin', right away, you know, soon as we started up on the porch, uh-uh, no way I'm goin' in there, and then — right then — that's when they started talkin'. Ain't said a fuckin' word till then — then! Then, it's hey, they're goin', 'What-samatter, Mis-ter Patter, somethin' in there you don't wanna see, huh? What don't you wanna see?'

"Listen, man, I know you don't believe me, 'cause nobody believes me, but I do not pretend to be anything but what I am, but that was bull-shit, pure and simple. I mean, what the fuck. If you want somebody to make a place for you, what the fuck would you drive him right up to the door for? Huh? That's stupid. I mean, stop the car, let the fucker out a quarter mile down the road, you know? See where he goes. You don't drive him right up to the fuckin' door, walk him around the *outside* of the fuckin' place, Jesus Christ. What's he s'posed to think, huh? Tell ya what I thought. Right away I thought what they want me to say is, I seen it from the outside."

"Don't stop now, Mister Patter. What else did you think?"

"Whatta you think? They got me, right? All they talked to me about the whole day before, the whole time, all they was talkin' about was dope, man, pot, that's all they wanted to know about, pot this, pot that, pot everyfuckin'thing. So if this was the place, what the fuck? Those two guys

150

musta got dusted over pot inside the cabin, what
else?"

"And?"

"And they started askin' me right away, who
did it? Who was there? Who was inside with
Stevens and Portiletto? Not what I seen. Not what
I heard. Not what time of fuckin' day it was, not
what was I doin' there, uh-uh. No. They didn't
ask me any of that shit. What they wanted to
know right then, man, was who, that's all, who
who who, like they was a coupla fuckin' owls."

"So you told 'em."

"Fuckin'-A I told 'em."

"Why'd you tell 'em Walczinsky?"

"Why do you think?"

"You tell me."

"C'mon. Why else? 'Cause I owed him like
three thousand dollars for pot I got from him,
man, and I knew he was lookin' for me. What
the fuck, huh? You was me and you bought like
three thousand dollars' wortha dope from somebody and the guy you're gonna sell it to, he rips
you off? Huh? You get ripped off — which is
exactly what happened — the guy I was s'posed
to sell it to, he ripped me off — you think Lester
was gonna believe me? With that story? Huh? But
it was the truth, man. It was not somethin' I
planned to do to Lester. I mean, I was good with
him. If I wasn't, man, why do you think he
woulda let me outta his sight with three thousand
bucks' wortha his dope? Bullshit. No way. If he
didn't know I was good for it, he wouldn'ta never

151

let me outta his sight, 'cause we done plenty of business together. But don't let nobody shit ya, Lester was far from the most honest guy himself, believe me."

"So, uh, what?" Balzic said. "You were afraid of him? And what, you believed he was gonna come lookin' for you and he was gonna kick your ass when you told him you didn't have the money, is that it? And here were these two cops lookin' for somebody?"

"Exactly, man. You gonna tell me they gave a fuck who they busted for that, you shittin' me? All in a day's work to them, man, no skin off their ass who it was."

"So, uh, screw Lester, right? Shame on him, right?"

"No no, you're makin' it sound like I set out to screw him, man, and it wasn't like that at all, swear to God. I didn't have nothin' against Lester except I owed him the three large, and I didn't know where I was gonna get it. Lester was not somebody you wanted to have mad with you, man. Lester's not real big, but he's quicker'n a rattlesnake. And in those days, he didn't ride nobody's shit. You fucked with Lester, Lester fucked back, believe me. He was cool when everything was right. I made a lotta money with Lester, smoked a lotta dope with him, had a lotta good times, but Lester had problems, man. He was seriously fucked up, and don't you believe for a minute he didn't take it out on the world. 'Cause he did. And I know, I mean, I can feel it in my bones, every time I see Lester, which ain't often, I mean, only times I see him is in court, but he never takes his eyes offa me, man. I know what he wantsa do to me. I don't blame him, but the guy he's got his beef with is not me. I'm not the one supplied me with all the details."

"The two state cops? What were their names by the way?"

"What were their names? Fuck them, man. They ain't the ones gimme all the details. It was his old man."

"What? Whose old man?"

"Lester's."

"Wait a minute, what did you say? Lester's *father* gave you the details?"

"I didn't stutter. Yeah. Lester's old man gave me all the details, man, it wasn't them fuckin' state cops. 'Cause soon as I said his name, Lester's, soon as Lester's name came outta my mouth, man, they had me back in the car so fast, and they drove me straight to his old man's station, took me inside, sat my ass down, had a little chitchat with Mister Chief of Po-lice Walczinsky, and then them two fuckers disappeared — none of this I knew at the time, understand? Huh? I didn't know where the fuck I was. Deer Mountain Borough Building, you shittin' me? I didn't know this cop was the chief there, man, you kiddin'? Or that he was *Lester's old man?* How the fuck was I s'posed to know that, you kiddin' me? All I knew was, after them two state cops split, man, they weren't gone ten seconds I'm gettin' dragged

153

downstairs backwards, this fucker's got me by the handcuffs and I'm goin' down the steps backwards, man. We finally get to this little office, man, he slams me down into a chair and bammo! Next thing I know I'm on my face on the floor and the back of my head is stingin', my fuckin' eyes're rollin', and I'm thinkin' I'm gonna throw up. Fucker jerks me up by the handcuffs, thought he was gonna tear my arms out, no shit, and he hauls my ass backwards down to one of his cells, he only got two cells, and there wasn't anybody in the other one, and I go flyin' inside, against the wall, smacked my head, ducked my face down, hit my forehead on the wall, now my head's hurtin' front *and* back, and this fucker's screamin' at me, tellin' me what a piece a shit I am and all dopers oughta die, my mother shoulda had an abortion, his wife shoulda had an abortion, I'm goin', whoa, what the fuck is this guy talkin' about, my mother shoulda had an abortion, his wife shoulda had an abortion, what the fuck is this?

"Well, he's gonna fix everything, he goes, don't you worry, he goes, you can just bet both cheeks of your ass on it. I remember he said both cheeks of my ass. And then he started, man. Turned me around and the first thing he did, he come at me with his right fist, I seen it comin', but there wasn't nothin' I could do about it, he had his middle knuckle stickin' out on his right fist and he got me right in the guts, man, right here, right below my breastbone, man, and he caught me

154

right when I was exhalin'.

"Jesus Christ, I thought I was gonna die. I could not get my breath. I just heard this awful fuckin' noise, and I'm thinkin', shit, man, that's me makin' that noise. Sounded like a donkey brayin', man, that's the only thing I could think of, a fuckin' donkey. And that was just the beginning. Believe me, that was just the start. Between him and that other fucker, man, I'm tellin' ya —"

"What other fucker?"

"The other cop, man. Showed up maybe ten minutes later, don't ask me how long, I don't know. Shit, he was worse than Walczinsky's old man — who don't forget I didn't know who he was at that time, okay? I did not know at that time he was Lester's old man. But that other prick, man, he was younger, and bigger, and stronger. Not that he enjoyed it any more. Uh-uh, nobody had a better time than the first guy. That prick really got off on it. Not that it makes a fuckin' difference, man, but I figured Lester out — I mean later on when I heard this other cop call this chief by his name, I go, oh fuck, why me?"

Balzic said, "So, uh, when did he start feedin' you details about the murders that the state cops had not told you? From what you said so far, all they did is show you where it happened, is that what you're sayin'?"

"Yeah, absolutely. He was who found 'em. The first cop I mean, I don't know who it was

155

found 'em, somebody trampin' around in the woods up there. But whoever found 'em, he was the first cop there."

"And they were found inside, correct? The victims?"

"Yeah, right. But he's the one told me where they were, how the bodies were layin' and how many times they'd been shot and how their pants were down around their ankles and whoever done it fucked 'em in the ass first so there had to be two of 'em, accordin' to him, you know, one of 'em doin' the fuckin' while the other one was holdin' the gun —"

"He told you all of this? The first one? The one you later found out was the chief? He's who told you in specific detail?"

"Absolutely. No way in the world I woulda known any of that stuff 'cause I wasn't there."

"He didn't feed it to you? He just told you?"

"No no, not like that, not like he just come out and told me, you know, one, two, three. He told me while the other one was beatin' me. I mean he was really fucking crazy when he was tellin' me about that, you know? How their pants were down and somebody had punked 'em, man, he was, oh shit, that just made him like, like he was frothin' at the mouth, he was like a fucking rabid dog, I'm not shittin' you. And every time I said it was Lester Walczinsky, he'd hit me, man. While the other prick was chokin' me, he'd whack me across my left arm, man, with this little blackjack. My left arm was every color of the fuckin' rainbow for about a fuckin' month. I still can't use my fingers good. I forget and reach for somethin', it goes right through my fingers."

"And you still at that time didn't know he was Lester's father?"

"Right, right, I didn't."

"When did you find out?"

"I don't know exactly. The other cop said his name. Neither one of 'em had nametags on. Soon as I heard the name, man, that's when I knew why I was gettin' the beatin', you know, 'cause who he wanted to beat was his kid, only he didn't know where he was, that's what I figured. 'Cause after he told me everything — you gotta understand — it wasn't like he was tellin' me like those state cops were doin' when they walked me around that cabin. It was like, so whoever shot them, punked them first — wham! Whoever shot them in the back of the head twice punked them in the ass first — wham! So not only was this all about dirty filthy dope, it was a goddamn dirty dope deal with a coupla faggot bastards shoulda been aborted — wham! And somewhere in there I heard the other prick call him Chief Walczinsky and the fuckin' light-bulb goes on in my head, you know, this sonof-abitch is crazy 'cause he thinks his son is not only a dope dealer, he's not only a murderer, he's also a faggot, and this crazy fuck was beatin' the shit outta me 'cause I'm the fool who gave up his son's name just to get outta the federal

157

shit I was in. And when I saw I was gettin' in worse and worse the longer I was there, I trieda tell 'em I didn't know nothin', the only reason I said Lester Walczinsky in the first place was just to get outta the federal system, but that just pissed 'em off more 'cause now they were callin' me a liar on top of everything else and they just beat me worse."

"So where'd you get the other name? You pull that one out of the air or did Chief Walczinsky give you that too? Or the other cop — whose name is what by the way?"

"Islip. Patrolman Martin Islip. Never forget that fucker if I live to be a thousand. That fucker went away one time for about five minutes and when he come back he had a knee pad on — you know the kind they wear when they play basketball? Only he had it on his elbow. And he stood me against the bars, facin' the bars? And he handcuffed me to the bars, way up high? And then that motherfucker went at my back with his elbow, with that pad on it . . . I thought I was gonna die. Went up and down my spine, high as he could reach, low as he could bend. I still feel like somebody's runnin' a hot wire down both my legs. Except for my toes. Can't feel nothin' in my toes. Seventeen years, man, I still can't feel my toes 'cause of that mother-fucker. Martin Islip.

"Best news I ever got in my life, honest to God, best present I ever got since I found out there wasn't no Santa Claus, almost enough to make me start believin' in God again, I heard that motherfucker's doin' ten to twenty for murder two. I'm snitchin' him out, man, to everybody I know, includin' screws, everybody. I'm prayin' somebody I snitch him out to gets in the same house with him, man, and makes him, honest to God, I pray for that. And I hope he dies the death of a thousand shanks."

"Well I'm sure you do, Mister Patter, but we have a problem."

"We? Who? You and me?"

"Yeah."

"Such as what?"

"Islip's sayin' you're a liar," Balzic lied.

"You talked to the sonofabitch? Where? Oh tell me, please, please tell me —"

"Forget about that. Fact is, Islip's sayin' you're a liar, says he knew you were a liar from the first minute he saw you. And you've been convicted of perjury, so the state agrees with him. And nobody's gonna get any argument about that from Lester Walin 'cause by your own admission he knows you're a liar too. And you've just admitted to me you lied to some federal narcs, and to two state cops, and then you lied to Chief Walczinsky and to Islip, you lied to 'em all. So why is anybody gonna believe you now? Because you got this ticket for drunk and disorderly in Ohio? If you're countin' on that, forget it, 'cause that's bullshit." Balzic wasn't a hundred percent certain that the ticket was bullshit because all he was going on was what Warren

159

Livingood had said about checking the citation out. What Balzic was doing was gauging Patter's reaction.

"Whattaya mean that's bullshit? That ain't bullshit. I was in Hubbard, Ohio, visitin' my aunt, I got blasted, and I got a ticket for it, man. It's proof. And that deputy attorney general, that Livingood, he got it, don't gimme that shit —"

"That deputy AG is who checked it out, and he found out the ticket's out of sequence and the date's been altered. State police crime lab is verifyin' that fact right now. So that's the problem we have, Mister Patter. And it's a big one. Too high for me to climb. So you're gonna have to come up with something else 'cause I don't think Chief Walczinsky is gonna corroborate what you're sayin' now, and Islip, as I already told you, he's not gonna corroborate your story. So you better have somethin' else for me."

"Well just tell me one thing, okay? Just one thing. You believe me? Just tell me that."

"Whether I believe you is beside the point, man. You do not have corroboration from nobody, nowhere, nohow. What I think doesn't count —"

"But do you believe me, that's all I'm askin', do you believe me? I know nobody else does, I'm askin' you, that's all, do you believe me or not?"

"I know you wanna get out real bad —"

"Who the fuck said anything about gettin' out, that ain't what I'm askin' you —"

"And I'm tellin' you, you got a history of tellin' people whatever they wanna hear in order to get what you want. That's not a good history to have."

"Then fuck you too. Fuck you, get outta here, get the fuck outta here, go on, I'm sicka lookin' at you. Story of my fuckin' life, honest to God, tell people the truth, nobody believes me."

"I'll believe you, Mister Patter, when you give me corroboration I can verify. You give me that, and I'll be the first one to stand up and cheer. You think of anything else, here's my name and number. Gimme a call." Balzic wrote his name and phone number on the back of one of Warren Livingood's cards and slid it across the table. "Meantime, good luck."

"Good luck?! Fuck you. Tell me where that motherfucker Islip is, I'll make my own fuckin' luck."

Balzic buttoned his coat, turned the tape recorder off, and thought about it. He put the tape recorder in his pocket after checking again to make sure it was off. Then he put his hands on the table and leaned close to Patter and whispered, "You wanna know where Islip is? I'll tell you where he is. You tell me some way I can check your story, I'll be happy to tell ya where he is. You make it possible for me to confirm what you said about him, I'll do better'n tell you where he is. I'll snitch him out myself."

"Man I told you everything," Patter said, nodding his head with ferocious disgust. "What the fuck else you want?"

"No you haven't. What you've told me is what you think is gonna work with me, and what I'm tellin' you is, it isn't. 'Cause the chief? Lester's father? He's had a stroke. Supposedly he can't talk, he can't write, he can't walk. So if there's nobody else involved but you and these two other guys and one of 'em's practically a potato and the other one's got absolutely no reason in the world to help you 'cause helpin' you just puts him in deeper shit, you followin' me? Then, Mister Patter, you better be the one who tells me somethin' that only you and Islip know about what happened durin' that time you were in their custody. 'Cause that's the only way I can go back to Islip and break him. So you think about it, real hard. But remember, if I can't verify it, it ain't worth my time to answer the phone, you hear me?"

Patter said nothing. He looked at the table and his shoulders sank. "Told you everything, man. Nothin' else to tell. Story of my life, no shit."

"The reason you think there's nothin' else, Mister Patter, is you're still tryin' to snow a cop. This time it happens to be me. You think you know better than me what I need to know, which I'm guessin' is what you think every time you talk to cops. In other words, you're not talkin' to me about what happened, you're tryin' to work me. Just like you tried to work everybody every single time you made a statement or gave testimony in this fuckin' farce. And that's not what you need

162

to do now. Just once in your life, you have to think about what happened — if it happened the way you say it happened — and what you have to think about is not what you think I wanna hear, but what actually happened, every little detail. You have to think about this as though you don't have one fuckin' thing to gain by what you say. Because in this case that's the only way you're gonna get what you want. The only way to get what you want is to stop thinking about what you want."

"I didn't tell you I wanted anything."

"Oh Jesus Christ. Islip? Remember? Coupla minutes ago you were practically beggin' me to tell you where he is. But now you think you don't want anything? Gimme a break."

Patter glared up at Balzic, but said nothing.

Balzic shook his head, turned and opened the door, and made his way down the narrow corridors to the front desk, where he turned in his ticket stub for his keys and pocketknife. He chatted with the CO briefly, briefly because he couldn't wait to get outside, and then hurried out into the cold, gray, wet afternoon.

Chin buried in his collar, shoulders bent against the wind, he hustled back to his car in the municipal garage, thinking that if Patter didn't take the bait about Islip there was no way in hell Patter was ever going to call. He'd asked Patter to do something Patter had never been able to do on his own: to see the world in some way other than the one that had caused his life to be continually

163

skewed and perpetually screwed; to see it separate from himself, as an object, a set of circumstances, a situation to be observed in every detail for its own sake. And Balzic knew Patter wasn't capable of that.

Besides, Balzic thought sourly, if somebody asked me to do the same thing I'd say they were being chickenshit. Only reason Balzic could give himself for asking it of Patter was that this time Patter was probably telling the truth. And if he was, then he needed something hard to bite down on every time he thought about why he was where he was and why Lester Walin was where he was. Sometimes I am a chickenshit, Balzic thought. No probablies about it. And someday I'm gonna pay for it. But not today. I hope.

After Balzic was cleared through the main gate at Southern Regional Correctional Facility, he turned right and headed for the visitors area, six cream-colored trailers fastened together with the inside walls removed and situated within a few yards of the gate. He saw two state police troopers and four corrections officers with their heads together, talking, pointing, writing, and taking pictures near the gate into the main building. Inside the visitors area, Balzic felt the floor giving slightly and then springing back with each step as he made his way to the caged office where the CO in charge was hunched over some papers. As far as Balzic could tell, the CO was the only person in the visitors area. This surprised him, as he'd expected to find the room jammed with sullen men, sulky women, and irritable children pretending to be happy families.

As he had done at the main gate, Balzic presented his shield and ID and a copy of his contract. The CO, scowling and edgy, was in no mood for small talk while he waited for somebody on the other end of his phone call to verify Balzic's bona fides.

The CO hung up and handed the contract back to Balzic. "You been here before, right?"

"Many times."

"So you know the drill. He'll be over in a coupla minutes. You can wait for him in the interview room."

"Yeah, thanks. Uh, you have a problem here today?"

"Why?"

"State troopers outside, nobody in here. I mean, this time of day, usually you can't find a seat."

"Yeah, we had a problem."

"Anybody get hurt?"

"Yeah. Listen, I got a report to finish here and it's gonna take me a while, so, uh, how about you just goin' down the interview room, okay? Waitin' down there? They'll be bringin' him over shortly. Shouldn't be too long, depends what kinda problems they're havin' with the lockdown."

"Sure, fine. Uh, one more thing. Is he a smoker, Islip, do you know? He allowed to smoke in there? Been a while since I've been here."

"Up to you, you want him to smoke, let him smoke." Then, rubbing his jaw briskly with his knuckles, he hunched over papers on his desk and was gone from Balzic.

Balzic walked to the far end of the room, opened the door to the interview room, and draped his topcoat over one of the two gray metal chairs on the near side of the rectangular gray metal table and sat on the other one. He took out his tape recorder and set it in the middle of the table and looked around. There was another chair on the other side of the table, but aside from that, the room, all institutional tan and beige and gray, was barren. It was lit by a pair of fluorescent tubes overhead. There was a window in the top half of the inside door, and a large window to the left of the door. Both windows had plastic blinds. There were no windows facing the outside, and no door.

A CO brought Martin Islip into the trailers. Balzic could hear the wrist and ankle restraints rattling as Islip shuffled across the springy floor. When they came into the interview room Islip was complaining about the restraints, saying he couldn't smoke. The CO ignored him and told Balzic to notify the CO in the cage when he was done.

"He have to keep those on?" Balzic said. "I don't think he's goin' anywhere."

The CO glared at Balzic. "He should be happy he's allowed to see the outside of his unit."

Balzic cleared his throat and became very interested in the settings on his tape recorder.

After hooking Islip's wrist restraints to the table, the CO hurried away.

"Who're you and what do you want?" Islip said.

Balzic looked at Islip but talked to the tape recorder.

"Uh, this is Mario Balzic, special investigator for the state attorney general. First interview with Mister Martin Islip, inmate here at Southern Regional Correctional Facility." Balzic checked the time and date on his Timex, recorded them, and said, speaking now directly to Islip, "This is in connection with a request for a post-conviction hearing filed by Lester Walczinsky, aka Lester Walin —"

"Let me stop you right there," Islip said in a patronizing monotone. He was large, two hundred and thirty or forty pounds, Balzic guessed, probably over six feet, with thick muscles in his neck, shoulders, and arms, muscles that couldn't be concealed even by the sweatshirt he was wearing over his jumpsuit. His black hair was cropped very close to his skull and speckled with gray above his ears. His face was roundish and smooth and made him appear much younger than he was. Balzic guessed Islip was at least in his mid-forties, but he looked ten years younger.

"I don't have anything to say about Lester Walczinsky," Islip went on in the same bored monotone. "His own father said he was a piece of dog shit and should've been aborted. I heard him say that myself many times, and everything I know about little Lester, believe me, nothing I

167

know about him would make me contradict anything his father said."

"What're you in here for, Mister Islip?"

"I was transferred here by the state Department of Corrections from Huntingdon Correctional Facility. You want to know why I'm here, ask them."

"Mister Islip, I woke up with a spasm in my back and nothin' I've taken so far is makin' it go away. You know what I asked you. Please answer it."

"Oh dear, little back boo-boo there? Take two aspirins and see me in the next life. Call the CO, I'm done."

"I'm not callin' anybody. I ask again, why're you here?"

"Why're you wastin' my time, you know why I'm here. What'd you say your name was again? Balzic? I know that name. Yeah. You used to be chief in Rocksburg, right?"

"That's right. I ask again, why're you —"

"Oh for crissake, the *state* says I murdered somebody. The *state* convicted me of murder in the third degree, which is a felony of the first degree, and the *state* has locked me in for no less than ten years and no more than twenty, all of which you knew before you left home, so what kind of fucking game are you playing here?"

"I just want it on the tape, that's all," Balzic said, giving Islip a crooked little smile.

"Well now you got it on the tape. Right after you also have me sayin' that I'm not gonna talk about Lester Walczinsky, so what're you gonna do now, hmm? I would've thought by now you'd be tired and sick of playin' robbers and cops. Askin' the same stupid questions to the same stupid people, where were you, who were you with, can either one of you prove that, what shit. How long were you a cop? Forever, Christ. I remember hearin' your name when I was in fucking grade school."

"Questions bore you, don't they? Askin' 'em, answerin' 'em, doesn't matter, does it?"

"Oh what, I'm gonna get your best psychological interrogation here, huh? Oh this is gonna be cute, go 'head, c'mon, put your best mind on it, lemme hear this. Who knows, when I leave my present position here, I may decide to go back into, uh, the criminal investigation field, so, uh, c'mon, show me somethin'. I'm open, I'm willing to learn."

"What're you doin', Islip? You writin' a scene for this movie you think somebody's gonna make about you?"

Islip snorted. "That's already done. I don't have to write anything. That's all taken care of. It's already makin' the rounds out there in Hollywood. There's been some interest. Strong interest, matter of fact. Nah, I really wanna hear this other thing, this theory you got about how questions bore me, askin' 'em, answerin' 'em, this is a new one to me. Just let me tell you somethin' before you get into this too deep, Balzic. I was the subject for two doctoral dissertations already.

169

Two guys wrote their dissertations on me in clinical psychology. Yeah, lower your eyebrows, it's a fact."

"Didn't know my eyebrows were up."

"You wanna do this kinda work, you need to get better control of your face." Islip was starting to get animated.

"Oh. I'll remember that. I will."

"See, fact is, I talked to those two guys, the first one, talked to him at least two months, four hours a day, five days a week. The other one wasn't what I call too quick, he took about three months. Point is, between the two of them, they asked me every fucking kind of psychological bullshit question anybody could've ever thought about askin' me, including Siggy Freud himself. But now here you are, *you're* gonna ask me somethin' new. Go 'head, this is gonna be real juicy. This is gonna be warm, and wet, and juicier'n hell."

Balzic shook his head. "They ever let you read 'em? Ever see 'em? Either one?"

"Read 'em? What the fuck would I do that for, I know what's in 'em. I'm the one that was answerin' the questions, remember? These things that bore me — according to you. I was there when they asked 'em, I was the one givin' *them* the answers, what the fuck would I need to read 'em for?"

"I never wrote a doctoral dissertation, so I don't really know, but somethin' tells me it's not just Q and A. Somethin' tells me there's a little analysis throughout, especially at the end. I mean that would just stand to reason, don't you think?"

"Oh, what, I was supposed to be interested in what those two geeks had to say? About me? After they gave it their best psychological analysis? Forget about them, they didn't know what you know. C'mon, I wanna hear how you have somethin' new to add to the study of human behavior."

"What did you say before? This was gonna be warm and wet and juicy? Is that what you said?"

"Somethin' like that, yeah, juicier'n hell's what I said. Oh. You gonna make some connection between somethin' I heard you say and with young pussy and, uh, feelin' good, huh? Oh, that's original. Lemme see. Cop psychoanalyst finds that incarcerated healthy males frequently associate intellectual pleasure with fantasies or memories of sexual pleasure. Oh Doctor Doctor, please do go on. Your brilliant analysis excites me so much, why yes, I do believe, oh my yes, it's true, I can feel it rising in me, I'm gettin' an erection at this very minute, oh Doctor Doctor, what could this mean?"

"Means you and Lester Walczinsky have somethin' in common."

"What?"

"Well what Lester told me is, while he was in solitary, what got him through solitary was, uh, while he was jackin' off, he used to fantasize about givin' his old man a heart attack."

Islip's eyes narrowed slightly and his lower jaw

crept forward as he tilted his head back. "Just one more piece of evidence to show what a sick fuck he was. Is. His own father told me what a sick fuck he is. Many times. Told me how he used to go around accusin' his own father of murderin' his mother, that's how sick he was. And I'm just glad his father isn't here right now to listen to this disgusting bullshit comin' out of your mouth. And I have nothing in common with sick fucks like him."

"I don't know," Balzic said, shrugging. "He gets off on hoping his father has a heart attack, you get off on the thought that you're smarter'n everybody else. Turns out you and him both get off on things that have nothin' to do with sex. Either one of those dissertation guys mention anything like that?"

"I guess you think you're funny."

"Who said funny? I never said funny. This is pathetic. You're pathetic. I think Walczinsky's — you should excuse the expression here — I think Lester's takin' a royal screwin'. And isn't that interesting, huh? That we associate bein' wronged with bein' screwed, which is another way of saying bein' fucked. Makes you wonder sometimes what women think about it, don't it? Well, maybe not you, but it makes me wonder."

Islip's heels started bouncing. His chin had slowly come forward until he was glaring at Balzic from under his brows.

"So whattaya think, Marty? Huh?"

"Mister to you."

"Marty, tell me, you think any of this is gonna get in the movie they make about you? Huh? You think anybody's gonna take a full frontal shot of some actor playin' you playin' with himself? Huh? Full frontal shot of a guy whackin' off while thinkin' of intellectual things? Like how would they do that in your script, huh? Would they have you humpin' yourself there while pictures of like what — triangles and square roots and hypotenuses would be floatin' over your head? Or would you be whackin' off to the words of the Gettysburg Address? Huh? Help me out here, really, I'm intrigued."

"Go fuck yourself."

"Now see there? There you go again. Let yourself get upset with me and whattaya say, huh? Go fuck myself. I don't get it, I really don't, all these associations with sex and pain, and, uh, intellectual stimulation and anger and rejection, man, it's startin' to get too deep for me I think, you know what I'm sayin'?"

"I said that a long time ago."

"Yeah, you're probably right. So, maybe I should get back to somethin' a little shallower, like, uh, listen, when did Lester Walczinsky's father, I mean he was your rabbi, right? Hired you, trained you, taught you all the little tricks — did he teach you that one about the knee pad on your elbow, or did you learn that one yourself?"

"Fuck you."

"There you go again. An expression of sex used to represent anger. I'm tellin' ya, sex is

173

everywhere with you, Marty, I mean it, really. It's everywhere on you. So, uh, the whole time you were the police patrolman in Deer Mountain Borough, I mean, you and Lester's father, you were it, right? You two were the entire department, right? There wasn't anybody else, right?"

"You know the answer to that."

"Yeah I do. I just wanna hear you say it, for the tape, you know?"

"Yes. For the tape. Chief Walczinsky and I were the entire police department of Deer Mountain Borough."

"From when to when?"

"From, uh, '76, uh, until '89."

"So, thirteen years you worked with him — until you were arrested and charged with criminal homicide, right?"

Islip said nothing.

"Mister Islip sits silently in response to the last question. I take his silence to mean he agrees with my arithmetic. So, uh, movin' on, Chief Walczinsky sent you through all the state police training, right?"

"Why you wastin' my time with questions you know the answer to?"

"And he made sure — I take that for a yes — and he made sure you kept up with your certification, right? And all your training, right? Traffic, domestic, firearms, self-defense, crime scene, all of that, right?"

"What the fuck's your point?"

"So he had pretty much control of your training, right?"

"You deaf — what the fuck's your point?"

"And he also pretty much had control of your finances, right? He wrote your fitness reports, right?"

"Who the fuck else would do it? He was the chief and there were only the two of us, you think I was doin' that? Jesus."

"Good cop, was he? Good rabbi? Huh? Good teacher?"

"The best."

"Well the best is relative, right? I mean, how would you know what the best is? He was your only, right? I mean, who'd you have to compare him to, right?"

"All the instructors with the state police training centers."

"Oh well sure, them, yeah. But they didn't teach you what he taught ya, right? The little things, huh? The little things even the best textbook instructors forget, you know? Despite all their good intentions. They got so much ground to cover, they can't get to those little things you only get from day-to-day experience, you know what I'm sayin'?"

"For the third time, what's your fucking point?"

"My point is, hey, I mean, they never taught you that little number with the elbow pad? The elbow in the spine, huh? That number you did on Edgar Patter? Remember him, Edgar Patter?"

"That's what this is about? That piece of shit? Get real. He's a certified liar. He's locked up for it for crissake. That piece of shit wouldn't know true from false if his mother's life depended on it."

"Well, maybe not, Marty, but he's who told me about you and the elbow pad. He's who told me how you cuffed him with his hands high facin' the bars, and how you stood beside him, and how you let him have it with your elbow, up and down his spine. How would I know about that if he hadn't told me?"

"Let me tell you what I think of Edgar Patter. The same thing I think about Lester Walczinsky. I think that when twenty or thirty niggers go lookin' for some white trash they wanna fuck to death, I hope those two are who they find."

"Oh my, there you go again, Marty. Now it's sex associated with murder. I can't keep up with you. Really, I don't know how to describe your mind. Certainly isn't lazy, I'll say that for it. Very active. Where'd you learn all these things? What kind of family'd you come from? Father died when you were very young, right?"

"You knew that before you left home, stop playin' this shit with me."

Balzic was making this up as he went. He had no idea when Islip's father had died, or that he had.

It was '76, wasn't it? Isn't that what you said — '76? When Chief Walczinsky became your rabbi? Huh? Your boss, your teacher, your men-

176

tor, the guy who told you what to do and whether you did it okay and how to do it better the next time? The guy who praised you, and blamed you, and taught you all the little ins and outs? The guy who made it official on borough stationery? The guy who decided whether you kept your job? And how much of a raise you got? The guy who said his own son was such a fuckup he wished his wife had aborted him —"

Islip lunged upward and shouted, "Officer! Officer! I'm done here! I want this visitor off my sheet. I don't wanna ever see this visitor again!" He tried to spin upward and away from his chair, but his wrist chain jerked him back into the seat. He kept shouting for the CO all the while.

The CO came bolting out of his cage, but slowed to a walk as soon as he saw Balzic motioning for him to calm down, there was no real problem. When the CO opened the door, he came in and said over Islip's shoulder, "What's goin' on?"

"I'm done here is what's goin' on," Islip growled.

"Mister Islip became upset, agitated you might say, by what I was askin' him, that's all. No problem for me." Balzic was sitting calmly, shrugging at the CO.

"No problem for me either," Islip said, smirking. "You know the rules. I don't wanna talk to the sonofabitch, I don't have to. He wants to talk to me that bad, he can get a fuckin' warrant and arrest me. Or he can get a fuckin' subpoena, one or the other. But without one or the other, there's not one rule in this world says I got to sit here and listen to this cocksucker."

The CO looked at Balzic and shrugged as though to say, He's right. Then to Islip he said, "I'll call for somebody to come get you."

"Jesus Christ," Islip said, "what's wrong with you? You're in full lockdown here and you're gonna waste everybody's time gettin' me an escort? Which is what I said to the CO who brought me over here. And he gave me the same dumb-ass look you're givin' me now. I don't believe you guys sometimes."

"This your first full lockdown here?"

"So? I've been in lockdowns before, I'm no cherry."

"You're no cherry?" the CO said evenly. "Well. Maybe they did it some other way where you were, but a full lockdown here means no inmate moves without an escort. We are in full lockdown. You are an inmate. You want to move you will have an escort. And you say one more word — one — you'll be talkin' to yourself for the next five days. And, uh, who I am is George Washington. And the reason you're not a cherry — the reason I know you're not a cherry is 'cause you're a cherry tree, you follow? Ah ah ah, don't say yes, don't do that, just nod, so help me, don't test me. Just nod."

Islip's chest and shoulders were heaving, but he managed to control his mouth. He nodded, turned, and glared at Balzic.

The CO disappeared back inside his office.

Balzic folded his hands in his lap and leaned forward. "You're the answer man, aren't you? Huh? That's why you don't bother with questions, right? You got all the answers. You know how everything oughta be and how everything oughta run and it's just so obvious to you you're right, you can't be bothered with questions, can ya? From people you think are stupid 'cause they can't see the answers written all over you, isn't that right?"

"He said he didn't want me sayin' another word," Islip said, nodding toward the door and the CO beyond it. "He can put me in restricted housing for five days, guaranteed, so I shut up. But there isn't one fuckin' thing in this world you can do to me, so shut the fuck up, asshole, okay?"

"Right on, answer man. Absolutely. There is not one thing in this world I can do to you — oh wait. Wait! There is one thing I can do to you. But before I tell you what it is, huh? Before that I gotta tell ya somethin' else. Talked to an old friend of mine. Walker Johnson. You don't know him, but he put me in touch with somebody I'm sure you do remember — Sergeant Rohrbacher, is that name familiar to you?"

Islip glared at Balzic and started grinding his molars.

"Don't remember him, huh? He was in charge of Troop B CID. His guys investigated your case, you remember him now? He was the lead investigator, you don't remember him?"

179

Islip continued to glare at Balzic and to chew his teeth.

"Well, right before I came down here, Marty, I called him up, had a long talk with him. Asked him, I said tell me about this guy — meaning you — tell me what you did. So he tells me. Honest to God, Marty, I have to tell you, I can't believe it, especially now that I know you're the answer man? Jesus, this was brilliant, what you did.

"When he told me, Marty, I nearly dropped the phone, I was stunned. The answer man, the man who knows how everything is supposed to run, the man whose rabbi was absolutely this outstanding teacher, taught you all the tricks, all the gimmicks, the ins, the outs, and what do you do, huh? I can't believe it."

"Don't."

"Oh, but I have to. 'Cause it's on the record. On many records all over the place. The answer man, the world's second-best cop after Chief Walter Walczinsky — you, you get the word your ex-wife is foolin' around — notice those two little letters, E and X? Your ex, as in a person you have no legal connection to? Oh God, this is so brilliant, Marty, I don't know if I'm even on your level that I should be tellin' it."

Islip jumped up growling, knocking the plastic chair over backwards, but the wrist chain stopped him with a jerk and brought him down into a half-crouch over the table.

"Ah ah ah," Balzic said, wagging his finger, "I wouldn't move till my escort got here I was you,

Marty. I would not wanna be testin' that CO out there. Course since you're the answer man here I probably shouldn't be tellin' you what to do. Anyway, first off, I don't have an ex-wife. I'm still married to the same woman I married so long ago I can't remember when I wasn't married.

"But back to you. I mean, when you hear your ex is foolin' around, you started followin' her, right? Followed her until you caught her with this guy you thought she was foolin' with, right? Your ex-wife this is — *ex?* And then you actually put all your police training and knowledge and skill — everything you learned from all those state police instructors and everything you learned from Chief Walczinsky? And you caught up with this guy at like three o'clock one morning? When you were in your police cruiser? And you pulled him over? And you walked up to the driver-side window? And you put your left hand on the roof of his car? Your left hand naked? As in there was no glove on it? So that it left an almost perfect print of your entire hand? And you shot this guy three times? With your service revolver? Twice in the chest and once in the head? And then you put your service revolver back in your holster? And you walked back to your cruiser, and you called Chief Walczinsky, and you called the coroner, and you told 'em both you found this guy along the side of the road, just like that, just doin' your routine patrol, and you saw the car, and there he was?

"Jesus, answer man, in my whole life I never

181

heard such a brilliant plan to murder your enemy. This should be in the murder hall of fame, I mean it. And the most brilliant part? I mean, I'm glad I didn't have to solve this case, honest to God, I woulda never thought of this. I mean, don't get rid of the murder weapon, right? Gettin' rid of the gun, that's for schmucks. Any schmuck woulda done that. But not the answer man. Oh no. Absolutely brilliant. The answer man kept right on wearin' it to work, every day, right? That was fuckin' outstanding — especially after you threw everybody off the track by puttin' your left hand on the roof of the car — while it was naked, while you weren't wearin' a glove.

"And the most brilliant part, I mean, when Rohrbacher told me this, I was just speechless, man. I literally could not talk. He told me — with the greatest admiration he told me this — he said that when he approached you and asked you to turn over your service revolver? Just for a routine ballistics comparison, remember that? Rohrbacher told me, and he was really impressed, man, with how absolutely totally in control of your face you were? He said you actually looked *sur-prised*. Yeah. *Sur-prised.*

"Oh oh, I think I hear your escort comin'. Yep, there he is. Listen, Marty, I'm really sorry we didn't have more time, I really woulda liked to see if maybe you coulda found it in yourself some way, you know, to share some of this with me."

Islip tried to pull himself up to his full height, as far as his wrist chain would permit, and he sneered down at Balzic, and said, "I'll share you somethin'. How about this, okay? How 'bout on your way out of here, a rabid raccoon runs across in front of you, and you have to swerve and you do a headfirst into another car, but you don't die right away. How 'bout you're pinned in there, and this rabid 'coon comes and starts chewin' on your face, eats your fuckin' eyeballs out."

"Well, thanks for sharin', Marty. In one way I wish you hadn't. But in another way, I'm glad you did. 'Cause it makes it easier for me now. I put a lotta guys in here. A couple of 'em are still here. And now? 'Cause of what you just said? Now I don't feel so bad tellin' you that there is one thing I can do to you. And I'm gonna do it, Marty. You guess what it is?"

"I hope the 'coon eats your dick off first. Before he eats your eyeballs out."

"Don't wanna guess, Marty? Huh? Why don't I just tell you, okay? I'm gonna snitch you out, Marty. The minute I hear this lockdown's over? I'm gonna call some of the guys I put in here and I'm gonna snitch you out to them. Bet your life on it, answer man."

"You done here?" said the CO who'd come to escort Islip.

"Yeah, we're done here, right, Marty? We done?"

"I wanna talk to the deputy warden of operations," Islip said. "I wanna talk to him now and I don't fucking mean a half hour from now, I mean fucking now!"

183

"He's busy," the CO said, unlocking the table hook, and leading Islip out and across the springy floor of the visitors area.

"I don't give a fuck how busy he is!" Islip was bellowing as he went through the door to the outside.

Balzic gathered up his recorder, put on his coat, and started across the floor toward the exit, but the CO in the cage called him back. "I take it as a bad sign when an inmate leaves this room and he's screamin' he wants to see the DWO."

"The who?"

"Deputy warden of operations. What was that about?"

"Don't know," Balzic said. "You'll have to ask him what he was screamin' about."

"Listen, mister, I've had a real bad day. A good friend of mine is in the hospital. And when you go outside, you're gonna see the chief of security and a whole bunch of state troopers conductin' an investigation, and soon as I finish writin' this report I'm gonna be out there with 'em, so don't pull my wire here, okay. What'd you say to that inmate? Did you threaten that inmate, 'cause if you did —"

"Yes I did."

"Huh?" The CO was incredulous. "You're admittin' it? What the hell's wrong with you? You're from the attorney general's office and you're admittin' you threatened him? You're supposed to say no, asshole! You tryin' to piss me off on purpose?"

184

"Hey, you asked me a question, I gave you the answer. Did I threaten the guy? Yeah I threatened him. Makes you feel any better, I have no intention of carryin' out my threat. Don't have to. 'Cause I do that, all I'm gonna do is get other people in trouble. But if I tell him I'm gonna do it, the only one's gonna get in trouble is him — himself, all by himself. And he's already doin' that. He's beggin' to do all the rest of his time in solitary, that's what he's hollerin' about. And I can't think of anybody deserves to be in solitary more'n that prick. And, as long as he's in there, who's gonna fuck with him? Nobody but him. So actually, what you could say is, what I'm doin' here is crime prevention, if you wanna know. And I feel pretty good about it. So, uh, you gonna do somethin' here, or can I leave?"

The CO grunted and shook his head, nodded toward the door, and said, "Leave. Now, okay?"

Balzic walked out and saw that the two state troopers and the four COs were still covering ground, talking, pointing, and gesturing, measuring, taking pictures, working another crime scene inside the razor wire. All in a day's work.

Balzic called Livingood half a dozen times at all of his numbers but heard nothing but messages on answering machines. Livingood called Balzic at home around nine that night.

"Mario, hope you have better things to say than I do," Livingood said, sounding like he was tired or starting to get a cold, maybe both.

185

"I probably don't. Just wanted to tell you a couple of things. First, I've interviewed Walczinsky, Patter, and Islip."

"Well, at least one of us is moving right along."

"That depends. In the words of Iron City Steve, I might be proceeding but that doesn't mean that I'm progressing. You don't sound exactly enthusiastic yourself. Or else you're gettin' a cold."

"I wish it was a cold. I've spent the last two days listening to one of my best interviewers get talked in circles by the Wabash DA. Official oppression, the DA says, is that what you guys're talking about? In a homicide investigation? The police beat a witness? While I was district justice? While I presided over the preliminary hearing? After I'd taken an oath to uphold the law? He hoped we had substantiation for these slanders because if we didn't he was going to have the testicles of the entire state of Pennsylvania in his hands — or the governor's, I forget which — probably both at one time or another, while, naturally, he was looking us both right in the eye like the pro that he is. Very controlled, very reserved, very much in command of who he is. So tell me, how'd you do?"

"Not real good. Edgar Patter has a great story, uh, only thing is, it's his word against two cops, and he's currently doing time for perjury — first person I've ever met who was actually convicted of that, and no, I'm not kiddin'. But, uh, anyway, since, of the two cops who supposedly fed him the information to convict Lester Walczinsky —

while they were beatin' it into him — I mean, of those two, one of 'em had a stroke and is now supposed to be pretty much a broccoli, and the other one, he's, uh, well, I pretty much fucked up the interview with him."

"Beg pardon? You did what?"

"Screwed it up. Went in with a prejudice, and he came on like the answer man, and I, uh, I lost my cool. Hey, I wish there was some other way to say this, but the fact is, I wanted to make the bastard miserable, so, uh, instead of doin' my job, I got carried away and started to ridicule him and, uh, generally fucked everything up. Got nothin' out of him."

Balzic blew out a sigh and waited, but Livingood said nothing. Balzic shifted from foot to foot for what seemed an interminable time. Then he said, "The only thing I can say in my defense is, soon as he came in and started blowin' bullshit about how he was the answer man, I knew I wasn't gonna get anything out of him. So instead of tryin' to do somethin' for him, tryin' to beat him with sweet talk, I just . . . I just did everything you're not supposed to do. Piss-poor interview is what it was —"

"Well if you truly believed you weren't going to get anything out of him, I suppose I can understand how you, I mean, I felt that way myself with this DA. You just get very very frustrated —"

"Yeah, right. Thanks," Balzic said, but he knew from Livingood's tone that he was just saying words. "But you didn't hire me to get frustrated, and — never mind. When you listen to the tape you'll know what I'm talkin' about. I mean I gave you that big speech about not wantin' to read other people's prejudices, and then I, uh, then I walk in there and all I can see is this prick bully who screws it up for every cop that's tryin' to do his job, and, uh, next thing I know, I just wanted revenge for that. Just wanted the prick to suffer, that's all, and I know — 'cause I knew immediately — there was no way in the world it was gonna happen in a courtroom. 'Cause it ain't. 'Cause nobody's gonna believe Patter. He's a born liar. And Chief Walczinsky wouldn't talk even if he could — if it's true that he really is a broccoli — and no way in this world Islip is gonna suddenly get a conscience. Pricks like him, I mean if they had a conscience they wouldn't be pricks."

Balzic waited for Livingood to say something.

"Hello? You still there?"

"I'm still here. Thinking. I still have to deal with the judge. Not that I have much hope there either, but, uh, we still have to do the drill. So. What's next for you?"

"Only ones I have left are, uh, the shooter and the woman — ah, I shouldn't be tellin' you this over the phone. Listen to the tapes, you'll hear — you listened to any of them yet?"

"Not yet. Haven't had a chance."

"I mailed them to that Pittsburgh address. You still there, right?"

"Not tonight. I'm too tired to drive back to

188

Pittsburgh. But that's all right, I'll get to the tapes soon enough."

"Where you stayin', which motel?"

"Haven't decided yet. Just encountered some truly awful food and actually what I'm hoping is I'll find somebody who knows how to make a hamburger, not that I'm optimistic."

"Good luck. Listen, I was, uh, sorta hopin' you'd already listened to the tapes I sent — ah never mind."

"Mario, I'll get to them soon enough, believe me."

"Well, okay. But listen. There's nothin' I learned so far that backs me up on this, but I know as sure as I'm standin' here, this Walczinsky didn't do these murders. I mean, I feel bad for the guy, but, Jesus, unless I come up with somethin' from the shooter, this Scumacci, I don't see how you're even gonna be able to swing the p-c hearing, I really don't. I'm gonna talk to this Missus Walczinsky, but even if she backs him up a hundred percent, his story is so cornball, I had a hard time keepin' a straight face. This is one of those times where everything I know so far, I mean, it's not only not provable, most of it's laughable. Nah, I don't mean that. None of it's laughable, it's not laughable, it's pathetic. I don't know what I mean. I'll keep in touch."

"Mario? Don't hang up."

"Yeah?"

"Did your mother cook for you? When you were a child?"

189

"Beg your pardon?"

"Did she?"

"Well, yeah, of course. Long after I was a child. Hell, she was still cookin' for us two, three times a week right up until she died. Why?"

"My advice to you is this. Eat something your mother used to make. Have a glass of wine. Talk to your wife. Listen to some music. Start over tomorrow."

Balzic held the receiver away from his ear and looked at it. "Uh, yeah. Okay. Maybe you oughta try that yourself."

"Wish I could," Livingood said. "Only time my mother ever went into the kitchen was to find out why Cook wasn't responding to the buzzer."

"Uh, didn't you know the cook?"

"Know her? My God, Mario, for the first six years of my life, Cook and Nanny were the only friends I had."

"Well, you know, maybe you can remember one of her recipes."

Livingood laughed. "You don't understand."

"I don't understand?"

"Yes. I don't think you can."

"Wait a minute. You assume that I not only know how to cook, but that I also remember one of my mother's recipes and also I can duplicate it, is that what you're sayin'?"

"Yes."

"But you also assume there's somethin' about you I can't understand? What?"

"Mario," Livingood said, laughing uncomfortably, "people like, uh, people like me, we don't cook."

"Uh-ha. That's what I thought. Cookin', uh, that's somethin' cooks do. Hey, I gotta go. Just remembered. Gotta pick up some, uh, some groceries. Bye."

"Oh, Mario, wait wait!"

"What?"

"Almost forgot. Good news. Scumacci's been transferred. I had nothing to do with it. Brought it all on himself. Seems he's got leadership qualities. Turns out he's one of the leaders of a racist group that's been causing a whole lot of trouble, and the staff at Pittsburgh decided it was time to break them up before it got worse. They've shipped him to Southern Regional."

"Aw man, that is good news. I was dreadin' that trip."

"Well dread no more. I have to go. Keep in constant touch."

"Beg pardon?"

"Oh I don't believe I said that. It's something one of my relatives used to say, keep in constant touch. Used to make me cringe. Now here I am on automatic pilot spouting that silly expression. Sorry. Keep me up to speed. Bye."

Balzic hung up and chuckled the whole time he was dropping another quarter in the slot and punching his home number. "Keep in constant touch"? "Keep me up to speed"? When Ruth answered he asked her if she needed anything from the Giant Eagle.

191

"Not for tonight," she said. "I already fixed dinner. You gonna be home soon?"

"Be there in twenty minutes. What'd you make?"

"Beans and romaine."

"Ouu, you mean with garlic and oil and a little vinegar, the way Ma used to make it?"

"Yeah. I needed to think about her today. So I tried to make it the way she used to make it. It's not the same."

"Sure it is, c'mon."

"No it isn't. It's good, but it's not the same."

"Well if you wanna put it that way, nothin's the same, everything's different every time you cook it, doesn't matter if you're a pro. That's what those Zen guys mean when they say you can't take the same breath twice."

"Mar, listen, I have to lie down, my knee and hip, my hip's really killing me."

"Yeah, well, it's startin' to get cold again, that's why. Temperature's droppin' fast. Go lay down, I'll be right there."

Next morning, Balzic was up and making instant coffee and toast long before Ruth stirred. He tried to pay attention to the strawberry preserves he'd gotten from one of the women who'd come to his retirement party, spread over toast made from his own bread, but his mind kept darting away to Mrs. Walczinsky. He kept thinking about what it would take to get her to counter Lester Walczinsky's obviously fabricated alibi,

192

despite his protest that it had started out as vengeance. Walczinsky/Walin could protest all he wanted about his motives for taking his father's wife to bed, but once he got her there his actions were never going to be seen in a court as anything but a bad alibi copied from a bad movie. On the other hand, as far as Balzic could see, the most credible thing about the alibi was that it had never been used.

After Balzic finished eating and washed his dishes and utensils and wiped the counter, he went to his office on the other side of the house, retrieved Lester Walczinsky's Polaroids, and put them in his briefcase. He buttoned his collar, ran his tie up, and carried the briefcase out to the window in the living room, where he glanced at the weather for about the fifth time, trying to make up his mind about how to dress. He took his wool topcoat, wool cap, and rubber overshoes out of the closet by the front door and put them on, and went back into the kitchen and wrote a note to Ruth that he was going to Deer Mountain Borough to interview a Mrs. Walczinsky. He didn't know when he'd be home. He'd call. "The beans and romaine really were delicious. As good as Ma's. She would've been proud of you."

On the drive out, he tried several times to go over what he thought might work with Mrs. Walczinsky, his approach, his attitude, specific questions, but he kept going back to how badly he'd handled Martin Islip. He couldn't let go of how really stupid he'd been with Islip, all purely for the satisfaction of knowing that the loathsome bastard would commit himself to solitary for the rest of his time. Sometimes satisfaction was all the reason he needed for doing something; other times even thinking about his own satisfaction just made him a jerk. Thing was, Islip really was an answer man, and Balzic had never been able to crack one of those. The more ways he showed them the wrongness of what they'd done, the more ways they found to explain that if he were only as smart as they were, he'd know how right they'd been, and that was that.

After a fifty-minute drive, the last third of it steadily uphill, Balzic pulled into the gravel parking lot in front of the Deer Mountain Borough Building. It was not quite freezing when he'd left Rocksburg, but here on this mountain it was ten degrees colder at least, and every time the wind gusted the temperature went whipping downward. He was indoors in less than twenty steps, but his face was stinging, especially the tip of his nose.

The only person he found was an elderly woman with a bluish tint to her gray hair seated at a desk on the far side of the counter that ran across the width of the room just a few steps inside the foyer. She was hunched over a computer keyboard and looked annoyed when he asked for help. He couldn't tell whether it was because of the computer or him. He was wiping his nose with the back of his left glove and holding up his ID case in his right hand when she finally pushed herself away from her desk and approached him.

"Justice Department," she said, scowling.

"Wonder if you could help me out. I'm looking for the wife of the former chief of police here. I don't have an address for them, I'm assuming she lives here in the borough, a Missus Walczinsky?"

"She lives in the township. We all live in the township. Borough's just a way some people thought they could get away with something."

"Uh-ha. And where could I find her, exactly, if you know?"

"Oh I know. I just don't know whether I should tell you."

"Uh-ha. And why would that be, ma'am?"

" 'Cause of who you work for. I hate everybody in Harrisburg. I especially hate everybody in the Justice Department. Isn't that who you work for?"

"Yes, ma'am, but all I wanna do is talk to this woman —"

"Used to be, out here, everybody minded their own business. Everybody got along just fine. Then these damn Jews come in, from Pittsburgh or someplace, wanted to build this resort. But they couldn't just build it, oh no, they had to come in start telling everybody how to build these roads they had to have, all these utility lines they had to have, water and sewage, hell, there wasn't anybody here had sewage, everybody had septic tanks, but septic tanks, oh no, that wasn't good enough for these Jews and their bureaucrat friends in Harrisburg, noooooo —"

"Ma'am, Missus Walczinsky, can you help me out —"

"You're so smart, find her yourself. Shouldn't be any big deal for a smart guy like you. All you guys from Harrisburg are smart. My husband argued himself to death, arguin' with you smart guys. That man was township supervisor for twenty-eight years, ran this township with Jerry Winters and Elton Smith just fine till those Jews brought their friends from Harrisburg in, told everybody how we were gonna pay for all these water lines and sewage lines these damn Jews just absolutely had to have, and everything had to be underground too, don't you know. 'Cause nobody would buy these houses they were gonna build 'less we got water and sewage and power lines underground, oh yes sir. Well we got the damn water and the damn sewage, and the damn power lines in a ditch and what my husband got was three heart attacks and the last one killed him!"

Balzic hung his head and said, "Ma'am, I'm real sorry about your husband. I'm real sorry I bothered you. Thank you very much for your time." He turned and ducked out before she could say another word.

As he stood on the gravel looking around he kept thinking if he'd just asked Lester Walczinsky where his father lived he could've avoided all that nonsense, but no, he hadn't thought to do that, that would've been too simple. Maybe he did belong in Harrisburg with all the smart guys.

He saw a convenience store about fifty yards up the road from the Borough Building, and for a moment he thought about walking there, but the wind gusted sharply and sent him diving into his car. Inside the store, behind the counter, there was just one clerk, a sandy-haired woman with no makeup and a complexion so fair she looked as though she would disappear before his eyes if he looked at her too hard.

Balzic spotted a pay phone and phone book dangling below it, but found no Walczinsky listed in the book, barely a quarter inch thick including covers. Now he was really starting to berate himself for not having gotten directions from Lester Walczinsky.

He approached the clerk and said, "You know where the chief of police lives? Chief Walczinsky? The woman in the Borough Building wouldn't, uh, she didn't seem to know, and he's not in the phone book."

"Oh he's not the chief anymore," the clerk said.

"He's not?"

"No. He's real sick. Had a stroke or somethin'. I hear he can't even walk or talk or nothin'."

"Uh-ha. Well I knew he was sick, but I thought he was still chief. Uh, would you happen to know where he lives?"

"Uh-uh, I don't. But Bob might."

"And, uh, where might I find Bob?"

"He's out back throwin' food away."

"Doin' what? Uh, never mind. I can just walk around the building and I'll run into him?"

"Should be you can," she said. "Just keep turnin' left."

Balzic pulled his collar up again and headed back out into the wind that was now gusting powerfully. Had to put his shoulder into the door to open it. He buried his chin in his coat and walked sideways around the building. When he turned the back corner, he saw what he first thought was a short, spindly teenager in a poofy blue parka struggling to jam plastic garbage bags into a Dumpster while holding onto his hat.

As Balzic drew near, the teenager spotted Balzic and looked as though he'd been caught stealing, but his face was not the face of a teen at all. He was at least sixty and very worried. Before he looked away, white was showing all around his irises, and then his head began going side to side as though he was searching for an escape route. Suddenly he lurched toward Balzic and began to talk frantically, but the wind blew his words away.

Balzic took him by the arm and shouted into his ear, "Inside, okay?"

The man said nothing, but his fear was unmistakable and he kept motioning for Balzic to go first, though he did nothing to remove himself from Balzic's weak grip.

The man tried to open the metal door in the back of the building but had to have Balzic's help to do it. Inside, in the storage room, the man began immediately to plead and protest.

"I was throwin' it away, honest. I wasn't gonna

198

give it away. If you want me to, I'll bring all 'em bags back inside and open 'em up and you can count 'em yourself. Everything, sandwiches, hot dogs, everything —"

"I don't know what you're talkin' about."

"Huh?"

"I said I don't know what you're talkin' about."

"Ain't you from the company?"

Balzic took off his gloves and brought his ID case out and held it up in front of the man, whose breathing was coming in shallow bursts. Immediately as he was reading the ID, his breathing started slowing. He slumped in relief and peeled off his soiled parka and ball cap. He appeared now to be even older than at Balzic's first sight of him. He was at least as old as Balzic, and probably older. He'd looked young only because he was so short and thin. Up close, his face was a crosshatch of tiny wrinkles and sparse white whiskers. Snow-white hair was growing thickly out of his ears.

"Scared the love of Jesus outta me. Thought you was from the company. Clerk used to work here told on me. Said she seen me 'stead of disposin' of the food accordin' to company regulations, said I was puttin' it out where anybody wanted it could take it."

Balzic shook his head. "All I wanna know about is if you know where I can find the chief of police, or the former chief of police. Name's Walczinsky? You know him?"

The man nodded several times, sniffing and

clearing his throat. "Really scared me out there. Thought you was them. Already warned me they catch me doin' that again, I'm fired."

"Uh-ha. Chief Walczinsky? Know where he lives?"

"Yeah. Just lemme have a second here, catch my breath." He coughed hard for a few moments, then cleared his throat, and said, "Go out here, go past the Borough Building, you'll come to a Y. Hang a left at the Y, then about a quarter mile down that road, you'll see a great big white mailbox, no name on it, just an American flag on the arm. That's his. Take that road, starts right there beside the mailbox, and go back about, oh, I guess, maybe a quarter mile, his place is on the right, back up against the woods. Can't miss it, nothin' else around. Police car'll probably be parked in front, 'less his wife's shoppin' or somethin'. But if you see two dogs, if they're out — he got two real big German shepherds, if they're out, don't get outta your car, I'm tellin' ya. Just blow the horn till she comes out, or somebody, whoever's watchin' him."

"You, uh, know the chief? You seem to know about him, you know him pretty well, do you?"

"You live here, you better know about him. And you better know about them dogs too." He turned his back to Balzic, reached back and pulled up his right pant leg, then he held that up and pulled his long underwear out of his sock, exposing his right calf, revealing an ugly reddish scar halfway down his calf. "I'm not gonna show you where the other one bit me. If I hadn't had that pepper spray, I believe they woulda killed me. Used to brag how he keeps 'em on a starvation diet. Those dogs've killed deer, they've killed sheep, goats, cats, other dogs. He laughs about it. Well, used to laugh about it. Guess he ain't laughin' too much now."

"So I should stay in my car, right?"

"If you got pepper spray, it'd be all right. But if you got Mace, that won't work on 'em, specially when it's blowin' like now. Pepper spray comes out in a stream — course windy as it is even that might not work — but if they got a hold of you and you could get the pepper right down on their nose? See, it don't just get 'em in the eyes, it gets 'em in their nose too and they can't stand that. I didn't have that with me, hell's fire, they was havin' a tug-of-war with me. I know I ain't very big, but I'll tell ya, that was the scaredest I ever been in my life, them two dogs yankin' on me different ways. But the pepper got 'em off and it kept 'em off till I could get back in the car."

"Well you had the spray, you must've known about 'em. What were you doin' there?"

"Oh at that time I was deliverin' for Digby's pharmacy. That was right after I lost my farm. It was Mister Digby made me take the spray, told me to keep it in my hand too. Believe me, he hadn't told me that, I'da had it in my pocket, and they come around the house like a coupla ghosts, they wasn't makin' a sound, just their paws, that's all I could hear. I'da had that spray in my pocket, I might not've been able to get to it. Wakes me up nights, believe you me, thinkin' how I might notta listened to Mister Digby."

"Didn't you try to do anything about it?"

"Like what? Oh. You mean like sue him?"

"Yeah. Or call the Game Commission, hell, I don't know."

"Game Commission can't do nothin' 'less they see the dogs bringin' a deer down, otherwise they can't touch 'em."

"Well, it's been a while since I had anything to do with dogs killin' anything. You coulda called a lawyer at least."

The spindly little clerk shook his head, smiled wanly, and said, "You may know who the chief is, mister, but you sure don't know him."

"I've heard about him."

"Well, there's at least one man I know swears the chief bragged how he sicced 'em dogs on a poor old soul he said was a Gypsy. Wasn't no Gypsy. Man lived over the mountain in a little house, farmed 'bout sixty acres by himself, never bothered nobody. His place wasn't too far from mine, where mine used to be. Talked to him every once in a while. He was some kinda Middle Eastern man, Armenian or Albanian or somethin', didn't speak real good English, but he wasn't no Gypsy. Not that if he was that woulda made it all right. Now I don't know if any of that happened. All I know is, I ain't seen that man for a long time."

"Ever think about goin' to his house, checkin' on him?"

The man shook his head and looked at the floor. "I been yakkin' enough already. Only reason I yakked much as I did was 'cause you scared me. Thought you was a company man. Every time I get scared I start yakkin', just a fault I have. Listen, I'm gettin' behind here. I got other stuff to throw away yet."

Balzic patted the man on the shoulder, thanked him for his help, and went back out through the store and out the front door to his car.

The man's directions were correct. Five minutes later, Balzic was sitting in his car, looking at the Deer Mountain Borough Police Department cruiser, a beige Ford LTD. Balzic looked around for sign of any dogs, rolled down his window slightly to listen for them, but neither saw nor heard anything except the wind blowing snow. Occasionally the car would rock when the wind gusted.

He blew the horn and immediately felt the car lurch to the left. At first he thought it was the wind, but then he heard the snarling as a gray and black shape hurled itself repeatedly at the passenger-side window, snapping and growling and smearing globs of saliva on the window after each jump.

Balzic nearly hurt himself winding his window back up as another gray and black shape came lunging up at him. The jaws snapping, the teeth and toenails clicking against the windows, the snarling, wild and deep, froze Balzic against the back of the seat. He jammed both hands on the horn pad and pressed.

Then, as instantly as they'd come, the dogs were loping away, tails low, out of sight around the house. Somebody was out of the house and on the front porch, a woman, her cheeks bulging as she had her right hand up to her mouth, but Balzic heard no sound. Balzic looked first at one window and then the other, watched the saliva dribbling down.

He started to get out, then closed the door again, rolled down the window, and shouted, "They gone for sure? Is it all right for me to get out?"

"What do you want?"

"I'm lookin' for Missus Walczinsky."

"What for?"

"Wanna talk to her about Lester."

The woman pulled a jacket closer around her shoulders and retreated a couple of steps. "What about him?"

Balzic started to ease out of his car, but stopped and closed the door again. He kept his eye on the corner of the house around which he'd seen the dogs disappear. He opened his briefcase and took out his blackjack, put his hand through the loop, and wrapped it once around his palm. Then he closed the briefcase, opened the door, and lurched out, holding the briefcase up in his left hand like a shield, then kicked the door shut, and hurried across the grass and dirt up the steps to where the woman was standing.

When he finally looked at her, his breath caught in his throat. He fumbled to put the blackjack in his coat pocket and to get his ID out, all the while unable to take his eyes off her. Both her ears were cauliflowered; the left one, worse than the right, was mashed almost flat. Her nose had been broken at least once, the cartilage pushed severely to her right. There were scars all around her eyes. She didn't have a tooth in her mouth. Her lips were scarred into cracks and puffs in a couple of places, and there was a puncture scar on her left jawline.

Her right hand, still fingering a silverish whistle, was near her mouth, while she held her coat closed with her other hand and studied the ID case Balzic extended to her.

"I'm here to talk about Lester," he said, after he'd composed himself from the shock of her appearance. Balzic thought of the Polaroids in his briefcase and began to doubt that this woman standing here in front of him was the same woman. The woman in the Polaroids with Lester was no beauty by any means, but all her features were readily distinguishable. Not so with this woman. Had somebody given her a mannish haircut, she would have passed for an aging professional boxer, one of those unlucky ones cursed with the urge to fight but none of the ability.

"All right if we go inside? Don't know about you, but I'm freezin' out here."

She nodded and led the way in.

The exterior of the house — while Balzic hadn't given too much notice considering his focus on the dogs — had been of white aluminum siding turned a dingy, streaky gray. The interior startled him almost as much as the sight of her. He had the feeling he was inside a furniture store, one that sold only seconds or repossessions or goods damaged in transit. While everything seemed fairly new, none of it matched, and many pieces of stuffed furniture were covered with sheets of plastic.

The woman disappeared into what looked to Balzic like the kitchen. He heard water running, and then in a moment the woman was back, her face filled out by dentures.

"You want some coffee or something?"

"Only if you got it made, or if it's instant. Don't make any just for me. Uh, you Missus Walczin-sky?"

She nodded and said, "Just takes a minute with a coffeemaker. I'm ready for my second pot, so I'm gonna make it whether you want any or not."

"Sure. Fine." He followed her into the kitchen. His mouth fell open. It was crammed with every cooking widget Balzic could remember seeing advertised on TV or in magazines in the last ten years. He saw at least three coffeemakers, one under a cabinet; three or four food processors of varying sizes; mixers; blenders; bread machines; pasta machines; juicers; milkshake mixers; many can openers, knife sharpeners, and bottle stoppers; and pots and pans, two and sometimes three to a hook on Peg-Boards affixed to three walls and from a metal rectangle descended from the ceiling. There were four knife sets in wooden blocks, and knives, cleavers, and sharpening steels jammed into slots on two sides of a foot-thick butcher block shoved up against boxes of dishes and flatware. Piled high on the butcher block were stacks of dishcloths and dishtowels, and underneath it were boxes of soap pads, metal scrubbers, artificial sponges, and dishwashing soap.

"Crazy, ain't it?" the woman said, watching Balzic look around.

Balzic had taken his coat off before he began his survey of the room and he was still standing with it held out in front of him when her question brought him back. "Beg pardon?"

"I said crazy, ain't it? All this stuff."

"Well, I guess that would be one way to say it. But then I don't know what you're gettin' ready to do here. Maybe you and some friends're gonna hold an auction or somethin'." He knew that was preposterous, but he couldn't think of anything else quick enough. He knew that what he was looking at could have come from only two sources: either the chief had commandeered it from thieves and was fencing it, or else it was tribute from local merchants. More likely it was a combination of both.

She made room for another mug around one of the coffeemakers, which was already bubbling.

"How you take it?"

"Uh, whatever way you make it'll be fine. Some days I like it white and sweet, some days bitter and black, depends on my mood. Uh, hate to keep askin', but, uh, you Missus Walczinsky?"

"I'm one of them."

"Beg pardon?"

"You hard of hearing?" she said, lighting a thin, black cigarette. "You keep beggin' my pardon. Is it 'cause you can't hear or 'cause you can't understand, which?"

"Well, to be honest, some of the things you say are, uh, not what I expect. I guess it throws me and I get to soundin' stupid. Whattaya mean, you're one of them?"

"Well there was one before me, and he killed her," she said matter-of-factly, bending down to see if the coffee had stopped dripping. "And there's at least one more livin' on a farm on the other side of the mountain, and one time he let slip he had one in a trailer park somewhere north of Johnstown. But he never said nothin' about her again, so maybe he was just drunk. You couldn't always tell with Walter. Especially when he was drinkin'. Everything he did and everything he ever wanted to do would kinda get mixed up."

"Uh, when you say the other side of the mountain, you say it like it's another part of the world, but this is all Deer Mountain, right?"

"Yeah, that's just the way some of us talk."

"So the eastern side, that's what you call the

208

other side of the mountain like it's a different place. Is it?"

"Yeah it is. It's all Deer Mountain Township, the whole mountain clear down to where Route Thirty cuts across Seven-Eleven, but the borough is just on this side. Over there, people just call that the township, or some of 'em call it the other side of heaven. Or the jokers, they call it the other side of hell. The people got on the wrong side of Walter, that's what they used to call it. If they can."

"If they can what?"

"Still talk. I'm havin' mine with cream and sugar, that okay for you?"

Balzic cleared his throat and tried to figure out how much of what she was saying was said for effect or because she'd taken so many blows to the head she no longer knew fact from fancy. "Any way's fine."

She stirred some cream into the mugs and brought them to the polished pine table and set one in front of Balzic. She said, "Sit down, table ain't goin' bite ya."

He'd been holding his tape recorder in his right hand since he'd draped his coat over the back of one of the six chairs. He took off his wool cap and put it on the seat next to him and then he sat. Then, putting the recorder in front of him, he said, "Missus Walczinsky, this is an official investigation, and I think, before I turn this thing on, I should warn you to be very careful what you say, do you understand me?

You've made some statements here that are, to be honest, I mean, they're outrageous. At the very least, in this very brief conversation we've had so far, you've accused your husband, a chief of police who as far as I know is still chief of this borough's department, you've accused him of murdering his first wife, and of bigamy, and, uh, you've implied that he had something to do with silencing other people. I really want to warn you, from now on, I caution you to think before you speak, before I turn this recorder on, do you understand me?"

She stood up and crooked her finger at him. "Come on along," she said, and led him out of the kitchen and down a short corridor to the last room on the far side of the house. She stopped at the doorway and pointed inside, motioning with her other hand for him to come on and look.

Inside was a bedroom turned into a hospital room, complete with electric bed, oxygen tanks, IVs dripping fluid into the left arm of a pale, gray man staring blankly at the ceiling. Waste bags were pinned to the bed, with hoses going up under the covers. The only signs he was alive were the shallow rise and fall of his diaphragm and the faint wheeze each time it fell.

"That the chief?"

"The one and only. Seen enough?"

Balzic nodded and started back for the kitchen. He waited for her to sit before he sat. She laughed crookedly and said, "My, ain't you the gentleman. Don't mind tellin' ya, you're wastin' it on

210

me, mister. And you can turn your thing on there, I don't care what I say. Course I s'pose I oughta tell you right now, I didn't believe half of what Walter used to tell me, 'cause I never knew whether he was usin' it to turn me on or to keep me in line, and sometimes it got real hard for me to know the difference, if you know what I mean."

Balzic pushed the start button and identified himself and then listed the other particulars of the interview.

"Special investigator," she said. "My my. I get a *special investigator*. I could almost think that was cute. There was a time I would've. Whatchu wanna know, Mister Special Investigator man?"

"Once again, I'm gonna remind you to be careful what you say —"

She jerked her arm up and pointed with her thumb toward the bedroom. "What do I have to do to make you understand he ain't no fun no more? He ain't no more'n one heartbeat from findin' out whether Jesus was lyin' or not."

"Ma'am, I don't know how to say this, because I keep gettin' this feelin' I oughta be Mirandizin' you, but, I mean, if you're a suspect in any crime, it's not one I'm here to investigate, but I really wanna try to impress upon you that you have to be careful what you say 'cause of who's gonna be listenin' to this tape. People in the state Justice Department're gonna be listenin' to this, and these people won't hesitate to prosecute you if you talk without thinkin' —"

She inhaled deeply and snorted and laughed,

smoke blowing every which way. "I been married to Walter since just before I turned nineteen. You think there's anybody in this world can do anything to me that's goin' scare me?" She leaned over her mug of coffee and said, "Honey, one time Walter got all pissed off 'cause I only had about six teeth left 'cause he'd either knocked 'em all out or busted 'em off at the roots? So without thinkin', I made an appointment with a dentist, and Walter, God, he started bitchin' about how gettin' a dentist to pull 'em was a hellacious waste of his good money — is that thing turned on for sure?"

"Yes."

"Well good, lover, 'cause I don't want nobody to miss this. Walter tied me down spread-eagle on the bed and went and got his pliers and yanked 'em out himself, one at a time, 'cause he was damned if he was gonna pay a dentist to do it. And then he got all pissed off 'cause I was sayin' I didn't think the bleedin' was gonna stop and he called up his flunky Marty and made him carry me to the hospital over in Johnstown."

Balzic felt his mouth dropping open, and he shuddered. "Jesus Christ."

"Jesus don't live out here, lover. He mighta used to at one time, but he moved on. Said Deer Mountain was a nice place to visit but he didn't wanna live here." She was smiling and smoking and running her tongue across her upper lip, and every once in a while she tilted her head back and lowered her eyelids.

"Special investigator," she said. "Is that a cop? Did you used to be a cop? You look like you coulda been a chief. I can tell. Some people, they just look that look. Like old flunky Marty, he coulda been a cop for a hundred years, but he'da never made chief, you know? Didn't have that look. And if you don't have it, lover, ain't no way you can buy it, borrow it, beg it, or steal it. Bet your wife has a lotta fun. You married, ain't ya."

"Missus Walczinsky, I'm here to talk about Lester Walczinsky, your husband's son —"

"Oh he was my son too, did he tell you he wasn't? He's lyin' if he said that. Course Lester lied almost as much as Walter. It's inherited I guess —"

"Missus Walczinsky, Lester's trying to get a post-conviction hearing, 'cause he says he was convicted on perjured testimony. Also claims he had an alibi for the time he was supposed —"

"You mean when him and me was back there?" She pointed with her thumb again toward the bedroom. "Smokin' dope and screwin' our brains out? Oh he had an alibi all right. Wouldn'ta made no difference, though."

"Are you talkin' about the first day of deer season, 1977? The Monday after Thanksgiving?"

"Oh sure, yeah. Me and him was back in the bed there almost the whole afternoon, from oh my, can't remember exactly, but he probably come in here 'bout ten in the mornin'."

"That was a long time ago, ma'am. You sure about that —"

"First thing you gotta do is stop callin' me ma'am, lover. Jesus, you make me sound like somebody's granny. I know I'm a mess, but I ain't nobody's goddamn granny, okay?"

"Fine, okay, Missus Walczinsky —"

"And don't call me that neither. Name's Letitia. Let for short. Which is short for let him do whatever he wants, lover." She was licking her upper lip again and tilting her head back and looking at him in that heavy-lidded way.

Gave Balzic the creepy-crawlies.

"Okay, Letitia —"

"Let, lover. It's easy. You can say it. Let." She started to get up, slowly.

"Sit down, Let. Now!"

She did. With a big smile. "Ouu, oh my, you have such authority, you have such —"

"Knock it off, Letitia. I'm not your father and I'm not your husband, so knock it off. I'm not playin', understand?"

"Or what, lover, huh? You goin' arrest me and put me in a woman's prison? God I would *love* to be in a woman's prison. Let some big ol' bull dyke get all excited over me. Walter used to make me all excited just tellin' me he had a new one and he wasn't goin' let me watch."

"New one what?"

"New domination video."

"Uh-ha."

" 'Bout the whole last two years, only way I could have one with Walter was if I dreamed he was some ol' dyke. Ain't that funny? Huh? The

214

way Mother Nature does you? The way she plays with your mind?"

"Back to Lester, okay? Letitia? Can we get back to Lester? How can you be sure what day it was seventeen years ago? What time? Most people can't remember what they had for supper yesterday."

"Oh, lover, supper's just plain ol' food. Sex and dope, honey, that's food for the gods, that's what Lester told me. And he was right, I do believe."

"Seventeen years ago, back in that bedroom where your husband is layin' right now, you and his son, Lester Walczinsky, you're tellin' me you had sex together? While you were smokin' marijuana? And you remember what time that was?"

"Oh better believe it, lover. I'll never forget that day. We musta smoked four joints. We'd smoke awhile, screw awhile, smoke some more, screw some more, it was the best fuckin' I ever did without gettin' beat up first. Lover, trust me, you never forget that kind of fuckin'. Least I never have. Anyway, Lester took pictures — though I ain't never seen 'em I'm sorry to say."

"Lester took pictures, that what you said?"

"Yes he did. Made me hold up this ol' newspaper. We was laughin' like crazy, I'll never forget that 'cause Walter's picture was on the front page. Walter was holdin' up this deer he killed the year before, he was so proud of that deer. Big ol' buck,

215

Walter killed it right while it was up humpin' a doe. Said it was the most fun he ever had killin' somethin'.

"And there we were, Lester and me, just screwin' each other's brains out and laughin' like crazy, you know, dope laughin', I mean you just don't laugh like you laugh while you're smokin' dope. I swear to God, that's why ol' square people make dope illegal. 'Cause everybody laughin' must piss 'em off or somethin', I never have understood why anybody'd make dope illegal except for that. It's gotta be the laughin' that makes 'em mad. That's what did it for Walter. Made him furious. Like, if he'd bring me some dope he took offa some kid, and then when I'd start laughin' he'd just start screamin' at me to stop. Walter, he — one of the worst beatin's he ever give me was 'cause I couldn't stop laughin' this one time. And he never did bring me no more dope after that, that's how I know it was serious. 'Cause in his heart and soul, I mean, all Walter is, is a prick. He don't really get no fun outta fuckin'. All his fun is in the beatin'. Sex ain't the cake for him, in other words. It's not really even the icin' either. Just the opposite for me."

"You never saw those pictures? The ones Lester took?"

"Sure I did. He was takin' 'em with one of them, uh, whatchacallits, one of them, oh, you know, one of them cameras shoots a picture out 'bout a minute after you take it? What do I mean, you know don'tcha?"

"Polaroid?"

"Yeah! That's it."

"And so you saw the pictures?"

"Yes."

"When he took them?"

"Well sure I did, yes!"

"And you remember seeing them? That day?"

"I'm tellin' you yes."

"On that day, there's no doubt in your mind about the time?"

"How many ways I gotta say it? Jesus."

Balzic opened his briefcase and took out the plastic bag full of the Polaroids he'd found among Lester Walczinsky's belongings. He took the pictures out one at a time and handed them to her.

She began to jump in her chair and squeal at the sight of them. "Oh! Oh! That little shitski, he told me he burned 'em, that little liar! Oh I wanted these! And he never come back and I never heard nothin' from him again and these are them, that little liar. Liar liar, pants on fire —"

Balzic repeated the day and the date again and again, and said, "You sayin' you're prepared to testify as to the time, day, and date those pictures were taken? And the place? And to identify both of you?"

"Well of course I am. What's the big deal about that?"

"There's no doubt in your mind about the time these pictures were taken?"

"There's a date right on the front page of the

217

paper, that's why he made me hold it up. And look there, you can see for yourself the clock right there behind us, on the shelf above the headboard?"

Balzic held up his hand. "These pictures could have been taken anytime after that newspaper was published. The next day, the next month, the clock could've been set for any time —"

"Uh-uh, lover. Couldn'ta been taken the next month, 'cause two weeks later, two weeks after Lester took these ol' pictures, he was arrested and in jail and he ain't ever been out since. So there was only those two weeks there when these pictures coulda been taken. And it don't make no difference anyhow. 'Cause whyn't you just ask me who killed them two dopers, huh? Ask me that, why don'tcha? Hell, you don't even have to ask me, I'll tell ya. It was Walter."

"Beg your pardon?"

"Walter. Him — you know, back there in the bedroom? The guy that's doin' his business in the bags? Him. He killed 'em."

"Your husband? The chief of police? The man I just saw layin' in that bed back there? Letitia, do you know what you're sayin'?"

"Course I know what I'm sayin', what do I look like? I told ya, Walter ain't no fun no more, all he is is work, that's all. I can go back there right now and pull my panties down right in front of him, and he won't even blink. So what difference does it make what I say he done or didn't do. Can't do nothin' no more. And I do

218

mean nothin'! I mean, if somebody calls that bein' alive, Jesus that ain't bein' alive."

Balzic hung his head for a long moment.

"Whatsamatter, lover? Am I spoilin' your supper?"

"All right if I have some water?" He started to stand, but she jumped up and rushed to the sink.

"Oh I got it, lemme get it, you just sit there, lover, let me bring it to you."

She returned with a smile as big as the glass of water and set the glass in front of him. "There. Want some ice in it?"

"This is fine." He drank half the glass, wiped his mouth with the back of his hand, and looked at her. "I have to ask you again, are you aware — do you know what you just said?"

"What do you want me to do, lover? Huh? You want me to take you out back'n show you where I buried his gun? Where he made me? Would that satisfy you? You be happy then?"

"He made you bury it?"

"Ain't that what I just said? Why you always askin' me everything I say, like I'm some kinda nut case? I'm tellin' ya, Walter come home that night —"

"Wait a minute, wait a minute," Balzic said, pushing his palms downward in the air. "You said Walter was out huntin' deer that day? That was the first day of deer season, right? And he was out huntin' — while you and Lester were back there?"

"Right, right. That's what he was doin'. That's

what he was s'posed to be doin'. It was while he was out huntin' that he come up on them two, only there was four of 'em. That cabin ain't but four miles from here. It's right before you get to the top of the mountain. I can take ya to it, you want me to."

"Uh-ha, later maybe. Back to him, what'd he say?"

"Said he watched 'em make the whole deal. And then these two other guys left. And bein' the good little ol' policeman that he is, he had their license wrote down. Both cars. And he was still all pissed off at me 'cause I couldn't quit laughin', from before? Remember? When I said he got all pissed off at me 'cause I couldn't stop laughin' from the dope? Well that was just like a week before. And I guess he took it out on them, only thing I could figure. 'Cause he never did say why he killed 'em. Just said he did. Said he fucked 'em both and then he shot 'em and took all their dope and money too — well not all of it. He left enough to prove it was a dope deal. Left enough to show the state cops what it was about. Then he just blamed it on them two was in the other car. He had their license, remember? I said that, didn't I?"

"Yeah. You did." Balzic put his elbow on the table and rested his forehead in his hand.

"Lover, you look like you ain't never heard nothin' like this before. You sure you're a — what are you again? A special investigator?"

"Tell me something. Did you say what I think

you said? About Walter?"

"You mean about him fuckin' those two? Oh yeah I said that. What, you don't believe me? That Walter would do that? Oh what you don't know," she said, shaking her head and smiling. "Walter loved humiliatin' people. Believe me that wasn't sex for Walter. That was him doin' his special pride'n joy, humiliatin' people. You ever see that movie *Deliverance*?"

"Yeah, I've seen it."

"You remember where those rednecks make 'em city boys pull down their pants and oink like pigs before they punk 'em?"

"Vaguely. It was a long time ago that I saw it."

"Oh my, then you don't know. Walter has his very own copy of that movie. It's the only so-called clean movie he owns. And every time he got down in the dumps he'd get that movie out, that's how I knew he was down in the dumps about somethin'. 'Cause every time he'd watch it and it'd come to that part? Walter'd just be rollin' around on the couch laughin'. He'd back it up and run it six or seven times and he'd be howlin' every time like it was the first time he ever saw it. That's the only thing I ever saw Walter really laugh about. Every other time he'd laugh it was all below his eyes. No matter how much noise he was makin' or how much his belly was shakin', you watch his eyes you'd know there wasn't nothin' ever really funny to him. 'Cept that part in that movie. That's the only time you'd ever see Walter's eyes laugh. He would truly laugh at that. He'd even get tears in his eyes his laughin'd be so real."

"So that wasn't sex in the cabin? With those two?"

"Oh no, lover. That was Walter havin' fun with those ol' boys before he killed 'em, that's all that was."

"Tell me somethin' else. If you know. How'd it happen — I mean, how is his son — why is his son doin' the time for this?"

"Oh it didn't just happen, lover. Nothin' ever just happened with Walter. 'Cept this buncha strokes he had. Didn't plan them out, I don't think. No. But, on the other thing? Well he just gave 'em Lester. See, 'cause of them two other guys in the other car? Remember? State cops could only find this one guy. I don't remember what happened to the other one, I'm positive they never did find him, but they found the car'n this fat ol' ugly dago boy was drivin' it. And Walter just beat him till he said he was who done it. And then they found this other stupid ol' clown, I don't know his name."

"Patter? Edgar Patter?"

"Told you, I wouldn't know his name. I don't know it. Walter never told me and I didn't ask him. All I know is, they beat him too. And somehow, in between them two, in between beatin' them two, Walter, I guess, he just decided he could take care of some other business that was aggravatin' him, so he just give him Lester's name. Told that ol' dago boy what to say and how to say it."

"Wait a minute," Balzic said, shaking his head rapidly from side to side as though that would make what he was hearing comprehensible. "You sayin' Walter gave his own son's name to this Scumacci, this guy you're callin' fat old dago boy, is that what you're sayin' now?"

"Why you lookin' so surprised? Everything I say you look so surprised. Listen lover, this fat ol' dago boy, they didn't even have to beat him real bad. Walter said he ate it up with a spoon, just *loved* it. 'Cause what was he? Nothin' but a fat little ugly nickel-dime drug dealer and now all of a sudden he was a real gangster killer dago, you know? Godfather crap. Walter told him he done it, and Walter said pretty soon he started believin' it, pretty soon he was practically braggin' how he did it. Who knows what makes people do what they do, lover, do you? I don't."

"Jesus, Mary, and Joseph," Balzic said, shaking his head. "Uh, those dogs, where are they now?"

"In the back probably. 'Less they're off runnin' deer. Why?"

" 'Cause I want you to go outside and show me where you buried this gun you said Walter used, 'cause I want to dig it up and I don't wanna be lookin' over my shoulder for those dogs."

"Well if they're out back, I'll just put 'em in the cellar. Wait a minute, I gotta check on Walter, see if he ain't quit breathin' yet. Oh I'm so glad you found them pictures. I always really wanted to see them again. Can I keep one? I'm gonna keep one, okay?"

"No. They're evidence."

She was halfway down the hall to the bedroom when she spun around and pulled one of the Polaroids out of the front of her slacks and held it up and stuck out her tongue at him. Then she put it back down the front of her slacks and giggled and disappeared into the bedroom.

In seconds she was back, walking toward him with a seductive glint in her eyes and an exaggerated thrusting of hips in every step.

"You gonna try'n get that picture back, Mister Special Investigator man?"

"Where're you from? Originally I mean."

"Oh you noticed I ain't from here, did ya? From the way I talk? I'm from Oklahoma, lover. Moved up here with my daddy when I wasn't but twelve years old. Daddy come up here to put in a natural gas line, he was supervisor of construction, don'tcha know. Finished that ol' job one day and fell over dead the next with a heart attack, and there was me and his fourth wife, stuck up in a trailer back in these very woods. You still wanna go outside? Gonna need a pick, lover, ground's frozen I'll bet down a foot."

"You got one?"

"Lover, there's enough tools on this property to start a chain of hardware stores. The way Walter loved tools you'd think he was some kinda handyman, but the only time I ever saw him use one was to get somebody to do what he wanted. Used to brag how he solved every burglary on

Deer Mountain from 1960 to 1970 with one little ol' solderin' iron didn't cost but six dollars. Five ninety-nine actually. Some poor nigger was hitch-hikin' through here, he confessed to all them burglaries. One little solderin' iron and one black asshole, that's what Walter said. Cleared all them burglaries."

"Jesus Christ," Balzic said. "What was his name?"

"You mean the nigger? Now how would I know that? Walter didn't tell me every little detail, lover, just the good parts."

"Oh Christ, c'mon, let's get goin' before I get sick."

"You are lookin' a little green, lover. Are you sure you're a cop? You don't act like no cop I know."

"Let's go goddammit! How would you know what a cop acts like? Only one you have to go by is that, that — shit, I don't know any words for him. I don't think there are any words to call him what he is."

"Ouu, you're gettin' all excitable, lover. Maybe you are a cop after all," she said, licking her upper lip and rolling her eyes at him.

Balzic grabbed his coat and hat, put them on, and put the tape recorder, still running, in his coat pocket. He took her by the elbow and said, "Get me a pick and shovel, and get those dogs out of my way, and show me where to dig. You think I might be a cop after all, huh, is that what you said?"

"Well you're actin' real authoritative now, lover, I'll say that for ya."

"If your husband's a cop, lady, I'm a fucking astronaut."

"Ouu! Oh I like that. Take me up in your spaceship and make me tell you everything I know —"

"Shut up and do what I said before. I want that gun! You ever look in a mirror? Huh? Take me up in your spaceship, Jesus Christ."

"Slow down, not so fast, I gotta go down the cellar first if you want a pick and shovel, I'm goin', I'm goin', just whoa down." She pulled away from him and went through a door and down a set of stairs.

Balzic waited until she came back up with a pick and shovel, both of them new but rusty. Then he followed her to the back door, which led out onto a deck. He started out after her, but stepped back in and said, "The dogs? Get 'em inside someplace."

She stepped out onto the deck, put the whistle in her mouth, and blew several blasts, her cheeks puffing and her face reddening each time. The dogs immediately appeared in the backyard as though they'd been lying below the deck. They began to run in small irregular circles, tails low, ears back.

Balzic stepped out onto the deck and watched her go down and drive the dogs with the soundless whistle through a door into the cellar. Then he crept down the steps, covered with snow, and followed her as she walked away from the house and to the base of a huge hardwood tree, an oak. Only reason Balzic knew it was an oak was because the ground around it was covered with acorns and acorn parts. Then something farther up into the woods caught his eye.

"Those what I think they are?" he said, pointing to a pile of deer antlers and skulls and hooves.

"Yeah. Dogs drag 'em back, leave 'em all over the place. Walter just used to carry 'em here and every spring he'd pour kerosene on 'em and burn 'em."

"Jesus, didn't he ever feed those dogs?"

"Walter said you train a dog with food, it'll leave you the minute somebody gives it food it likes better. He didn't believe in wastin' food. He believed in pain. And fear."

She pointed to a spot about six feet away from the base of the trunk and said, "Well you want to know where to dig, lover, there it is. Goin' be like bustin' through concrete, I'm tellin' ya."

"Just keep those dogs off me, okay?"

"Don't worry 'bout them dogs, lover, they're smart, but they can't open doors I don't care what them people that watch Lassie movies think."

Balzic was glad he was wearing gloves. He knew that if it were the summer, he might be dumb enough to tackle this with his bare hands and wind up with a case of blisters that would take a month to heal. Now, all he had to worry about was tearing muscles, tendons, or ligaments in his back, arms, and shoulders. He tested the pick's heft several times and tried to decide how hard he wanted to go at this. He couldn't remember the last time he'd done this kind of physical labor. What he was fully aware of was that no matter how easy he tried to take it, he was going to pay for it tomorrow and for many tomorrows afterward. That's why people said getting old wasn't for sissies.

It took him a half hour to clear out a hole a foot square approximately and a foot deep. He'd shed his topcoat. His forehead and upper lip were stinging cold as the wind whipped the perspiration dry there. He kept on only because Letitia kept saying it wasn't much deeper, the ground was nearly frozen when she'd dug the hole in the first place. He didn't ask her if she was sure he was digging in the right place.

Five minutes later, the pick bounced off something metallic and ten minutes later, he had it in hand, rusted and dirt encrusted, a Smith & Wesson .38 Special with a six-inch barrel. Balzic put his coat back on, took out his tape recorder, and described what he'd just done and where. Then he blew out a long breath and felt his pulse hammering in front of his ears. He took many deep breaths on his way back into the house and still more between gulps of water trying to get his pulse back to normal. Then he asked her to get him a plastic food bag, preferably one that had a space for writing on.

"So you think Lester's goin' get out now?" she said, bringing him a bag.

228

"Not for me to say. All I do is talk to people and dig up evidence. Up to other people to decide that." He wrote on the outside of the bag where and when the contents had been recovered, and initialed it. Then he put the gun inside, zipped the bag closed, and put it in his briefcase.

"One more thing, then I'm gone," he said. "People are gonna be talkin' to you from now till whenever. From the attorney general's office, the state police, the DA's office, the public defender's office, I might even be back. I hope for everybody's sake you were tellin' the truth. I hope you weren't pullin' an Edgar Patter."

"A who?"

"An Edgar Patter. That's the second poor sonofabitch you said Walter tortured. You know? To get him to say Lester was who murdered those people? Every time Edgar Patter opened his mouth a different story came out. I sincerely hope you're not another one like him."

"Why would I be? Ain't nothin' to be scared of now."

"Oh so what're you tellin' me now? That all the rest of the times Walter beat you up, it didn't scare you?"

"Oh you don't know nothin', poor baby. Every time Walter beat me? That was a turn-on, lover. That was foreplay. That was like other women need candles and music and chocolate candy. I wasn't afraid of gettin' beat, honey, I don't care whether you think I'm a sick puppy or not, I ain't gonna try to say I ain't, but, lover, when it comes to dyin' I'm no different than anybody else. I'm just like you about dyin', honey, I'm scared to death of dyin'. I'da told any of this before Walter had his strokes? You know what woulda happened to me? Can't you guess? Lover, I'da said any of this before now, Walter woulda hung me up in the cellar, honey, and filled every hole in my body with his solderin' irons and turned 'em on. You might not believe there's any difference between what we used to do and what he woulda done, but believe me, lover, there is. All the difference in the world. So you bring on whoever y'all wants to bring. What they hear next month is what you heard today, I ain't no Edgar whatever his name is. Ain't got no reason to be."

Balzic gathered up his briefcase and cap and headed for the front door. Outside he said to her as she was standing in the door frame, "That picture you got in the front of your pants is evidence. You go ahead and make all the copies you want, but that picture belongs to the state, it doesn't belong to you. So when you finally get a subpoena and you show up wherever you're supposed to go? You make sure you have that picture with you, you hear? 'Cause I don't wanna stand up in front of a judge somewhere and say I got eighteen of somethin' when I only got seventeen, understand?"

"Oh you give up way too easy, lover. Sometimes you have to fight for what you want, don't you know that?"

"Lady, I'm havin' one of the worst fights of my life. At this very minute."

"You are?" she said, inching forward, pouting out her cracked and puffed lower lip. "Why what over?"

Balzic looked at her for a long moment. "I don't think I could explain it to you. That man in the bedroom back there? If only half of what you've told me about him is true, you have no idea what a struggle I'm havin' to get in my car and drive away from here."

"Oh my, lover, sounds to me like you wanna do somethin' to him."

"Yeah. To you it probably would sound that way."

"Know what I think? I think you just heard somethin' you have never, ever thought about in your whole life and you purely don't know how to deal with it, that's what I think."

"Right now, Missus Walczinsky, what you think about what I think is beside the point. I just wanna caution you about one more thing. If there are any records in this house — police records? Any records your husband might have kept in this house, anything at all, citation books, notebooks, letters, copies of warrants, anything that looks like official police records, I caution you, I'm warnin' you to make it your business to protect those records. 'Cause the first chance I get after I leave here I'm gonna sic everybody I can in the Justice Department on that man. There will be people here with search warrants, I promise you. Don't throw anything away. Don't destroy anything."

"Oh, lover, save your breath. I could burn the house down ten minutes after you leave and what could you do about it? You gotta stop warnin' people and such. Walter used to say warnin's just a threat. He said — I mean it was like it come down the mountain with Moses — Walter said never ever threaten nobody. It just gives 'em time to interfere with what you wanna do."

"Your Walter was a regular philosopher, wasn't he? How long was he the chief here?"

She shrugged. "I don't know. All his life I reckon. Heard him say he been chief since he was eighteen."

"Jesus Christ. How old is he now?"

"Sixty-somethin', I don't know. All he ever said was you was only as old as you felt and he felt like he could whip a rattlesnake and give it two bites head start."

"Yeah. Figures." Balzic started down the steps, but stopped and looked around for the dogs. He felt in his topcoat pocket for the blackjack, got it out, wrapped the strap around his palm, held his briefcase like a shield in front of him, and ran down the steps and to his car. Once inside, he looked back up at the doorway.

Letitia Walczinsky had taken her teeth out and was laughing at him.

Balzic went about twenty miles out of his way to Southern Regional to get to the Game Commission office in Fort Ligonier, where he presented his ID and tried to file a complaint about two German shepherds running deer on Deer Mountain, in both the borough and the township.

The Game Commission officer listened patiently until Balzic finished talking and then said, "You've come to the wrong place, sir. We don't handle dangerous dogs — unless one of our people sees a dog in the act of bringing a deer down, we can't touch them. What you're talking about, sir, you need to talk with a dog warden. That's Agriculture Department, that's not us."

"It's not you? It's Agriculture?"

"That's correct. Let me ask you, these dogs, would they happen to belong to the chief of police up there, Deer Mountain?"

"Yeah. As a matter of fact they do —"

The game officer shook his head and chuckled. "I can't tell you how many complaints we've had about those dogs. And everybody gets all irritated and annoyed with us when we tell them it's not our bailiwick. Check out the dangerous dog law, sir, you'll see what I mean. That's strictly Ag Department."

"Well's the dog warden ever gone up there?"

"I think you should talk to him about that. I don't want to get into that. His number's in the book. In the blue pages."

Balzic shrugged, thanked the game warden, and went back outside, where he stood looking at the frozen dog slobber on his windows and wondering why he knew so little about dangerous

dogs and who handled them. Then he got in and
drove off in search of a pay phone, and after a
minute or so, it occurred to him that the reason
he didn't know about the dangerous dog law was
that the city of Rocksburg had always hired private firms for animal control for as long as he'd
been chief. Anytime he or any member of his
department had had a problem with a dog, they'd
immediately called the animal control officer the
city had hired, and that was the end of it.

Balzic spotted a pay phone in a gas station and,
after filling his gas tank, called the dog officer.
He got a recorded message asking him to leave
his name and the number and a brief description
of the problem, ending with the dog warden's
promise that he would return the call within
twenty-four hours.

Balzic eased his frustration about the dogs
somewhat by anticipating his interview with the
convicted shooter — the purported convicted
shooter — of Joseph Portiletto and James
Stevens, one Hubert Scumacci. Balzic had
known Scumacci since he was a pudgy juvenile
delinquent who'd attacked his grandmother with
a pair of scissors, and had subsequently given
no indication he was going to do anything but
persist in his juvenile obsessions.

When the COs, one on each side, brought Scumacci into the interview room, Balzic was putting
a new tape in his recorder. He watched while they
put Scumacci in the chair, attached his handcuffs
to the loop bolted into the table, and stepped

back outside. Balzic looked at Scumacci for a long moment, at his shaved head, his Fu Manchu moustache, his prison tattoos over all his fingers and hands, crude blue graffiti testifying to his wildly defiant opposition to authority. Balzic snorted a laugh.

Scumacci cocked his head and squinted his tiny, blackish-brown eyes. "Somethin' funny to you? Whoever you are?"

"I've thought to myself, ever since I heard I was gonna have to talk to you, I said, don't tell me there's another human being in this world with that name. Can't be. Can't be two Hubert Scumaccis on this planet. And I was right. 'Cause here you are. The one, the only, Hubert Scumacci. Hubie Scum himself. Don't remember me, do ya, Hubie?"

"Nobody calls me that anymore. Last person called me Hubie Scum watched some associates of mine separate him from his balls."

"Ouu, associates? Wowsie. Hubie Scum has *associates* now? Used to be all you had was other piles of protoplasm stuck to you 'cause you were all covered with grease. But look at you now, ouu, all what? I don't wanna say all grown-up 'cause I know that's not true. But anybody can see you're not just another roly-poly juvenile delinquent, uh-uh, now you're a, a what? A large economy-size delinquent. I hear you're so bad, they couldn't contain your badness down there in Pittsburgh. You're one of the bosses of some racist empire, gonna take over all the prisons, some shit like that, that's what I heard. But now that you're sittin' here, Hubie? Know what you look like to me, huh? Look like all the other stupid-ass skinheads I've ever seen, Hubie, think they shave their head and get some tattoos, that makes 'em a *bad* man. So when'd you change barbers, Hubie, huh?"

"I don't know who you are, so that means there's no way I could've put you on my visitor sheet —"

"Forget all that, Hubie, you're tryin' to talk like you're still in Pittsburgh, like you still got some power. You don't have any power, Hubie. You're just another number here, just another fucked-up juvenile delinquent put on some weight and height and turned into a fucked-up con. Still don't remember me, do ya?"

"Am I s'posed to?"

"Let me refresh your memory. I can't remember where you started out in this world, Hubie, but when you were about fourteen some UFO dropped you off in Rocksburg. Went to live with your grandmother, you remember that? You remember her?"

Scumacci said nothing. He pushed his tongue against the inside of his upper lip. His eyelids lowered. Then he licked his lips and looked away.

"It startin' to come back now, is it, huh? Startin' to remember who I am, aren't you? Right, right, I'm the guy had to take your grandmother to jail till we got you out of her house 'cause she'd rather sleep in jail than go back to

236

her own home, long as you were there. Wouldn't file a complaint till after she got outta the hospital. And I'm who had to talk her into that, remember now? I'm the one told her she was in danger long as you were there, and the next time you might get a brainstorm to tie her up while she was asleep instead of just attackin' her. Remember what you did to her, Hubie, huh?"

"Fuck you."

"Ouu, Hubie, you're so manly when you curse like that. You're such a manly man. What did you do to your grandmother, Hubie, huh? That sweet lady good enough to take you in after her own daughter put you out, huh? Can you say the words, Hubie? Can you even get the words out of your mouth what you did to her?"

"What do you want?"

"You remember me yet?"

"I remember. Just forgot what you looked like. So what?"

"Just wanted to hear you say it, that's all. Just wanted to hear you say you remembered me."

"So I remember you, big fuckin' deal. What do you want?"

"So we had you locked in four years for that, right? Any of that counseling ever take, Hubie? Huh? Apparently not."

"Don't talk that shit with me, Balzic, that was a fucking joke. Half them counselors're fags."

"Oh so you really do remember me. I'm flattered, big, bad-ass dago gangster like you."

Balzic took his ID case out, slid it across the

237

table for Scumacci to see, and pulled it back after Scumacci had read it and lifted his eyes.

"So? So now you're big-time with all those dickheads in Harrisburg, so what?"

Balzic pushed the start button on the tape recorder.

"This is the first interview with Hubert Scumacci, inmate at Southern Regional Correctional Facility, Mario Balzic speaking, Special Investigator, Attorney General's Office, Pennsylvania Department of Justice." He checked the time and date on his Timex, recorded them, and said, "I'm interviewing inmate Scumacci in connection with what is commonly referred to as the Deer Mountain murders. You familiar with this case, Hubert?"

Scumacci snorted. "It's what I'm doin' the time for, asshole, why wouldn't I be familiar with it?"

"Uh-ha. Well, I know you've told your version of what happened that day, first day of deer season, first Monday after Thanksgiving, 1977, but just for the record here, and briefly, too, don't go into any great detail for the moment, just give me a quick rundown of what happened at the cabin there, would you do that please?"

"That's what this is about?"

"What it's about officially is this is an interview pertaining to a post-conviction hearing motion that was filed by the man you say was the shooter in this case, that's what this is about, Hubert. So whyn't you just give me a quick one two three of the events there that day, all right?"

"Well you want the official version or you want the real version, which one you want?"

"I wanna know what you told the state police, and the people in the DA's office in Wabash County, and what you testified to in court, all the prelims, the trials, the mistrials, how many times, four, five, six?"

Scumacci leaned forward. "I don't get this. Why they'd pick you to ask me this stuff, huh? I mean, everybody's gonna know you're prejudiced against me."

"What, you think I'm carryin' a grudge against you? Huh? You think I harbor some belief as to your innate badness? Get real, Hubert."

"You always had it in for me, you prick. Every time I had a parole hearin', somebody'd read the letter they got from you. You never showed up, but somebody was always readin' a goddamn letter from you."

"You think I'm prejudiced against you, Hubert, is that what you think? For tryin' to cut your grandmother's breast off? While she was asleep? With a pair of scissors? You think because everything failed with you? Huh? Counseling, chemicals, everything everybody tried with you, nothin' worked — you think because of that, there's somethin' in me that I want you off the streets forever, huh? Because of somethin' personal between you and me?

"Tell me, Hubert, if you can remember, what did you do three months after you got out of juvenile detention, huh, you remember anything you might've done then? Like go after some woman in a bar? Huh? With a pair of scissors? Try to cut her breast off while she was playin' the jukebox? That sound familiar, Hubert? Woman almost died and she still didn't file a complaint against you. Amazing. And two years later, Hubert, huh? Did it again, didn't ya? Another woman, another bar, another jukebox, another pair of scissors, but same old Hubie Scum. And here you sit, lookin' baffled about why I kept writin' letters to the parole board. Hey, Hubert, maybe it *is* me. Stupid fuckers let you out, and now look where we are, huh? Almost back where we started."

"Little bit different this time, asshole. This is life times two for murder in the commission of another felony."

"Ouu, oh, that's right, you've moved on up, I forgot. Graduated to the real world of large badness, yessir, not kiddie crime this time, nosir. So tell me about this large crime, Hubert. The official version first, then whatever version you feel like tellin', and then I'll ask you some questions, okay? Why don't you just start now, okay?"

"I don't think I have to waste my time talkin' to you, asshole. I already told what's-his-face, that Livin-whatever —"

"Livingood?"

"Yeah, him. Already told him and some other asshole that I was gonna take back everything I said about Walczinsky, so what do I have to talk to you for?"

240

"C'mon, Hubie, you know the drill as well as I do. We keep askin' 'cause guys like you keep tellin' different stories. Every time you talk, somethin' new pops out, somethin' different."

"You got me mixed up with that dickhead Potter."

"Patter?"

"Potter Patter, what the fuck's the difference."

"You went to the cabin with him, you were in the drug business with him, you didn't know his name?"

"Gimme a break, Christ."

"Well you musta called him somethin'. What'd you call him?"

"Shithead, what do I know. I can't remember."

"So okay. So who was the other guy now? If it wasn't Walczinsky, who was the shooter? You are gonna testify it wasn't Walczinsky, right?"

"That's right."

"So who was it?"

"Billy Band."

"Band? Billy Band? Oh, you mean William Banditti. Didn't he just get killed in Rockview a coupla months ago?"

"Six weeks ago."

"Got stabbed by another inmate, right?"

"No he got *shot* by another inmate, what the fuck."

"Uh-ha. So where were you when you got this word he was killed?"

"Pittsburgh."

"Where were you before you were in Pitts-burgh?"

"Rockview."

"And naturally, when you were in Rockview, you renewed acquaintances with your old buddy there, Billy Band, right?"

"Naturally."

"Talked over old times, good-old-bad-old days when you and him were practically a two-man crime wave, right?"

"We talked. Yeah."

"And naturally you talked about how he dusted those two chumpos on the mountain there, right? Deer Mountain? You and him? You talked about that, didn't ya? By the way, how much money'd you take off those two, huh? And how much dope?"

"Why you goin' through all this shit, man? I've said all this stuff a million times —"

"I told you why, Hubie. And you know why. 'Cause I'm tryin' to trip you up, catch you in a whole bunch of inconsistencies, you know the drill. Just answer the questions and stop whinin'. Mad-dog killers like yourself, they don't whine, c'mon. Fu Manchu moustache, man, I'll tell ya, Hubie, you really are startin' to dress the part, you know? I mean, I'm sure people who don't know you, they hear what your rap is? They take a look at you, they must think, man, this is some dangerous dude, some real bad-ass dago gang-ster, cut your heart out, grind it up, make meat-balls out of it, and eat it with rigatonis."

"I was the accomplice, asshole. In the commission of two felony murders, I was the accomplice, I was not the shooter."

"Oh that's right, I forgot. *You're* not the mad-dog killer. Billy Band, *he* was the mad-dog killer, you were the wheel-man, the getaway guy, right? Or wouldn't he let you drive either?"

"I was drivin'."

"Uh-ha. And when you went in the cabin there, where was Potter? You remember where he was? When you and Billy Band were in there humpin' those two chumpos, before he shot 'em and you two both robbed 'em? Where was Potter?"

"Patter don't you mean?"

"Potter Patter, you said it yourself — what the fuck's the difference? Where was he — while you were humpin' those two?"

"I never humped nobody."

"Oh. Oh, Billy Band humped 'em, I see. Well, was he humpin' 'em both at the same time? What's he have, uh, did he have two dicks? Huh?"

"He did Stevens first and then he did the other one, that, uh, Portilletto."

"And what were you doin', huh? Holdin' the gun on 'em? Did you tell me how much dope you scored? Did you tell me or did I forget?"

"I didn't tell you. I told ya I told everybody and his mother about a million times."

"Well tell me again, go 'head. How much?"

"Two keys."

"Two keys, wow. Holy shit. And how much money? Huh?"

"About fifteen large."

"Wowsie. Fifteen thousand dollars. Whoa, Hubie, you really are large-time. Really are a large-ass dago gangster. So when the state cops picked you up the next day, I mean, how much money did they find on you, huh? I heard all they found was like three hundred bucks. And about like, uh, what, an ounce of grass? What happened to the rest? You stash it someplace?"

"We moved it, what do you think?"

"We? You and Billy Band? You moved the dope? Sold it, is that what you mean when you say moved it?"

"What the fuck else would I mean, Jesus."

"Ahh, sure. Coupla fast movers like you two, I don't know why I should be surprised. Course you woulda moved it. What else'd you steal it for? So how much'd you get for it?"

"I don't know. Billy did that. I got busted before I heard."

"Oh, right, so you were locked up? From that day forward, you never got out on the street again, right? Double felony murder like that, there was no bond, so you didn't know how much you got ripped off by Billy Band. Course he was the shooter. And you saw what he did to those two before he shot 'em, right? So you were not really prepared to argue with him anyway, right? And anyway, even if you were prepared to argue, you were locked up, so what could you do about it, right? If Billy Band rips you off, so what? You ripped them off, right? And now somebody

244

dusted Billy Band, right? Finally, after all these years. After he dusted those two chumpos? So it looks like it's all workin' out even, huh, whattaya think?"

"I don't know what you're talkin' about."

"Sure you do, Hubie, I mean, look at you. Shaved your head, grew that moustache, got all those tattoos, been liftin' some weights, runnin' your mouth, braggin' behind this terrible rap sheet you've got — hey, you're not just a tit-cuttin' psychopath anymore, Hubie. Uh-uh. You're not just a roly-poly juvenile delinquent anymore, nosirree, you are large-time bad for sure. You jump in with the tattooed white boys inside, you learn how to talk the talk and walk the walk, and the next thing you know, you're gettin' transferred around the system for bein' a real bad boy — excuse me, a real bad man. Hey, I'm impressed. I think your next tattoo, I think you should get the word *evil* tattooed right across your forehead there, right above your eyes, so everybody'd know for sure, all they'd have to do is look at you and they could see it, wowsie! Hubie Scum is evil. Says so right there on his forehead."

"What's goin' on here?"

"Oh you know what's goin' on here, Hubie. Look into my eyes, c'mon. What do you see? C'mon, c'mon, look!"

"The fuck's wrong with you, whatta you doin' here?"

"Tell me somethin', Hubie. And this time, don't lie. This time, tell me the truth. When did

245

you decide to take it back, huh? When did you decide to cop Billy Band to all this bullshit, huh? You decide that after he got killed? Or did you decide that after you found out you were gonna get transferred here? After you found out Lester Walczinsky was already here? When did you have this sudden revelation that it wasn't Lester Walczinsky that was the shooter, huh? That it was Billy Band? When did the divine light of truth shine upon you, Hubie, tell me, I wanna know when that happened."

Scumacci's heels started bouncing slowly, the chains rattling. He looked away and started blinking, and then his head started rocking in time with his heels.

"Hey, Hubie, listen up here. Stop tryin' to tune me out. 'Cause, Hubie, we both know, don't we, huh? We know you're not evil. We know you're no bad-ass dago gangster. We know what you are, Hubie, don't we? We know, both of us, you and me, we know you're still nothin' but a small-time, fat, juvenile delinquent. We both know you're nothin' but a scissor boy. Like to cut women's breasts off. Startin' with your own grandmother. That's all you are, Hubie, all you ever been, all you're ever gonna be, I don't care how many tattoos you get, I don't care how you grow your hair or don't, or what you shave or don't shave, I don't care how much large bad shit you talk, you're still what you always were. And you know how I know that, don't ya, Hubie?"

Scumacci's heels were bouncing faster, and his

head was rocking faster, and now he was rolling his neck trying to work some kinks out.

"C'mon, Hubie, how do I know that?"

"You're so fuckin' smart, you fuckin' tell me. How the fuck should I know?"

"After the state cops picked you up, Hubie, where'd they take you?"

"You're the one talkin' here, not me."

"They took you to the Deer Mountain Borough Building, didn't they? Huh?"

"If you say so."

"I'm sayin' so, Hubie, 'cause it's true, isn't it?"

"If you say so."

"You know, I could almost feel sorry for you, you know that? I could almost work up some real sorry for you."

Scumacci said nothing. He kept rolling his neck and stretching it, and the bouncing of his heels was steady now. Steady and quickening.

"You know why I could almost feel sorry for you, Hubie? 'Cause you almost pulled it off. People always talkin' about jailhouse conversions, always talkin' about people gettin' religion inside, hallelujah, but there are all kindsa conversions in here, right, Hubie? I mean, look at you. You almost made it. Took yourself from a small, fat, dago juvenile delinquent and almost turned yourself into some kinda large, bad-ass, dago gangster guy."

"Aw fuck you."

"No I'm serious, Hubie, you almost pulled it off. 'Cause you were there that day, Hubie, no doubt about that. You were on Deer Mountain that day, you were in and out of that cabin, there's not a doubt in the world. That's how you got suckered into all this bullshit. You were there, you bought some dope, you smoked some, who knows, but when the real shit went down, Hubie? Huh? When the real bad shit went down, the shit you're doin' this time for? Hubie, you weren't anywhere around there."

"I guess you're gonna tell me *you* were. Right. That's fuckin' hilarious."

"Oh no, I'm not gonna tell you that, Hubie. That would be a joke, uh-uh, that wasn't me that was there. But I know who was. I know who killed those two poor bastards. And not only that, I know who told you what to say about it. So how 'bout it, you wanna help me out here, huh? You wanna give me backup on what I already know? What we *both* already know, whattaya say?"

"I already told that Livingood, already said I was gonna say who it was. I already said I was gonna say it wasn't Walczinsky, the fuck you want from me? You want me to open up a vein or somethin'?"

"Still ridin' Billy Band, huh?"

"What difference does it make who it was, long as I say it wasn't Walczinsky? Huh? What difference?"

"I'll tell you the difference, Hubie. Ever hear the words 'official oppression,' huh? Ever hear those words?"

"No."

"Never heard 'em."

"Just said no, the fuck you want?"

"Just think of this, Hubie, okay? Just think of you in Deer Mountain Borough Building, you do remember some state cops takin' you there, is that right? You do remember that?"

Scumacci said nothing. His heels stopped bouncing.

"And then after a while, the state cops, they left? Correct? And you're left behind there, correct? With those two local cops? You remember them?"

Scumacci was suddenly motionless except for the rising and falling of his paunchy stomach; the period between each rise and fall was growing noticeably shorter the longer Balzic talked.

"And all the while you were there with those two local cops, huh? The whole time you were with them, they never once, not either one of them, they never once ever said that name William Banditti, did they? Either one of them, huh?"

Scumacci's eyes began to dart around the table, but, except for his rising and falling stomach, he was still motionless.

"But the name they did give you, over and over and over, remember? The name they gave you wasn't Banditti. The name they gave you over and over and over, every time one of them whacked you around, what name was that, huh?"

Scumacci said nothing, his eyes continuing to dart, his breathing becoming noticeably quicker and shallower.

"You know what it was, what you want me to say it for?"

"I know it. But I want you to say it. Say it now."

"Lester Walczinsky."

" 'Cause you weren't there, were you? Huh?"

Scumacci said nothing. He was starting to make small, barely audible grunting noises, part snort, part cough, part belch.

"You weren't anywhere near that place when those two poor bastards got dusted, am I right?"

"Yes. No."

"Which is it, yes or no?"

"Yes I wasn't . . . I wasn't there."

"So you — of your own knowledge — you don't have any idea who was there, isn't that right? I mean everything that happened to those two, Stevens and Portiletto, everything you know about them was put in your mind by somebody else, isn't that true?"

Scumacci nodded.

"You gotta talk, Hubie, this ain't a camera."

"Uh-huh. Yeah. Yes."

"So everything you know about that day after you bought dope from those two, everything — you know 'cause you were told, either by one or the other of two police officers from the Deer Mountain Borough Police Department, is that true or not?"

"Yes. It's true."

"And of those two police officers, which one gave you most of the information? That you know about what happened to Stevens and Portiletto? Did one give you more information than the other?"

"Yeah. Just one."

"And this one who gave you this information, did he identify himself to you in any way? Did the other officer call him by name or rank, for example, or did he tell you himself who he was?"

"Yes. The other officer."

"What did the other officer call him that identified him in your mind?"

"Chief. Once or twice he called him somethin' else. Papa Bear, I think. But mostly he called him Chief."

"And did he have, either one of them, did either one of them have nametags on that you could see?"

"Yes."

"And you saw those nametags?"

"Yes."

"And do you remember the names on those tags?"

"Yes."

"What were those names?"

"One of 'em, uh, he was Icelip."

"Icelip, is that how you heard the other one call him? Is that how you heard him pronounce it?"

"Yeah. And it said it too. His nametag."

"Where was his nametag, you remember? On his collar, where?"

"On his shirt."

"Where on his shirt?"

"Right above his left pocket."

"What'd it look like?"

Scumacci shrugged. "It was black. Shiny. White letters, I don't remember."

"And while you were gettin' beat, while you were lookin' at their nametags, and while the one you believed was the chief — they were the only two police officers present?"

"Only ones I saw."

"And while they were beatin' you, the one who kept givin' you information about what happened and who was there, what was his name? Did you see it on his nametag? Or did you hear the other officer call him by somethin' other than Chief?"

"Same as the one he kept givin' me."

"The name they kept givin' you? Huh? Lester Walczinsky?"

"Not *them*. Just him."

"The one who gave you that name, right, he's the one who had the same name on his nametag? Is that what you're sayin'?"

"Yeah. Yes."

"So what you're sayin' now is, you didn't just dream that name up, did you? That name, Lester Walczinsky, that name was given to you repeatedly, is that right? By police officers who were beating you?"

"Yes."

"Like how many times were you given that name over what period of time? How long were you there?"

"Fuckin' forever, I don't know."

"Yeah I know, musta felt like that, but, uh, how long? You ever see a clock? Or a watch?"

"Uh-uh. It was when they was gettin' tired. Started jokin' about how it was a good day's work, some stupid shit like 'at."

"What time did they say?"

"Like around eleven o'clock. Somethin' like 'at."

"Eleven at night?"

"Yeah. Somethin'. At night."

"Where you were, were there windows in the room?"

"No."

"So you couldn't see outside?"

"No."

"So you didn't know whether it was daylight or not?"

Scumacci shook his head. He was sagging. With each question and each answer he seemed to slump lower into the chair.

"Did either one of them say anything like, say, twenty-three hundred, or twenty-three hundred hours, or anything like that?"

"No."

"They said eleven o'clock?"

"Yeah."

"What time of day did the state police pick you up?"

"Morning. Real early."

"And they interviewed you?"

"Yeah."

"For how long?"

"I don't know, coupla days."

"Uh-ha. Before they picked you up, were you smokin'?"

"You mean dope?"

"Yes."

"Sure."

"A lot?"

"That's what we bought it for."

"So you were still flyin' when the state cops picked you up?"

"Probably. Sure."

"So you didn't know how long you were in their custody, or when they took you to Deer Mountain Borough Building, right?"

"Right." Scumacci belched nervously.

"In the ride over, was it light out? Was the sun shinin'?"

"I don't remember."

"You think you were still high when you got to the Borough Building? In Deer Mountain?"

"Coulda been. Probably. Sure. Smoked about four joints that night. Smoked a coupla more the next day."

"So you really had no idea about the times you were anywhere, right? Over the next coupla days?"

Scumacci shrugged.

"So when you heard those two police officers talkin' about eleven o'clock, they coulda been talkin' about eleven in the morning for all you know, right?"

Suddenly, Scumacci sat up and bristled. "Listen, you asshole, the way they were beatin' me, the last thing in the world I gave a fuck about was what time it was. You know anything about dope, huh? Know how it makes everything bigger or better, you know anything about that? Well lemme tell ya somethin', it makes it hurt worse too when somebody's poundin' on ya!"

"If you say so."

"I say so!"

"Okay. So it was eleven o'clock in the morning, the day after the state police picked you up. The state guys interview you all day, the next morning they take you to Deer Mountain, the dope you smoked two days before, it's still in your system, so by what, eleven o'clock they had you convinced you were there? Is that what you're sayin', huh?"

"Right."

"And you were the driver, and the shooter was Lester Walczinsky, they had you convinced of this, right? And you were standin' right there with him and you watched Lester Walczinksy sodomize these two dope dealers, and then you watched him shoot them until they were dead, is that the story you were given?"

"Yes."

"And you were given lotsa details, weren't ya? Like give me one now. That nobody woulda known unless they'd been there, give me one of them."

"He told me what kinda underwear they were wearin'."

"Stevens and Portiletto?"

"Right. Yeah. Yes. Stevens was wearin' white briefs, and Portiletto had boxers on. Some kinda red and blue somethin'. Just some kinda pattern, wasn't nothin' you could tell."

"Wasn't apples or cherries or fish or somethin' like that, was it?"

"No. Just some kinda pattern they put on boxers."

"So while they were giving you these details —"

"Just the one was doin' 'at. Not the other one."

"Not this Icelip?"

"Right. Not him. The other one."

"Well while he was doing this, what were you thinkin', huh?"

"The fuck you think I was thinkin'? I wanted to get outta there. Thought those motherfuckers was gonna kill me."

"If you didn't agree to say what the one was tellin' you to say? Who did he want you to say it to? Anybody in particular?"

"Anybody? What, you crazy? He wanted me to tell everybody. Wanted me to tell the whole fuckin' world what a faggot dope dealer Lester Walczinsky was."

"So you finally agreed to do this?"

"I was tellin' 'em all along, right from the git-go, soon as the motherfuckers hit me the first time, I said, whoa, stop, man, stop hittin' me,

256

youns two don't have to hit me, and they kept hittin' me anyway, and then this motherfucker, he went away and he come back, he was carryin' this wooden box, this old fuckin' telephone, this wood box with bells on the outside, and he started unrollin' these wires, I said whoa motherfucker, you ain't hookin' me up to that, uh-uh, no fuckin' way, whatever you want, man, I been tryin' to tell youns, whatever you want me to say, hey, I'm good for it, I'll say it, whatever youns want, I'll say it, I'll say it in a heartbeat, fuckin'-A, man, you want me to say it was your kid, fuck yeah, I'll say it, whatever youns want, only just don't start gettin' no idea about wirin' me up to that fuckin' box —"

"He told you it was his kid? He told you that?"

"Yeah. I just said that. Ain't that what I just said?"

"I know what you said, Hubert, I just want you to be absolutely clear about what you're sayin'. And I wanna be clear. So tell me. Did he tell you it was his kid —"

"He told me about a hundred times, yeah, it was his kid, Lester Walczinsky. Said his kid was a dope-dealin' faggot and oughta be in prison for the rest of his life 'cause executin' him was too easy."

Balzic settled back and sighed. He thought for a moment about what he should say next. He reached out and pushed the stop button on his recorder, and studied Scumacci's face for a long moment.

Scumacci's face was flushed. He kept thrusting his chin upward, drawing down the corners of his mouth, rolling his head from shoulder to shoulder, trying to stretch kinks in his neck.

Finally, Balzic said, "We have a problem, Hubert, don't we?"

"I don't got no problem. Maybe you got a problem, I ain't got no problem."

"Yes you do, Hubert. Maybe you haven't thought of it yet, but you're goin' to, sooner or later. Eventually, it's gonna come to you, how much of a problem you have."

"I don't know what you're talkin' about."

"Think about it, Hubert. You're gonna get subpoenaed to testify at Walczinsky's hearing. So am I. And we both know there's a tape right here, right inside this little machine, this little box sittin' on the table between us, and we both know what you just said, and we both know that what you just said isn't anything like what you said to Livingood. So, uh, you see the problem yet?"

"What problem? Don't matter what I say. Whether I say what I told 'at Livingood, so what? So what if I say what I said here? So what if you play the tape? So what if both of ya swear I told youns both somethin' different. Long as either way it comes out Lester's off the hook, so what?"

Balzic stood and put his topcoat on, and his cap, and put his tape recorder in his pocket. "Remember what I said before, Hubert? About how I could almost work up a sorry for you, huh? You remember that?"

"So? I don't need your fuckin' sorry, so what?"

"I don't have to work it up, Hubert. I feel real sorry for you."

"Aw fuck you, huh? Who asked ya? What, I'm supposed to think you ain't an asshole anymore just 'cause you're feelin' sorry for me all of a sudden? What, you're doin' me some kinda favor? Huh? Fuck you, you're still an asshole."

"See ya, Hubert. Thanks for your cooperation. I mean that. And good luck. I mean that, too."

"Good luck, Jesus. Get lost, I make my own luck. Get the fuck outta here."

Balzic went to the CO in charge of the visitors area and told him that he was finished with Scumacci. It wasn't the CO who'd been there the day Balzic had interviewed Martin Islip, and when Balzic asked about the disturbance that day and about the CO who'd been injured, this CO said that all he knew was what he'd heard and he hadn't heard much. Balzic knew better than to push it. He said good-bye and hurried back to the main gate as a cold drizzle turned to snow, thick heavy flakes slanting out of the north. By the time he started his car, the ground was covered.

On his way home from Southern Regional, he stopped at the state police Troop A crime lab and helped a clerk book the pistol, no longer encrusted with frozen dirt, the dirt now turning to mud from having sat in Balzic's car for the last couple of hours. Balzic asked the clerk to tell the ballistics people to get it firing again as quickly as possible because it was very likely the only evidence that was going to overturn a wrongful conviction. The clerk listened politely and dutifully said he would pass the message on, doing his best not to look at Balzic like he was a total jerk because they both knew this pistol was just one more drop of water in the river of evidence that flowed into the crime lab every day. They both knew it would get evaluated in its turn, and not a second sooner, no matter who said what.

Back home, after hanging up his topcoat and cap and taking off his overshoes, Balzic kissed Ruth on the hair as he walked past her while she was talking on the phone. He went into the bedroom, got a pair of fresh rechargeables out from under his side of he bed, went to his office, slumped into his swivel chair, and put the new batteries in his recorder, thinking hard about what he wanted to say, and how.

After five minutes or so, he pushed the start button and said, "To G. Warren Livingood, Deputy Attorney General, Department of Justice, Commonwealth of Pennsylvania, from Mario Balzic, Special Investigator, same department, uh, March 6, 1994, uh, subject, uh, recommended investigation of Deer Mountain Borough Police Department by the Justice Department, uh, over the tenure of Walter Walczinsky, borough chief of police, uh, now incapacitated.

"Paragraph. It is, uh, my strongest recommendation to you and to the attorney general of this Commonwealth, uh, that the Justice Department begin an immediate investigation into every criminal prosecution that was initiated by either Deer Mountain PD Chief Walczinsky acting on his own, or by former Deer Mountain PD Patrolman Martin Islip, currently incarcerated in Southern Regional Correctional Facility at Rocksburg, Conemaugh County, uh, or by Islip acting on his own, or by both of them acting together as duly authorized officers of the law in Deer Mountain Borough, Wabash County, Pa.

"Paragraph. After interviewing, on your direct order, certain persons in connection with the petition of Lester Walczinsky for a post-conviction hearing, it is my belief that during the tenure of the those two, especially Walczinsky, God, outrageous . . . outrageous. Ha. Shit, there isn't a word strong enough for what this, uh, scratch that, uh, for these continuous acts of official oppression, yeah, that's what I wanna say, for these acts in violation of Title 18, Pennsylvania Consolidated Statutes, uh, Section 5301, lemme see if I can remember it here . . . ah shit, uh-uh, hang on, can't remember shit, gotta get my Title 18 here, I'll be right back. . . .

"Okay here we go. Section 5301, official oppression. Quote, A person acting or purporting to act in an official capacity or taking advantage of such actual or purported capacity commits a misdemeanor of the second degree if, knowing

261

that his conduct is illegal, he, colon, subsection one, subjects another to arrest, detention, search, seizure, mistreatment, dispossession, assessment, lien or other infringement of personal or property rights, semicolon, subsection two, denies or impedes another in the exercise or enjoyment of any right, privilege, power or immunity, end quote. Can't imagine why I thought I could remember that. Anyway.

"Paragraph. As to the specifics, I believe that even a cursory investigation will conclude that said acts of official oppression will include, but will not be limited to, uh, reckless endangerment, terroristic threats, assault, aggravated assault, attempted homicide, homicide, subornation of witnesses, intimidation of witnesses, et cetera.

"Paragraph. I believe the Pennsylvania State Police should be ordered to impound all official police records in Deer Mountain Borough PD, including but not limited to, case records, dockets, phone logs, citation books, mug shots, personnel records, budgets, equipment requisitions and inventories, especially firearms for ballistics comparisons, property room logs and inventories, et cetera, plus all copies of court documents for cases cleared. Failing that, I believe the office of that PD should be sealed until such time as the records can be impounded. Or until such time as the Justice Department determines that said records should be impounded.

"Paragraph. I believe the PSP should execute warrants to search the residence of Chief Walter

262

Walczinsky on Deer Mountain, including the house and grounds and all other buildings and vehicles, for the purpose of seizing any and all records, official records, notebooks, diaries, correspondence, phone logs, audiotapes, videotapes, et cetera — oh firearms! Don't forget that, firearms, anything pertaining to the prosecution, conviction, and incarceration of any person or persons that can be found, uh, for the purpose of determining whether such prosecutions and convictions were legitimate. Uh, based, that is to say, on complaints that were represented as being legitimately investigated and legitimately filed and presented to the district attorney of Wabash County for trial.

"Paragraph. The foregoing recommendation is based on the statement, much of it unprompted, uh, don't want to say unsolicited, that's stupid — it's based on the statement I took from Chief Walczinsky's wife Letitia, which, when you listen to the tape of my interview with her, you can hear that much of this information she just blurted out. When you listen to the tape, you will hear me warning her, cautioning her as to what she was saying. You will hear her disregard my cautions. At one point, for example, she said her husband had at least two other wives — which you can hear for yourself so I don't know why I'm going into any of the details. Anyway, Letitia Walczinsky is, as far as I could see, the sole caretaker of the chief, who's in what appears to be a vegetative state, which is my opinion and I'm certainly no medical expert. But from what I could see, he gave no indication he was aware of anybody's presence when I observed him in bed in his house.

"Paragraph. I believe also that with the ballistics comparison made on the revolver I recovered at Chief Walczinsky's residence at the direction of his wife Letitia, also which you can hear on the tape I made during that interview, uh, I believe that with the comparison of bullets taken from the bodies of James Stevens and Joseph Portiletto, and with the weapon which — Jesus, I don't know if it's even possible that weapon can still fire, I mean, I dug it out of frozen ground, which, according to Letitia Walczinsky, who claims she buried it, which you can hear on the tape, that pistol's been in the ground for seventeen years, well above the frost line. I don't know if it's possible to make that thing fire again, which, uh, if we can't, ah shit.

"I have to finish this later. I need some wine. I mean, sometimes, Warren, no shit, you learn things, which the minute you learn 'em you wish you hadn't. Today was one of those times. I didn't really wanna learn all this, uh, this . . . fuck, I don't know what to call it. I just hope with every drop of blood in me, good cholesterol, bad cholesterol, triglycerides, whatever, all of it, I hope the ballistics people in Troop A crime lab can make that thirty-eight fire again, 'cause if they can't . . . shit, I gotta finish this later. This is too hard right now. . . ."

He shut the recorder off and went into the kitchen, intending to pour himself some jug chablis out of the carafe in the refrigerator, but Ruth interrupted him by handing him the phone.

"Who is it?"

"The dog warden. Returning your call."

"You wanna pour me some wine, please? I could really use about eight ounces of cold wine." He took the phone and said, "Balzic here. Thanks for callin' back. I didn't quite get your name on your machine, what is it again?"

"Mazurek. John. And you're with the state Justice Department, is that correct? Special investigator?"

"That's correct."

"Well what's your problem, sir?"

"Uh, problem's not mine exactly, though for a coupla minutes today I thought it was, but, uh, there's a coupla dogs runnin' deer. I observed, uh, many racks of antlers, I didn't count 'em, but there were, oh, I'd say at least a half dozen. Plus lotsa skull parts, hooves, rib cages, partsa hides, and so on, on this property in Deer Mountain, township I guess it was, but maybe it was the borough. Pretty confusing up there about where one stops and the other starts."

"Well lemme stop you right there, sir."

"I'm listenin'."

"Unless you or somebody else sees that dog in the act of killing a deer, there's really not anything anybody can do about that. Now, see, if the dog bites a person, or a domestic animal, see, then

265

we can move on, but this deer business is very tricky stuff. I'll bet you called the Game Commission first, didn't you?"

"Matter of fact, yes I did. Went to see them."

"Well I'm sure they told you the same thing I'm telling you, because they refer complaints to me all the time. Let me tell how this works briefly and then we'll see what else you have to say, okay?"

"Well before you do that, why don't I just ask you a specific? You ever responded to a complaint about dogs on Deer Mountain? Is that part of your turf?"

"Yes it is. Oh wait. Are you going to tell me about that police chief up there? Huh? And his two German shepherds?"

"Yes I was."

"Well save your breath, sir. I've gone to the dance up there twice, so to speak, and I've come home alone both times, and I'm not about to go up there and get jerked around a third time."

"I don't understand."

"It's real simple. What you're talking about, what I tried to deal with on two separate occasions, was, uh, one totally corrupt human being and one, I guess the nicest thing I could say about him is he's just scared out of his mind, or else he's being blackmailed by the other guy."

"You talkin' about the chief of police there?"

"That's exactly who I'm talking about. And also the district justice I took the complaints to — twice. See, that's what I started to tell you

266

before, how this works. I get a complaint, I make my investigation, and if I think it has merit, why then I have to take it to the district justice where the owner of the dog lives. He's who makes the determination of whether we're dealing with a dangerous dog, see? And I did that twice with that chief up there, and both times I just got, I mean, in the face of overwhelming evidence that I had collected, that district justice, that sonofabitch, he just threw it back in my face. Oh, the second time was a nightmare. Accused me of, uh, of conducting some sort of, uh, witch-hunt, some sort of official vendetta against the chief. Which was preposterous. I had no idea who he was — I mean before the first complaint. Afterwards, oh, now that was a different story, what I learned when I was collecting my evidence, that was an altogether different matter, I'll tell you."

"Uh, this district justice you're talkin' about," Balzic said, "would that be the same guy who got himself elected district attorney?"

"That's him, that's the one. Man's either a total coward, or else he's the victim of blackmail, there's no other explanation. I've never run into anybody — before or since — so cowardly in his dealings with me. I'll be the first to say the law's a tricky thing when it comes to dogs, but I almost quit over that. I took that all the way up to the secretary of the department. I have a log of phone calls and registered letters I sent up the chain of command, hell's fire, I even thought about writing to my state representative, you know, as a private citizen, you know, asking him to ask the, uh, your people, Justice, to make an inquiry. Hell it just occurred to me — that's not what this is about, is it?"

"Oh no. No no, I was involved — am involved, uh, in something else, and I had to interview the woman, uh, the chief's wife, and uh, these damn dogs, Christ, they came out of nowhere — and I'd been warned about them, but Jesus Christ, they attacked the car. I was inside the car with the doors locked and the windows up and I don't mind tellin' ya, I wasn't feelin' very damn secure. One of the few times in my life I ever wished I was carryin' a gun."

"Well sir, I do carry weapons. Lots of 'em. Pepper sprays, stun gun, a pistol and a shotgun, twelve-gauge pump with double-O buckshot, and after the second fiasco I went through up there, when that miserable coward accused me of carrying on an official vendetta, I'll tell you, I thought long and hard about going to the chief's property and killing those dogs myself. And killing him if he tried to interfere with me. I don't like violence and I hate it every time I have to supervise the destruction of a dog, I truly do hate it, but sometimes it has to be done. And the only question I have for you, sir, and for your department, if you don't mind my saying so, is what took you so long? I begged you people to do something about this man three years ago. Three years ago, sir! I wrote more than thirty letters, every one of them registered, to your department,

I can't tell you how many memos I wrote to my supervisors, how many phone calls I made, Jesus —"

"Sir? Sir? Mister Mazurek? Sir?"

"What?"

"I just came on board here. Not even a week ago. I never got one of your letters —"

"Well somebody did! Somebody signed for every one of 'em, I have the green cards! Every damn response was a buncha baloney about how I should work through my own department, what crap."

"Sir, I give you my word, I am writing a report to my supervisor, that's what I was doin' before I walked in here to the kitchen and my wife handed me the phone, and believe me, from what I've learned, I agree with you one hundred and ten percent, but all of what you're sayin' is new to me, sir. But I'll tell you what I'm gonna do, if you'll go along with me."

"What's that?"

"If you send me copies of everything you sent to the Justice Department and to your bosses, I guarantee you, I will include them in my next report to my boss, how's that? That okay with you?"

"Well you just give me your address, sir, and I'll have everything I ever did on this on a UPS truck tomorrow morning, after I get 'em notarized."

"Fine. You do that, and I guarantee somebody will be talking to you."

They thanked each other for their mutual concern and cooperation and said good-bye.

Ruth had gone into the living room while he was on the phone, but she came back in when she heard him hang up.

"God," she said, "you okay? You look terrible. You gettin' something? Let me feel your head."

He set the wine down and held out his arms to embrace her. "I ain't gettin' anything. I just need a hug. Bad."

She crept forward into his chest and looked up at him. "What's the matter?"

"Just talkin' to people, that's all." He looked down at her and shook his head.

"What?" When he didn't answer, she said it again.

"You will agree, right, we have been havin' our problems, right? Huh?"

"Yeah. And?"

"And sometimes, uh, you know, I been actin' like the world's biggest asshole — wait wait, don't agree to that real fast, okay?"

"Okay. I won't. You sure you're not gettin' something?"

"Like what, the flu you mean? No no, just listen, okay? I'll tell you, I'm not gettin' anything."

"I'm listening. Just be sure and tell me when it's my turn to talk, okay?"

"I will, just wait a minute here, I'm tryin' to say somethin'."

"Trying to tell me what? How we have such a

wonderful thing goin' here? Right here in the frozen north? In our little oasis in Rocksburg? 'Cause you've just been out talking to some poor woman whose husband or boyfriend or father or son or whoever just beat the crap out of her, haven't you?"

"Or whoever?"

"Yeah, whoever. I mighta left somebody out. Whoever's been beatin' the crap out of her, all over her house or apartment or trailer, where he probably just now threw her out of, and you, big schtunk that you are, you're all full of guilt 'cause of how you've been talking to me lately, and now you wanna tell me how lucky you are to have me —"

"That's pretty much what I was gonna say, yeah —"

"And how lucky I am to have you, right? Right?"

"Well I wasn't gonna say that exactly, no —"

"But you were thinking it."

"Aw sometimes you're a pain in the, uh —"

"Pain in the what? Huh? Pain in the where?"

"Aw c'mon."

"*You* come on. If I'm a pain in your ass — which is what you wanna say except you know you'll feel worse if you do, sometimes, lover boy, sometimes you're a pain in my whole body. For instance," she said, her eyes dancing impishly, "you know when was the last time you took me to bed? Made love to me? Huh? A month ago." She dragged out the last three words.

271

"What? Wait a second, I'm tryin' to tell you what a good thing we got goin' for us here and you're talkin' how long it's been since what? Since I took you to bed?"

"That's exactly what I'm doing, big boy. You thought you were gonna come in here and make a little speech about how lucky we are just 'cause we have each other, and I was going to get all dreamy-eyed and drooly —"

"Hey. We *do* have a good thing goin' here, Ruth. Ruth, Ruth, listen to me — hey —"

"You listen," she said, smiling, shaking his shoulders playfully, "if I hadn't learned how to use my hands about twenty years ago, ha! If I had to wait on you, who thinks we got this great thing goin', ha! I'd have about two orgasms a year it was up to you —"

"Oh what're you talkin' about, two a year, that's crap —"

She shook him again, her eyes agleam with mischief. "If I hadn't discovered Betty Dodson's books, if I had to sit around waitin' on you, I might as well be a divorcée —"

"Aw come on," he said, trying to pull away. But she wouldn't let him. She began to sway her hips against him, her eyes kept up their dance. And he knew he didn't have a chance.

"I'm wondering whether you even know what to do anymore," she said, "been so long since you've seen me naked."

She was having fun with him and he knew he deserved it, but because it was about sex it made

272

him cringe inside. "Aw c'mon, Ruth."

"You come on," she said, smiling and making her eyes go wide. "Gawd, Mar, it's just talk, there's nobody here but you and me. And I've shut off all the hidden cameras and tape recorders. We're actually alone here, and nobody's gonna ever know that your prissy little ears are hearin' this."

"Prissy ears? What kinda crap is that, prissy ears. I do not —"

"Oh you don't, huh? Then listen to this, okay? Huh? If you think you still know how to do everything, then whattaya say, big boy? Huh? Why don't you give me one right now, whattaya think? Think you still know how to give me one? Hmm?"

He closed his eyes and sighed. "Boy you really are somethin', you know that? You really are terrible sometimes. I'm tryin' to tell you how much, uh, how —"

"What? What're you trying to tell me? Can't say it, can you? Say it. I wanna hear you say it, c'mon say it."

"You been into the wine today or somethin'? Huh?"

"Oh what, I have to be into the wine? To wanna go to bed with you? Big schtunk! I missed you! You were gone all day, I missed you, it was wonderful! And you missed me too, don't say you didn't. All the while you were out talking to this woman, whoever she is, you were missin' me, weren't you? Say it, Mario, I know that's what you wanna tell me. Say it!"

"Sometimes you're fuckin' impossible —"

"That's right! Damn right I'm impossible. Exactly! And that's why you love me 'cause today whatever you were doin', it wised you up to that. That's why one of us has to get out of the house, Mar. 'Cause if one of us doesn't, if we're both here all day, lookin' at each other, it starts to look so possible around here all the time, we forget to make it happen, Mar. That's what's been goin' on around here. We're walkin' around here taking each other for so goddamn granted — stop looking at me like that. You're thinkin' this is some corny crap. It isn't! It isn't, Mar, it's the truth, and you know it. If you never knew it before, you know it now. I don't know what you learned from that woman, but it was something big, I can see it in your eyes. I don't think I even wanna know what you learned. But you learned somethin'. I'm sorry for her, but I'm glad you learned it."

"What I learned today, yeah. What did I learn today? I learned today, man . . . what I learned today was sometimes you can learn things that make you sick you're alive."

"And sometimes these things you learn, Mar — correct me if I'm wrong — but sometimes these things can make you so sick you're alive, you actually wanna do somethin' about the way you live so you don't really get sick, don't you think?"

He held her away from him for a second, then

pulled her back into his chest. "I love you, Ruthie. I really do. You're the best —"

"Damn right I am."

"Oh a little modesty here, don't you think, huh? Just a little?"

"Oh the hell with modesty," she said, giggling. "We're alone here, Mar, you know? Modesty isn't what we need. What we need is to remember that we're alone here, you and me. We're alone! And we don't have much time, and how do we want to spend the rest of it? Huh? Gettin' on each other's nerves? Or remembering that we're alone here and that we don't have much time, and it's a sin to waste even a second of it, Mar, it's a sin, I'm telling you. It's a sin when two people who love each other as much as we do — at this time in our lives? To waste time jumpin' down each other's throats like we've been doing for the last three months? It's a sin. It's the worst sin there is. It's anger and pride and sloth all rolled up into one."

"Well thank you Sister Ruth. Hold it a second while I pass the tambourine."

"I'm serious, Mar. We get all full of ourselves for how much we think we do for each other, and then we get mad 'cause we don't think we're appreciated, and then we go pout and say the hell with it, and then we say it's okay to get lazy about trying to keep it up, it's all your fault or it's my fault. I read somethin' once I wish I could remember who said it. Said everybody gives credit to people for building new roads, but that's the easy part 'cause there's always a lot of adventure and glory in building something new. The hard part is maintaining the roads 'cause all that is is work."

Balzic grinned down at her. "Damn. I'm impressed. Lemme put my tambourine away, get my oil can, missus, see if I still know how to lubricate your earthmover."

"Your oil can's on my side of the bed," she said. "Where it's been for a month —"

"Yeah yeah, right, and if it wasn't for this, uh, who the hell's this Betty person?"

"Betty Dodson," she said, pulling away from him and walking out of the kitchen.

"Who's she? Where you goin' now?"

"I need to take a shower," she said. "Haven't had one since yesterday, that's how lazy I'm getting."

"I knew I was smellin' somethin'. Who's this Betty person again?" He grabbed his glass of wine and followed her into the bedroom and sat on the bed.

She spoke to him through the half-closed door to the bathroom. "She's a writer. An artist. I really like her drawings. She draws people making love. And genitals. Vaginas and clitorises. Really interesting. I know I'm not ever gonna get a vote about this, but if there's such a thing as a contemporary saint, she'd be my choice. Believe me. I'll bet she's relieved more stress in this world than Herbert Benson ever thought about relievin'."

"Herbert who? Who the hell's he now?"

"He's one of the guys wrote *The Relaxation Response*. All the stuff you say about meditation, you of all people oughta know who he is."

"Oh man, what I oughta know and what I do know, shit . . . You ever seen a woman with cauliflower ears?"

"What?"

She'd turned on the shower, and Balzic shouted that he'd tell her later. He set the wine on top of his chest of drawers and started peeling off his clothes. When he was down to his shorts, he sat on the end of the bed and fell back and closed his eyes and immediately saw Letitia Walczinsky's left ear and wondered why people called that a cauliflower ear, it didn't look anything like a cauliflower. Looked like an ear with all the cartilage busted, didn't look like any damn cauliflower. Wonder if Letitia Walczinsky ever heard of Betty Dodson. Draws vaginas? And clitorises? What the hell's she readin', man. Been married to her so long I can't remember when I wasn't married to her and she's lookin' at pictures of vaginas and clitorises? This woman'd get her vote for sainthood? Man. Question isn't about wastin' time. Question is if there's enough time left for me to find out who I'm married to. . . .

"Mario," Ruth said, shaking him. "Mario? Hey, Mar, you wanna wake up or you wanna keep on sleeping for a while? Maybe we can make love later, huh? What do you wanna do?"

Balzic blustered around, rolled on his side, and then sat up. "I think maybe I need a shower, feel better, I think."

"Why don't you? Go 'head, you will."

"Oh yeah, right, I know your game. You just wanna get me outta here so you can look at those dirty pictures'n do it yourself."

"They are *not* dirty. They are the exact opposite of dirty. Unless you're one of those TV preacher-creepos."

"How come you never showed 'em to me?"

" 'Cause you never expressed any interest, that I could see."

"Well I'm expressin' interest now," he said, scratching his belly.

"If you'd stop scratchin' your belly and got a shower and brushed your teeth and shaved, maybe I would show 'em to you."

Balzic shook his head. "I shaved this mornin'. Man, today has been one strange day. This mornin' I was talkin' to a woman had cauliflower ears and tonight I'm talkin' to my wife who's gonna show me dirty pictures."

"They are *not dirty* I said! Get your shower. G'on, get movin'."

"Don't go 'way, I'll be right back."

"Oh yeah, you'll be right back. Try not to fall asleep in there," she said. "That's okay in bed but it's kinda dangerous in there."

"Not half as dangerous as gettin' to know my wife." He went into the bathroom and turned on the shower.

"That's right," she called after him. "That's exactly right. I'm the most dangerous person you know." When he didn't respond, she said to herself, "And if you weren't so damn scared of me, it might be such fun. Am I that scary? God, I hope I'm not. . . ."

Lester Walczinsky's post-conviction hearing was convened in Wabash County Courthouse, Judge E. Howard Sonnett presiding, on Monday, June 20, 1994, almost two months after Balzic had his third interview with Letitia Walczinsky. Sonnett had been assigned to the case because Judge G. Merle Fraelich, who'd presided over Walczinsky's conviction in 1977 and retired in 1980, had died in 1993.

Attorney for the Commonwealth was F. Elliot Mueseler, first assistant DA of Wabash County, who was replacing T. George Humbolt because Humbolt, the then district attorney of Wabash County who'd directed the prosecution of Walczinsky, was now a judge and himself the subject of Deputy Attorney General G. Warren Livingood's continuing investigation into the events surrounding the prosecution and conviction of Lester Walczinsky, as well as other persons convicted on evidence collected and testimony given by Walter Walczinsky.

Livingood was sitting in the first row of the spectator section directly behind the petitioner's table, behind and to the left of Public Defender Robert Piano and to the right of

Lester Walczinsky.

Balzic was sitting in the last row of the spectator section, alternately examining the woodwork around an otherwise empty courtroom and watching dust stream upward through the sunlight coming from windows high above the empty jury box. He almost nodded off listening to Piano reading Walczinsky's petition into the record, along with the affidavits and other documents in support of the petition. It had been a long drive out from Rocksburg on an especially humid day, which had clogged Balzic's sinuses, and he was even drowsier because of the antihistamine he'd taken. He'd also awakened with throbbing pain in his right elbow which had no understandable cause except that a couple of days before he'd really had to strain to open a jar of pickled beets.

Next thing Balzic knew, Livingood was nudging him in the shoulder.

"Huh? What? What'samatter?" Balzic croaked, his lips and mouth feeling like he'd been chewing cardboard.

Livingood leaned down and whispered, "Sonnett doesn't want you in here while Scumacci's testifying. Or anybody else for that matter. Besides which, you're starting to snore."

"Scumacci here already? Thought you guys'd be arguin' affidavits all morning."

"We have been. You didn't start to snore until a couple of minutes ago. Sonnett wants you out."

"Okay, I'm gone," Balzic said, yawning and

standing. After he was out in the corridor, he rolled his shoulders frontward and backward five times each, and watched a woman on her knees polishing the brass kickplate on a door to the law library across the corridor. He asked her where he could get some coffee. She told him there was a coffee shop in the basement but not to take the elevator.

"Why not?"

" 'Cause it's throwin' fits again, hon. I was stuck in there for a half hour yesterday. I keep tellin' 'em to fix it, I can't walk these steps no more. They don't fix it, I'm gonna have to quit'n where'm I gonna get another job? No air conditioner in there neither. Just that little-bitty fan. And when the elevator quits, the fan does too. I was wringin' wet when they finally come'n got me. Take the steps, hon, believe me."

"Can I bring ya somethin' back? Huh? Coffee? Tea?"

"No thanks, hon. I got a Thermos. But, uh, you could play me a number if you wanted to."

"Beg pardon? I could do what now?"

"Play me a number. Six six six. On the old stock."

"Play you a number, huh, is that what you said? Instead of buyin' you coffee? And just where would I do that?"

"Down in the coffee shop, hon. Just tell her it's for me, she'll know."

"Uh, you, uh, you wanna give me some money? How much you wanna play?"

"Well were you just kiddin' when you said did I want a coffee? Were you gonna buy it or not? 'Cause if you'da bought it, hon, it's forty-five cents. Then you could maybe put a nickel to it, you know, and make it half a buck even. You don't have to, hon, just if you want to, I just thought you said you were gonna buy me one, that's all."

"Uh-ha," Balzic said, scratching his ear. "Fifty cents on trip sixes. Isn't that some kinda special number, the, uh —"

"Devil's number, yeah, hon, that's what they say. I think if the devil's as powerful as everybody keeps sayin' he is, he oughta be able to make his number hit once in a while. You'd think. But I been playin' it for two years now and it hasn't hit once yet. Course I don't play it all the time."

"Can't imagine why not."

"Nice as I keep everything shinin' around here, you'd think somebody'd wanna buy me coffee every day, but they don't."

Balzic walked away shaking his head, and went down four flights of steps to the basement and found the coffee shop. He bought himself an iced tea, and, after getting his change, slid two quarters back across the counter. "Six six six. For the charlady on the third floor."

The lady in charge of the coffee shop dropped the quarters in the front pocket of her smock and said, "Seven down, three to go."

"Beg pardon?"

"I just said seven down, three to go. You're trip

sixes. That just leaves sevens, eights, and nines."

"I don't get it — oh. Well. Ha. Isn't she the sly one," Balzic said, saluting the coffee-shop lady with his iced tea and starting back up the steps.

Back outside Sonnett's courtroom, Balzic saw a short, slender woman smoking by the window at the far end of the corridor beyond the law library. Something about her jogged his memory but he wasn't sure what it was. She was wearing a white pantsuit and red high-heeled shoes and carrying a small red purse. Her hair was combed forward around much of her face. It took him a long moment to recognize Letitia Walczinsky. Dressed up, she looked very different from every time he'd seen her in her house. He was starting toward her when the door to Sonnett's court opened and Livingood came striding out, looking ruffled. Annoyed almost.

Balzic immediately turned back toward Livingood. He'd never seen Livingood looking anything but calm, totally in control, so much so that Balzic had started thinking Livingood was one of those people who wouldn't permit himself to be anything but calm and controlled.

"What's goin' on?" Balzic said.

"You were right," Livingood said. "You said this was going to be a waste of everybody's time, and you were right. It is."

"I'm right about what? Scumacci?"

"Yes. Sat there and took the Fifth exactly as you said he would. Which I said he would not."

Balzic shrugged.

"Sonnett just finally asked him if he had any intention of answering any questions today — or ever, and that smug little psychopath smiled and said, 'No, Your Honor, not about this.' Then Sonnett started saying what about your statement, what about this tape, and Scumacci, exactly as you predicted, just flat denied he ever made that statement to me or to you or to anybody ever — that he was going to recant."

Balzic shrugged again. "So, uh, just move on, right? The sooner you move on, the better."

"Why didn't you argue this a little more strongly with me?"

Balzic sidled close to Livingood and, lowering his voice, he said, "Hey, look. The question isn't why didn't I argue this with you, the question is, if you think this guy deserves a new trial — which you said plenty of times to me he did — the question is, what're you doin' out here in the hall talkin' to me? Get back in there where you belong."

"Piano's arguing for a contempt citation right now, I've got a few minutes to stretch my legs."

"Well see? Hey. You want me to argue somethin' with you? Tell Piano knock it off. Scumacci gets cited for takin' the Fifth, all that's gonna do is make him a bigger problem inside than he already is. You didn't wanna listen to me before, hey, you're the boss. But now you're askin' me why I didn't argue stronger? Okay, I'm arguin' now. All a contempt citation's gonna do is add more bullshit to the macho mystery he's already created for himself. Piano talks the judge into citin' him, they may as well take him down to the nearest tattoo shop and get a medal tattooed on his forehead, the silver cross of contempt, with clusters. Plus it's just gonna cost the taxpayers more money.

"Hey, Warren, fuck Scumacci. You got the gun, you got the bullets, you got the ballistics guy from Troop A lab —"

"Speaking of whom, have you seen him yet?"

"No. He'll get here, don't worry. And when he does, he'll say which bullets came outta which gun and went into which skulls. And you got that woman standin' right down there at the end of the hall, who's gonna say who gave her the gun and where she buried it, so forget Scumacci, tell Piano to shut up already. And forget Patter too. You're just wastin' time with these guys. 'Cause what you can't do is you can't be losin' sight of the real problem here. Lester Walin's doin' time for one reason and for no other reason — just because he happened to be his father's son. But he's not the only one. I sent you a dozen tapes since I started goin' through that prick's records — you listened to 'em?"

"I've listened to some of them, yes, but not all of them —"

"Well somebody better start listenin' to 'em, Warren, I mean it. 'Cause that's the problem here. Not Scumacci. There are people that bastard put away — there are six guys I'd bet my right arm on they never did the crime they were convicted for. Only thing they had goin' against 'em was the shit luck to be that bastard's jurisdiction when he decided he wanted to have some fun. And now that the sonofabitch is dead, hey, all that does is give me more incentive to stay on somebody's case, Warren, I mean it. I'm sorry if it has to be yours, but I'm warnin' ya, I'm not gonna get off. State owes these people. There isn't anything worse than what happened to these poor fuckers. You want a for instance? The latest one?"

"I don't need any more of those, Mario, thank you —"

"Oh, excuse me but yes you do. Listen to this. Talked to this guy two days ago. Poor fucker's doin' ten consecutive convictions for burglaries that happened while he was workin' in the maintenance department at Northwestern University, which is in Chicago, Illinois, which I checked with about seven phone calls and two faxes, one from Illinois DMV of his driver's license and the other one from security for his campus ID, which also included his fingerprints. Only wrong thing he ever did was decide he didn't wanna take the turnpike through Pennsylvania, wanted to see somethin' else besides traffic on his way to Philadelphia. Happened to stop for gas in Deer Mountain when that prick Walczinsky decided he was bored. Just ran him in, tortured him for two days, and cleared all these burglaries the prick was probably doin' himself.

"And I did this before lunch yesterday, Warren. Meanwhile, this poor fuck's been in Southern

Regional for twenty-six months now, and he's got ten more months before his first parole hearing if nobody does anything about what I found out! Jesus Christ, Warren, somebody gotta tell the people here in the public defender's office about caffeine, you know? How it wakes you up!"

Livingood stood there and took it, then said with a wry smile, "Incredible. Seems only minutes ago, you were snoring."

"Hey, let's stick with the point here, okay? Which is, the prick's dead, we can't do anything to him, but we gotta do somethin' for these people he fucked over —"

"I hear you, Mario. Let me get back inside and see if I can redirect our focus." Livingood went back into the courtroom without another word.

Balzic had just started down the corridor again to talk to Letitia Walczinsky when he heard somebody laboring up the steps, breathing hard. Even though Balzic had known the man for years, he suddenly couldn't recall his name, even though he recognized him as one of the ballistics people from state police Troop A crime lab.

The man waved to Balzic and approached him and said, "Mario, they haven't called me yet, have they? I hit a dog." He set his heavy case on the marble floor and wiped his face with a damp handkerchief. "Woman was standing right there, right alongside the damn road, she was looking in her mailbox, the dog just turns around and walks out right in front of me, never got my foot off the gas, never touched the brake, honest to

God. What time is it? You know what time it is? Battery quit on my watch this morning. That's what I was thinking about, where can I get a battery, the damn dog just walks right out in front of me. Woman got all hysterical, Jesus. Can't blame her, oh God."

"Want some iced tea?" Balzic said, holding out his plastic cup. "Just drink outta that side, don't turn the cup around. I don't have anything, cold or anything. Go 'head."

"Oh. Thanks." The man took the tea and drank several swallows. Then he sighed. "Usually I don't like sugar in my tea, but this tastes good. Thanks — did you say what time it was? God. I told the woman I'd buy her a new dog. She hit me. Right here." He pointed to his left wrist. "Said I'll buy you a new dog and she hits me. With her fist! I didn't know what else to say. I've been dealing with people shooting people for twenty-four years, I hit a dog, I run over a dog, it's an accident, no way I could've stopped, I feel like I committed murder. I don't know if I can testify."

"Finish the tea, go 'head. C'mon, sit down," Balzic said, touching the man's elbow and nodding toward a bench against the far wall.

"Mario, I have to find another way back. I can't drive past there. I keep hearing her scream. The dog just gave this one little yip or yelp or whatever, but the woman, my God, she screamed such a scream, I never heard anything like that. Do you know another way? Back? I

288

don't think I can go that way."

"Hey, we'll ask around, somebody'll know. Drink the tea, go 'head, finish it. You want more? I'll go get you some more."

Just then the door to the law library opened, and the charlady appeared, pushing her cart of cleaning supplies. She cocked her head at Balzic and said, "Did I hear you say you were goin' downstairs, hon? Say you were gonna get somebody a tea? Wouldn't wanna play me a number, would ya?"

"Already played you one, remember?"

"I remember. Just need one more, hon, and I'll have 'em all covered."

"You're up to trip nines? Already?" Balzic laughed.

"Yeah, hon, trip nines already. Father, son, and holy ghost. But just if you're gonna buy him a tea, you know, just if you're goin' anyway, don't do it just for me. But if you're goin', you know, that'd be nice."

"Yeah, I'm goin'. Sure." He patted the ballistics man on the shoulder and told him he'd be right back.

Balzic started down the steps, thinking, Trip nines? Father, son, and holy ghost — is that what she said? What the hell's that about? Some people put it in the collection plate, some people give it to their bookie, is that what that's about? Hey, granted, they're both long shots, and if all you got to look forward to every day is polishin' and moppin' and dustin' all day long, why not? Maybe she'll get lucky. Everybody needs to get lucky once in a while. Wouldn't it be lovely if all it ever took was a coupla quarters?

Course, she tries to run this number on me every day I'm here, we're gonna have to have a little conversation. . . .

The employees of G.K. Hall hope you have enjoyed this Large Print book. All our Large Print titles are designed for easy reading, and all our books are made to last. Other G.K. Hall books are available at your library, through selected bookstores, or directly from us.

For information about titles, please call:

(800) 223-2336

To share your comments, please write:

Publisher
G.K. Hall & Co.
P.O. Box 159
Thorndike, ME 04986